The Snake-oil Dickens Man

Ross Gilfillan is a magazine journalist who lives in Suffolk with his wife and three children. *The Snake-oil Dickens Man* is his first novel.

'A quality romp set in the America of the late 1860s ... Robustly written, and with plenty of Dickensian resonances, Gilfillan's first novel is an ingenious and entertaining read.' *Mail on Sunday*

'Weaves a fascinating tale ... The atmosphere of 1867 is brilliantly captured.' *Oxford Mail*

'Compulsive, quirky, beautifully constructed, a read that has you wondering why no one has ever tried it before.' *Birmingham Post*

THE SNAKE-OIL

DICKENS
MAN

Ross Gilfillan

FOURTH ESTATE • *London*

This paperback edition published in 1999
First published in Great Britain in 1998 by
Fourth Estate Limited
6 Salem Road
London W2 4BU

A catalogue record for this book is available from
the British Library.

ISBN 978-1-85702-814-0

Typeset by
Avon Dataset Ltd, Bidford on Avon B50 4JH

To my wife Lisa
and Fae, Tom and Alice

Prologue

Ces Américains qui aiment tant à être dupés
Baudelaire

No one does something for nothing any more.

So the smart money says, anyway. If this is true then I suppose there is no reason why I should not be well recompensed for the hours I will sit at this desk, removed from spheres of more certainly remunerative activity. There are infinite ways in which wealth can be acquired with much less expenditure of effort than by the writing of a memoir. No, the profit I hope for here will be of another kind. I relate what follows not for pecuniary gain but rather that I might by the process of autobiography come to understand more of myself and see the beginning of the thread that has woven the thing that now I am.

Let me begin as I mean to continue – honestly – and say right out that I am not as I seem. No doubt you know me by my reputation and my office but even were we strangers, you might observe my English-cut suit and my fancy waistcoat and hear my knowing tones and mistake me for a man of consequence. And if I'm offering you some deal that's going to make you rich quick and won't jeopardise your capital one little bit then that's exactly how you would have me. For all the world, I am prosperous, refined and respected. I am solid and that is all you need to know.

1

But perhaps what you now see really is me. Perhaps money has made me one of you: just as prosperous and as solid as any of the speculators, private investors and city tycoons I have lately lived off so well. All I know for certain is that once I thought I was different and that this journal shall be my testimony.

At this distance it is hard for me to credit that I was once a veritable slave to a low hotelier; that I was employed by Elijah Putnam as an agent of his own ambition and that I let my mother be abominably abused. Harder still to acknowledge that I owe my present eminence to an individual whose philosophy was markedly at odds with those who hold propriety and the law in reverence.

But now I have arrived at a time in my life when I would leave off pretence and apply myself to the task of understanding of what I am made. I shall begin today while my wife is in Mississippi, opening up the house in Natchez. She hardly needs two whole months to ready the place for Christmas – only an excuse to decamp from Washington DC. (She has never enjoyed playing the part of the politician's wife.) However, her absence affords me ideal opportunity to begin my work. To this end I am seated at my great oaken desk, my inkpot brim-full and my nib poised above half a ream of white paper, fully resolved that I will not be distracted by my present great responsibilities or by the formless stain of black ink which despoils the oak and has proven the match of brush and polish alike.

But where to begin? A natural place might be with my mother and father but if I had known their histories in the first place this one would not be worth the candle. Nor was sense made of my childhood until its term had expired. Rather, I must overleap my dim origins and begin at a place which now seems pregnant with some significance, although I can offer no more apt beginning than this, with which you will surely be familiar:

Whether I shall turn out to be the hero of my life, or whether

2

that station will be held by anybody else, these pages must show.

And so to make a start.

Chapter One

I

I HAD BEEN reading to Mr Putnam, same as I always did, right after supper and before I climbed the ladder to my bed beneath the rafters. I guessed he had something on his mind because this night he let me choose.

'We'll have the one about the feller with high hopes,' I said, and settled down on the hard chair by the lamp and began to read.

Pip was still on the marshes, beside the graves of his five little brothers, when Mr Putnam, who had been quite unusually restless throughout, fidgeting and biting his fingernails, said, 'That's enough, boy. You must know it by heart. I had hoped you might have read us the latest part of his new one.'

I wanted to tell him that I had never liked that book and that when I had read its opening pages, which he bid me do as soon as the first instalment landed on American soil, I had been terrified out of my senses. I told no one that for weeks afterward, my bed became a boat whose dreadful occupants were black and faceless figures who sculled the river at night, fishing for the bloated corpses of suicides. I went to replace the volume but he heard my tread and sat me down.

'Stay,' he said. 'On reflection, it occurs to me that the book will do very well for tonight.'

I took it up again and read of a marshland that I thought must bear resemblance to that which spread out beyond the limits of our own town – for how different can bogs be? – and of the hulks, which put me in mind of the captured ships tethered by the quay, here in Hayes, Missouri, and of the ranks of rebel prisoners that had shambled through the town only months ago. And of Magwitch; I thought I knew him, too.

I read mechanically, the narrative familiar and my mind more fully employed on matters closer to home. There was that about Mr Putnam tonight I was certain signified an urgency to communicate something to me. But it wasn't my place to ask and I read on and let him bide his time. Pip had returned to the forge and to Joe, but also to his terrible sister and Tickler and still Elijah said nothing. He only continued to grip the copper head of the weather-worn old stick that he had come to rely and rest upon now that his eyes had untimely closed upon the world.

As I turned the pages, I saw he was no longer attending to the words I read but seemed instead to be listening to other voices and was murmuring and nodding in tune with conversations to which I could not be privy. I stopped the reading and he was immediately sensible of the closing of the book. I expected him to remark my temerity but instead, he waved me away and said only that it, whatever that was, would wait until another day. I snuffed out the lamp and found the handle of the door.

My eyes were still accustomed to the bright light and I was feeling my way along the black hallway, when I collided with a bulk I knew straightaways was Merriweather. I had run into him hard and he cuffed me, as I knew he would. I made to let him pass, thinking how it might teach him to be less mean with his gas, when he took me by the collar and whispered so close I could tell the grade of the whisky on his breath:

'What did he say? 'Bout the lawyer he had up with him today?'

I said he hadn't mentioned no lawyer to me, just gone and giv'n me my lesson, same as always. My sight had gotten used to the obscurity in time to see that this wasn't going to satisfy the old goat tonight. I tried to dodge a blow he aimed at my head but either I was too slow or he wasn't as drunk as I had judged because he caught me one, bang upon the temple and the black hall was lit up in flashes of lightning.

Even as a child, I had never considered Merriweather a strong man, but, reeling from his lucky blow, I couldn't fail to notice that he had hefted me up by my shirt-collars and now had me pinned against the wall. He hissed spittle in my ear:

'Mighty queer a man would see no visitors in three weeks and then spend three hours tucked up with a lawyer, ain't it? And say nothing to no one?'

'He didn't mention no lawyer, I swear,' I said.

'You wouldn't lie to me, would you?' and his stubby little finger poked my face so that my eye bulged. Again, it came to me that even a skinny stick like me could maybe take a fat runt like Merriweather if push came to shove. He must have known the direction my thoughts were taking because he spat out the name that always brought me up short and I swore I would never lie to him, though I reckon I must have lied my way through every day at Merriweather's Particular Hotel.

I don't know that he believed me. I have learnt since that you need to look steadily into the pits of a man's eyes before you can be certain he has swallowed your line and that sometimes the act of looking itself is all that is needed to gull your mark. Merriweather's eyes were normally the most polished and plated of any soul's windows. They blinked ignorance and stupidity when faced with subjects beyond his purview of money and the baser forms of gratification and were slits of suspicion and avarice at most other times.

Tonight, though, they had been digested in the general pitchy gloom of that unlit hallway and I awaited his pleasure and my doom. He let go his grip and when he spoke he sounded mollified. Maybe he was just pleased with the bull's-eye he had landed me.

7

'Course, I reckoned he'd not be discussing his business with you anyways. It'd be me he would come to. But, for the sake of insurance, you be sure and tell me if Mr Putman ever mentions anything concerning that lawyer. Anything at all, you hear?'

I heard, for now, anyway. I waited until Merriweather had descended to the saloon and somewhere between stepping upon my ladder and crawling onto my old straw tick mattress, I swore that just as soon as I could arrange it, things would be different.

II

I knew quite soon what it was that Elijah Putnam had come so close to divulging to me that night. He had been sick for several weeks and he must have thought himself a lot worse than we did because he had indeed called in a lawyer and he had made his will. He was unwell, we all knew that. His failing sight, that had been so poor he had utilised my services as reader, amanuensis and discreet guide whenever he made a rare excursion from the hotel, was now entirely gone.

Elijah appeared to interpret his blindness as a terrible and significant portent, an indicator that his illness was progressing towards its final stages and that the next time he beheld a scene that was bright and clear and full of colour it would be in the Kingdom of Heaven.

By the next day I had clean forgotten about Elijah's strange preoccupation, his suggestion that he had something to reveal to me and the behaviour of Merriweather in the hallway. My daily routine was one that left no time for idle imaginings.

I rose, as usual, to the sound of the roosters in the yard and shimmied down the stairs to the front hall where I unlocked the doors and swept the front step. I hung out the sign that advertised that we had vacancies and that our vittles were always hot and fresh, which stretched the truth a little, and fixed up the saloon. I washed up the glasses, righted the chairs, collected up the stubs of cigars and cleaned out the spit-boxes.

Next I made a swift inventory of the stock and made sure that Irving, who kept bar, hadn't been cheating. Not that Merriweather considered this a bad business practice – it was he who saw to it that I qualified every bottle of liquor we kept – it only became a problem when someone else got the benefit.

By the time the saloon was shipshape there were stirrings in the kitchen. I wouldn't get anything to eat before I had prepared the table for the commercial gentlemen's breakfasts and assisted in the laying on and clearing away of the plates of ham, pickles, salmon, shad, liver, steaks, sausages and other sundry items that these voracious salesmen and drummers demanded every time they sat down to board. I had emptied the pail of leftovers into the hogs' trough and helped myself to bread and butter before changing out of my overalls to run errands in the town. We all had to look our best in town; Merriweather's wasn't called the 'Particular' for nothing and appearance counted for a lot.

There was a mirror in the porch, which was there for the gentlemen to set themselves aright before sallying forth to engage the town's merchants. The glass swung on a central pivot and depending on how he placed it, a fellow could check the arrangement of his neckwear and hat, or the shine on his shoes. I always inspected my turnout thoroughly in case I should, accidentally on purpose, run into Cissy Bullock.

I can't say that using the glass ever boosted my self-esteem. My store-bought clothes were good enough when they were gotten me, but now I had grown and the pants were too short, the sleeves the same and the ill-fitting stove-pipe hat, which Merriweather passed on to me, now served mainly as a challenging target for small boys with slingshots. But I thought that no mere apparel could mitigate the physiognomy with which I had been cursed. The deep-set blue eyes were much too big and doubtless I appeared as if perpetually amazed. The nose was sharp and much too small and my lips, I was told by a schoolfellow, were like a girl's. This montage of errors was crowned with a tangle of tumbleweed that served as hair. I mustered what dignity the application of a little bears' grease would afford and took up my basket.

On that occasion, the morning after the encounter with Merriweather, I had a small list of items to buy, a couple of letters to mail and some bills to settle. Then I planned to attend to a little business of my own: I traded in the gossip of the commercial gentlemen; in this way some merchants were able to hold out for better terms when they came to dealing with our guests and I was able, sometimes, to make fifty cents or even a dollar for myself.

Meantime, I would need cash to transact the business of the hotel. I could hear Merriweather in conversation in his parlour and considered postponing my departure. I preferred to encounter him on other ground; there had been times when a summons to Merriweather's parlour had occasioned terror. It wasn't that the room with its huge and heavy furniture and a crimson wallpaper such as Satan himself might have picked out was ugly and reeked of the sweet and stale smell of Merriweather's cigars. Nor that he had beaten me in that place. There was something else about that room, some childhood memory that time had erased, but whose palimpsest was still traceable on the adult mind, which made me strangely awkward and uncomfortable whenever I addressed Merriweather in his private sanctum.

Merriweather was breakfasting in his shirt-sleeves, his black moustache twitching and collecting crumbs as he ate buttered toast and listened to what Silas Amory, the newspaper editor, was saying. 'Now this town has the railroad, we need to give the city folk a reason to use it, get 'em coming into the town. Trading, settling, starting up businesses. It's not happening yet. Tell me, Merriweather, has the railroad brought you the business they said it would?'

Amory's slight and angular figure perched upon his chair. Only his small dark eyes showed animation as he awaited Merriweather's reply. I thought he looked like a thieving magpie, intent on stealing morsels from the hotelier's plate. Merriweather sneered and swallowed. 'Waal, I allow it might have done that,' he said, reaching for his cigar-box, 'had not

10

the railroad company gone and erected its own hotel hard by the depot. They never said nothing about that and I call it low-down and irregular.'

'Sharp, too, though,' said Amory. 'So I guess you have to lower your prices to secure the custom.'

'That I do, and allow for some little expenditure on advertising that fact, too. There just ain't enough people coming through this town. Not for us all to turn a good profit.' He swallowed some coffee and said, 'What this place needs is a magnet of some kind. I don't know, s'posin' someone was to let on, to a newspaper, perhaps, that a little gold had been found in the creek?'

'We'd get the wrong kind of people,' Amory said, 'and they'd be gone soon as they knew the truth.'

'I reckon you're right at that. This business needs some kind of a shove, though. Couple more years like this one and I'll be looking for a job at the Central Pacific.'

'Bad as that?' said Amory.

'Close to it,' said Merriweather. 'You know I got a little capital left. It ain't much but maybe the time has come to venture it. Find some sure-fire investment opportunity. How about precious minerals?'

'Nothing sure about that line. Lot of people lose their shirts. You might reconsider that matter we spoke of last fall. I'd still welcome a backer if you'd like to make your investment in me.'

'You?'

'I'm running for mayor whether or not you stake me, Melik. I'll get the money if I have to put the *Bugle* in hock. But if you come in with me now, you won't see no new hotels going up in Hayes. When I'm mayor I can put all kinds of interesting business your way.'

I cleared my throat and asked Merriweather for the money and I thought I saw Silas Amory damning me with his eyes.

'Gaul-durn it, boy, allus asking for this or that. I tell you, Silas, this boy has drained me of a sizeable fortune since I took him 'n' his mother in, nigh on twenty years ago. Twenty

11

years of feeding and clothing. Sizeable, I tell you. Ah, but that's the cross a true Christian has to bear, I suppose.'

'Well, you got yourself a wife into the bargain, kind of,' said Amory, with a leer to which Merriweather refused to respond. Instead, he spat out the end of the cigar and snapped, 'Charity, Amory. You seen her, as ill-educated a crittur as ever crawled from the swamp. What I done, I mostly done for charity. Never mind what people might say. '

'So long as you don't go extending your charity to other women hereabouts.'

Merriweather choked on a crust, and his features broke into a leer that was quite as lascivious as Amory's. He said Amory was a card and no two ways about it and then he pulled out his purse and warned me to account for every penny. I took the money and skedaddled down the steps. Old Henry, who had worked in the neighbouring livery stable for ever, probably, was being walked around to the front door by his chestnut mare.

'That for me?' I said.

'No, t'ain't, as well you know,' Henry said. 'It's hired to the gennulman as arrived late last night.'

'Well, ain't you got some broken-down old nag you could lend me? I have to go to town.'

'Elsa an't broken-down, jest old,' said Henry. 'An't your learnin' taught you no respect for age?'

'I'll try and acquire some,' I told him. As I started for town, I tried to summon up instances in which I had considered that respect was due. I was probably of a cynical disposition then but my short history had given me few occasions to be otherwise. I was twenty-four years old and young men of my age had already established themselves in lines of work and some were succeeding in their own concerns. Others were married.

I walked on towards town, lamenting my own single state, which I considered was partly the fault of older folk. I would most certainly have married Cissy Bullock and maybe now be lying in her arms had not our secret liaison and moonlight encounters been brought to an unsatisfactory close when Mr

Bullock discovered us on their porch one night. I was returning her from a dance where we had contrived to lose her Aunt Louise and reckoned her folks would all be asleep by that time. Events had been taking a romantic course and I was hopeful of pressing my suit.

But Pop Bullock had found us and he was furious. He rounded on me like a mad dog. Foolishly, I tried to explain and lost all my standing. There wasn't anything that needed excusing. I had behaved honourably and didn't deserve this. But he had a head of steam up and was hollering for all the neighbourhood to hear, 'I guess I've heard more than I ever want to about you and yours. Particular indeed! No one respectable goes up there any more. Travelling gentlemen and sharpers maybe but church folk don't and my daughter won't neither. You come around here again and I'll fill you full of buckshot, understand?'

Pop Bullock had forbidden any further congress between Cissy and me and that was all because of the way Melik Merriweather ran his affairs. Or at least, so I believed at the time. I kicked stones down the track, like each one was a little granite head of Melik Merriweather. That morning I had been galled that he had ridiculed my mother as if her son had not been standing before him. 'As ill-educated a crittur as ever crawled from the swamp,' he had said.

Merriweather never gave a damn that my mother couldn't read or write and had at best a basic understanding of life. I supposed he was just excusing himself to Silas Amory. But that she and I came from the swamp was undeniable. The oldest, faintest memory I have is the smell of the swamp. I don't even know if it is a real memory. Maybe it came later, when I knew a little more, but that makes no odds: the stench of something rotten is too strong and too pervasive to be dismissed as fancy. The odour is sickly sweet and I seem to know it again – in the air on the marshes where the trees are stunted and toppled and the roads are still mud and corduroy – or strangely, in the stale smoke that is ever-present in Merriweather's parlour.

Other memories are of equally doubtful provenance. Sometimes I think I remember the stage coach in which I know I travelled from Cairo but I know that can hardly be as I was still a babe in arms when I was taken away and installed with my mother at Merriweather's Particular Hotel.

Within sight of the town, I was sensible, suddenly, of the thunder of hooves. I had been so lost in thought as I approached the church and burial ground that marked the town's limits that I didn't hear a thing until horse and rider were upon me and had nearly run me down. The Particular's chestnut mare with its rider, cloaked and masked for the dust, galloped past. It wasn't common to see anyone in a great hurry in these parts and I watched until he was out of sight.

III

Before my eyes were opened I was the lowest creature of evolution and I'm sure Mr Darwin would have recognised in me then some hairy antecedent of my present evolvement. My lot was better than that which had lately belonged to slaves and also than that of most new freedmen but I was a child strangely and harshly circumstanced and what might be supportable now, was infinitely less so then.

You will wonder how this came to be and to answer that I must go back to the beginning of all things and return to the smell of the swamp, which might or might not be my oldest surviving memory. There is that and I can summon its noxious vapour even now but what else of that time survives? Not much. The mingling of images and impressions and half-remembered speech that I retain must date from two or three years after I was brought to the hotel as a babe in arms and in what order they occurred I have not the slightest idea. But they are as follows.

I am pulled from my mother's arms and someone is crying, no, howling and whether it is me or my mother who keens so piteously, I don't know. This, I now believe, must have been the moment I was taken from my mother to live at the house

14

of Elijah Putnam. A woman's hands grip my wrists as she teaches me to use knife and fork. She leans across my shoulders, her breasts brushing my neck and her sweet-smelling breath whispers encouragement in my ear and I am grateful. The same woman is talking, loudly enough for me to hear clearly from the top of the stairs on which I sit, 'Don't take him away from me, Elijah, he's all I have.'

And I remember the smoking and acrid-smelling remains of the house in which she died: the blackened doorframe and uprights that still stood among great heaps of charcoal and ashes and the half-burned artefacts and knick-knacks I rescued from the ruins and were my damaged records of a time when I had been happy.

There is the schoolroom, too, in which Elijah Putnam, appearing little different in my memory than he did when last I saw him, strides up and down between the desks. Stopping at my own with much greater regularity than at others, he points out this or that in a book or corrects marks I am making on a slate. There are many schoolroom memories: of reading aloud before the class or standing upon a chair with a sign about my neck that advertises that I am slothful; of my classmates finding me alone one day and taking their turns to cuff me about the ears . . . *Teacher's pet, teacher's pet* ringing in the ears they stung so long ago.

It must have been soon after Mrs Putnam died that I left my room at his house and first slept beneath the roof of the Particular Hotel. My history is quite distinct after this date. After living a relatively ordered and peaceful life with Mr and Mrs Putnam, I found myself plunged into a chaotic world in which my function appeared to be to scrub floors, fetch and carry wash-basins, empty chamber-pots, change bed-linen, polish the boots, help the cook, wait on and clear away the tables, run errands, help Henry with the livery horses, clean the saloon and do any number of jobs, all at once, that would probably have taken three people to get done anywhere else.

I don't know when I first encountered Merriweather but he seems a part of every memory I have of my new existence at the hotel. My life was quite suddenly, utterly changed. It seemed no stranger to be working my hands to the bone in the role of unpaid factotum to a hotelier than it did to find myself receiving personal tuition from Elijah Putnam, who had retired from his position as schoolteacher and had taken rooms in the Particular, to which I repaired every day.

But it wasn't the work, exhausting as it always was, that made my days so miserable. I think I could have borne that well and enjoyed some parts of it, too, had I known that Merriweather were not always somewhere about the building, ready to box my ears or make threats of violence that would be directed not at me but at someone else and these I feared more than anything Merriweather might do to me.

I knew that the woman who worked mostly in the laundry and whom I sometimes caught stealing along the corridors was my mother. She cut the strangest figure of the establishment. It wasn't just her worn-out appearance: she was taller than her posture suggested, her hands wrinkled from her work, rather than by nature, although what age she had then attained was hard to guess. Her clothes were patched and stained and she and they smelt strongly of the wash-house.

What was more extraordinary was the way she carried herself – like a whipped animal. She kept closely to herself and could even sometimes be heard running ahead of footfalls in an effort to conceal herself from any approach. She rarely met a glance and her eyes that were normally cast down were often shielded anyway by the wild mess of lank locks that fell about and often concealed her physiognomy. It could be a shock for a stranger to catch her with her face unobscured and find that she was actually pretty.

I discovered that this was my mother not long after I moved from Elijah's house to the Particular Hotel. I had been helping Mary Ann, the cook's girl, to knead the dough. The kitchen was warm with the baking and Merriweather, whom I had already identified as an enemy to children, was playing at cards in the saloon. I was happy to be there with Mary Ann. She wasn't more than a few years older than I was and had become my only ally in this inhospitable place.

There was fun to be had when Cook wasn't about and as she was napping, the bread-making had become a great game. Water was splashed and flour was spilt. Just as we were becoming so riotous that Mary was saying 'Hush, you'll wake Cook', I caught sight of a figure in the corner of my eye and stopped everything, fearing Cook or Merriweather had caught us fooling.

But it was the woman I had seen skulking in the corridors. She hastened through the kitchen and out into the yard. Mary Ann looked up from her dough and muttered something like, 'They hanged the witches at Salem,' and giggled. I was shocked.

'Is she a witch?' I asked. She certainly looked like one.

'Aye and a terrible one at that,' said Mary Ann. 'You seen all them cats in the graveyard?' I had. There was a whole colony of feral cats there. 'Them's her families and she dances nekkid with 'em on dead men's graves, come a moonlit night.'

'Has she ever put a spell on you?' I asked, terrified to find such awful danger so imminent.

'She sure has. Turned me into a bullfrog one day and I had to hop all the way to th'pothecary, get some help.'

I don't know if we were overheard or whether chance had played its part but when we looked through the door the woman was to be seen sweeping the back porch.

'She's got a broom too!' I exclaimed, weak with horror.

'I'm so scared I could just faint,' said Mary Ann. 'I never seen her with her magic broom afore. Likely she'll murder us here or take us with her on her broom and do it in the forest. Oh, Billy, help me!'

'What can I do?' I said, scared stiff but unwilling to let down my only friend. 'Shall I get a gun?'

'Guns is no good 'ginst witches,' said Mary Ann. 'You gotta go right up to them and look straight into their eyes. Then you gotta say, "Listen, witch, to this my spell, get thee gone or burn in hell." And then you says, "Begone old hag, begone!" '

'You sure?' I asked, and Mary Ann said it had never failed

17

yet and the last witch they had, vanished in a cloud of smoke.

From where we had ducked down under the kitchen table, I could see the woman passing and repassing the door, sweeping the fall leaves back onto the yard. I had no doubt that this was indeed a powerful witch who might at any moment look up from her labours and make me into one of the hogs which were then squealing beyond the stoop.

I looked at Mary Ann who was pouting and appearing awfully frightened and I knew what I must do. I emerged from under the table and edged about the kitchen to where the door stood open. I looked once again at Mary Ann who signalled me to go on. Mustering my courage, I stepped out on the porch. There was no one there. Relief flooded my soul. 'She ain't here, Mary Ann,' I called. 'That witch musta seen me coming and took flight.'

Then the woman, who had been around the side of the house, turned the corner and looked at me. Her hair had been brushed off her face, whose still-youthful appearance seemed ill-fitted to her crone's hands and stooped posture. Her green eyes were unusually bright and, to me, menacing. There was nothing to do but defend myself. I said something that approximated the incantation Mary Ann had taught me. I don't know exactly what but it seems to me I called her a witch and an old hag more often than had been prescribed.

She remained where she was, still looking intently at me. I wondered if I had transfixed her and whether at any moment she might disappear in smoke. The spell seemed to be taking hours to work and I said, 'Get thee gone, hag,' louder and louder and still she stood there. Maybe in my panic I was finally shouting the words because the next thing I knew, Merriweather was standing by me, looking mightily amused and saying, 'So you've met your mother, have you?'

I hardly need to tell you that I was terrifically shocked at this fantastic revelation. *I*, the son of that monstrosity? I had known that Elijah and Mrs Putnam were not my natural parents, whom I had vaguely understood were both dead. To find that my mother existed under the same roof and that she was as I saw her was a shock of cataclysmic proportions.

I was revolted but whether by her weird appearance and my newly-discovered relationship to her or by my stupid and heartless behaviour, I was too young to know. Whichever it was, such was the revulsion I felt that I concurred willingly with Merriweather's dictate that I should at all times avoid her society.

And so, for the first year or so, I saw little of the woman they told me was my mother. I worked as usual, performing the same routine chores and becoming adept at anticipating what needed to be done to keep the business running smoothly. Merriweather let up on beating me and began to lean on me instead. I won't say I was happy but I was becoming accustomed to my lot. But sometimes, as I performed some mechanical and dull task such as blacking the boots of the guests, I would be unable to stop my mind from returning to that woman and wondering about my own origins. But this was never productive and my curiosity stopped short of breaking Merriweather's injunction and overcoming my own disgust, to talk to the woman herself. Besides, I had much to occupy me now and the times at which I had leisure to consider the oddities of my birth were few. Increasingly, I found my evenings taken up with the hours of tuition I was receiving from Elijah Putnam.

Boys will accept a *status quo* easily, especially when they have never known anything different and I don't think I ever properly questioned why Elijah Putnam had singled me out for special attention at his school. Perhaps I assumed that it was because of the affection I was due as his ward. Nor did I find it strange that upon the death of his wife, he should throw up his position of schoolmaster and move into the rooms on the second floor of the Particular Hotel.

But move he had and even after years of infesting the place, it still looked as if its occupant had never intended these apartments as his permanent residence. There was insufficient shelving for his books and these stood in piles or collapsed in heaps about his chair and on top and underneath of the table.

He had a big globe, whose dominant colours seemed to be red and blue. There were several oil lamps, whose wicks it was always my first job to trim and so our sessions of study were never interrupted by the going down of the sun.

What never ceased to puzzle me was why Merriweather was compliant with Elijah's strange and often inconvenient scheme. Just when we seemed at our busiest and I was hurrying this way and that with dinner or tending to newly-arrived horses, the bell would ring and Merriweather might curse but he would always send me upstairs where Putnam would be waiting, book in hand. I could only figure he was pandering to the whim of his only resident guest.

Elijah Putnam had been a part of my life for almost as long as I could remember and yet I really knew very little about him. It was his gentle wife Rosalie I remembered first and who was, for a tragically short time, my mother. Elijah had been then an indistinct figure backgrounding those days and he only showed an interest in me when I grew a little beyond my infancy.

One day in particular I remember. I have always thought of it as the day he discovered me. I had been sitting by Rosalie as she plied her needle amongst a design that included a small house with roses around the door and flowers in its garden. The fall sun was shining low and yellow gold through the trees that shaded the lawn beyond the window. It was a little after the time we were used to expecting Elijah home from the schoolroom and Rosalie had been remarking his tardiness, when the door swung open and Elijah himself strode in.

She put down her sampler and stood to greet her husband but he ignored her proffered kiss and took me up in his arms, an action that both surprised and alarmed me. He carried me to the window where the rays of the setting sun dazzled me and then he turned my head this way and that and seemed to want to see me anew from every angle. At last he put me back upon the sofa and stood, peering down at me, with his hands upon his hips and his chest thrust out. He was smiling broadly and, because his countenance was more usually of a severe set, the effect was remarkable.

'Well,' he said, his thick red hair shot through with the dying rays of the sun, 'this changes everything.'

IV

And presently I will tell you of how everything changed. As people often remark, it is a curious story. But no doubt you remember a masked rider astride the Particular's chestnut mare and would rather follow him, because he was fast. When I met up with this man, he was in company with one of the most singular individuals it has ever been my fortune to meet.

The morning had been one of routine as I hurried about from one store to another, settling accounts, gossiping with shopkeepers and chewing the fat and plugs of tobacco with young men of my acquaintance. When I had done all I had to do I availed myself of a little leisure and strolled down Main Street, gravitating towards the environs of Cissy Bullock's house. It was a striking residence, its clapboarding newly white-painted and its garden still in bloom. It was one of the few larger houses to escape molestation when the Yankees had ridden through the town a few years ago and that only because it became the temporary headquarters of a General Crabtree. Traces of the General's occupation could still be seen, Cissy had told me, in the cigar burns on her father's desk and in the light squares of wallpaper against which had once hung some valuable paintings.

There was no sign of Bullock himself so I swung a leg over the picket fence and edged around the corner of the house to the source of the music that floated on the air. Through an open window I could see Cissy sitting at the piano. She had on a pretty lemon dress; her hair, that she usually tied up, was let down over her shoulders and it seemed to me I could smell her soap from where I stood. I never saw any picture that looked half as pretty nor mountain stream look an eighth as pure as Cissy did then as she gave herself up to the music,

21

unaware of my proximity. What torture it was to stand within inches of my beloved. I yearned to make my presence known.

But to have done so would have brought trouble not just for me but upon Cissy herself. Bullock might be anywhere about the house and I contented myself with listening to the nocturne and astonishing myself with the brilliance of her hair and delicate tones of her skin until I heard footsteps in the hall. At that juncture, I withdrew and retrudged through the town, heedless of the puddles and mud, oblivious even to the locomotive that must have crashed over the rails right by me, spitting sparks and cinders as it braked for the junction, where I found it, minutes later.

Our chestnut mare was tied up by the tracks still snorting and breathing hard after her exertion. I was curious about her rider and walked alongside of the train from which folk were alighting and carrying off trunks and I peered through the windows wondering if maybe our guest had ridden hard to make the train and be miles away before we discovered his unsettled hotel bill. The man seemed not to be aboard though I was unsure if I would have recognised him anyway. I only saw him once the night before when he had inquired whether there was a printing shop in town and nothing about his appearance or demeanour had been memorable.

I must have been possessed of more striking aspect than he, as when I turned from the last window I found the man I sought standing before me.

'Pardon me, but ain't you the manager of the brick hotel? I'd have knowed that hat anywhere. Mighty fine. Unusual, too.'

I admitted that you didn't see many like it, any more. Was there something I could do for him, I asked.

'Well, yes, I think there is,' said the man, who I now noticed was rangy and tall, with wispy wires of hair that escaped from under his hat like stuffing from a chair. 'I'm in urgent need to speak to someone in authority at that hotel and who knows this town like the back of his hand.' I assured him that I was such a man and he took me by my arm and led me back to the mare. A man was standing in a buggy, distributing

22

handbills to a small crowd of people and declaiming about something I hadn't time to get the sense of. The man at my side said, 'That's a very important man, in that air fly. Very important for you and this here town. He'll 'spect your best room. It's free, ain't it?'

I assured him we had a good room vacant at that time. He mounted the buggy and whispered something to his companion, who wished the dispersing crowd well and turned to me.

'Your servant,' said the second man in a voice so rich and deep that I heard in it something of the quality of polished mahogany.

Perhaps you have at some time been in the presence of someone whose whole effect is to make you feel underdressed, under-educated and under-prepared for the occasion? Such was the case then, as I took in the magnificence of the man who now extended a manicured hand. I guessed that he was perhaps fifty years old but he may have been younger or older. His hair was long but well-groomed and he wore what must have been a new city-style of hat, for we had none such here. His suit fitted him no worse than his skin and he gripped a polished, expensive-looking, leather valise. Something glinted upon his waistcoat as he pulled out and glanced at a fancy silver watch.

When he regarded me again, I was impressed by his deep-set, pale blue eyes, which I can only describe as being like beams that shone right inside my head.

'I am honoured to make your acquaintance, sir,' he said to me. 'This is a great day for your town.' And, with some gravity, presented me with a handbill on which I read the portentous type: *P.T. Barnum. Greatest Show On Earth. Astounding Moral Circus, Museum and Managerie. Prop. Phineas T. Barnum. As Exhibited Before the Royal Courts of London and Paris.*

There was more of the same but I was only conscious of my heart thumping beneath my shirt and the dazzling eyes of the man whom I took to be the world's most brilliant showman, P.T. Barnum.

'Mr Barnum!' I breathed with no less reverence than a courtier addressing Queen Elizabeth or the Sun King. The thin man laughed but the other held my gaze and only slowly did his eyes crease and did I discern a merry twinkle. But I thought that he said, 'Not in person, I regret,' with no less imposing a manner and in my mind some small doubt still lingered.

'I am Henri D'Orleans,' he said. 'And this, John Wilkes. We are advance agents for Mr Phineas Barnum's great travelling museum and we are here to make the necessary preparations for its visit to this town.'

'Barnum's show, here?' I said.

'And very soon. We shall require the services of someone who can show us the lie of the land. We will need certain amenities arranged in advance of Barnum's arrival. And, of course, we must be shown some place where we can throw up the tents and exercise the animals. I hardly suppose you would know of such a person?'

I did and while I rode the chestnut mare back to the hotel, allowing Mr Wilkes to converse with his partner in the fly, ('You run along ahead, boy, and tell 'em the Barnum men is coming!') my mind was churning with the excitement I then felt and that I knew would be shared by all when I told them the great news. Just wait till Merriweather and everyone else heard that Billy Talbot was bringing P.T. Barnum to the Particular!

I expected to create a stir, for the impresario had been much in the news, and a hotel guest who had visited Barnum's American Museum in New York had been greeted with wheel-eyed amazement when he arrived back in town with his tales of performing animals, amazing automatons, astounding tableaux, panoramas and dioramas of scenes from the Creation to the Deluge, incredible human freaks of nature, rope-dancers, jugglers, ventriloquists and any number of scientific and mechanical marvels of the age. It was entertainment beyond possibility.

P.T. Barnum had been news for twenty years. He had the

24

valuable trick of ensuring that anything he did was of great interest to editors of newspapers. Who in the country had not by then heard of his celebrated protégés General Tom Thumb or the Swedish nightingale, Jenny Lind? His American Museum had been successful far beyond its home in New York and when he mounted the whole shooting match on wheels – because that was how it seemed – it was a magnet, a dollar-attracting lodestone for miles around, wherever it pitched up. Even his setbacks and reverses, his crashes and his fires were big news.

We all wanted to know what he would do next – there was no stopping Barnum!

Chapter Two

I RODE THAT poor horse hell for leather back to the Particular and jumped off by the front steps, fully expecting to be received like the messenger from Marathon. I found Merriweather where I had left him and poured out my news in one long and unpunctuated narrative. Merriweather was suspicious and sceptical but Amory said he'd had reports of Barnum's juggernaut rolling through a neighbouring state and thought it might be due at a city not fifty miles from us the following week. Now he considered it, Merriweather recalled that he had seen a handbill bearing Barnum's name in the street but hadn't stopped to pick it up.

I said, of course it was Barnum. They'd only have to look at him to know that. And they could do that now because here was the buggy stopping right outside. Merriweather flicked aside the curtains and peered out. Irving, whose excitement had propelled him into the parlour after me, said:

'I tell you it's Barnum hisself!'

'Barnum don't look like that.'

'How d'you know? You seen pictures?'

'No, I ain't seen no photographs, but why would he claim to be this Dorlyon?'

'Well, I heard tell, one time he went and sat in the seats of his own cirkis, jest like he was a reg'lar customer and when they was all applaudin' and calling out for Barnum, he jest sat where he was and never let on.'

'Kinda thing he might do, then?'

'Sure is. Exactly so. He's checking us out, making sure this town's the one for his show. Looking over this hotel too, I reckon.'

'Appears the part, I must say,' said Merriweather. 'Fancy clothes. And what's that on his finger? A diamond?'

'P.T. Barnum ain't the man to wear paste,' said Irving.

'Well, Barnum or no Barnum, it don't do to keep customers waiting,' said the hotelier and hustled Irving out the door. Then he checked himself in the glass, sent me about my work and made his own regal entrance.

II

I didn't see Mr D'Orleans again until dinner-time but I could tell the impression he was creating from the orders that were being sent to the kitchen. Mary Ann and the cook were preparing for dinner like it was Thanksgiving at the White House. I had come to help out but finished up only getting underfoot and Mary Ann loaded me up with a great bundle of bed-linen and sent me spinning across the yard towards the wash-house. My mother was there, as she always was, stirring sheets and shirts in the big copper tub. She said, 'Lo, Billy,' but she kept on stirring, her hair all over her eyes, as it ever was.

'You all right, Ma?' I said, for I had taken to using this appellation and from that you may deduce that my relationship with her had considerably improved from the day I had attempted to exorcise her from the back stoop.

'I guess I am,' she said.

'Don't look it, Ma,' said I, 'Merriweather getting at you agin?'

'That man,' she said.

28

'He ain't beat you again, has he?' I said. 'Because if he has . . .'

She stood up from the wash-tub and straightened herself. Whenever she did this I was surprised to see how much taller she was and how proud she could appear when she didn't stoop and wasn't so timid and servile.

'You listen to me, Billy,' she flashed, 'I don't want you meddling with nothing that happens 'twixt Melik and me; 'taint none of your business. Someone's going to get hurt if you do that. Understand me now.'

Anger and burning frustration flared like foxfire, as it always did whenever I tried to touch upon the roots of things and asked why Merriweather was so blamed keen to keep us both at the Particular.

I said, 'I don't know that I do understand, Ma. It's awful hard when he threatens you. He does it to keep me in line. What if we was both to go away from here? What then?'

'Some things jest ain't possible,' she said, with grim simplicity, 'and that's one of 'em.'

'I wish I could change your mind.'

'Don't worry yourself over me. Merriweather ain't so bad.' She plunged her arms into the water and began to pummel one of his shirts. 'Any case,' she said, 'where could we go? Here, I got shelter and food.'

She paused a moment and then said, 'But you're getting to be an ejucated fellow, Billy, I can see you gotta look out for something better.'

I couldn't tell her the nature of the threats Merriweather had made against the eventuality of my deciding to quit him and his hotel, so I let the matter drop and helped her with the laundry. After we had done, I said maybe we could talk more when I came to see her later. My mother occupied a room in a lean-to behind the wash-house and I had taken to visiting her for an hour; not mainly for conversation, because she wasn't one for that, but to teach her to read and write. But it was beginning to look like she was either word-blind or quite as stupid as Merriweather said and the worst of it was, I could

29

never seem to make out which. As I left the shed, she said, 'T'aint just Merriweather, Billy!'

'What do you mean, Ma? Who, then?'

She held out her arms which were lividly red up past the elbow and her hands, wrinkled as a corduroy road, closed me to her bosom.

'Nobody, Billy. I didn't mean that,' she said. 'Only sometimes little people get swept into a corner by the big folk and once they get themselves in that corner, there just ain't no escapin'.'

III

D'Orleans and Wilkes were seated before the most sumptuous table I had ever laid at the Particular. I served them with turkey and chicken and ham and pork and every kind of vittle we had in the larder. Then I brought the wine and was startled, as much as injured, when Merriweather struck me hard for bringing out the second-best. He sent me to fetch bottles from his own stock, apologising to his guests all the while. When I had set wine and a box of cigars upon the table, Merriweather ventured to pull up a chair and address the opulently-attired Mr D'Orleans.

'I'm told you are agents for Mr Barnum,' he said, with a smile you might have hung cups on.

' 'Deed we are,' said Wilkes, through his own chip-toothed grin. 'Our job's to make sure everything's fine and dandy when the travelling museum comes to town. I'm in sole charge of advance publicity. Maybe you seen some of them bills I posted?'

Merriweather nodded but his eyes were fastened upon Mr D'Orleans who continued to eat, quite daintily; eating and observing, but so far without saying anything.

'And a nation hard job it is,' the thin man was saying. 'Barnum demands the best and only the best will do.'

'Barnum's is a pretty bully show, ain't it?' said Merriweather.

30

'Why I should say it is,' said the man. 'Best since C'ligula. It's been laid before the kings and queens of Europe. Barnum give 'em the best seats hisself.'

'Old Barnum must be making a sizeable pile of money,' observed Merriweather, eyeing D'Orleans' ring.

Here Mr D'Orleans slowly ground out his cigar and spoke.

'The trick, as I'm sure you appreciate, is in spending money to make money.'

Merriweather nodded, eagerly.

'If Barnum thinks whales are what the public wants to see, he catches them and shows them at the museum, regardless of expense. Barnum has men scouring the earth for fantastical novelties that will pull the city crowds through the doors of his American Museum or the country folk after his travelling circus. Do you know how much it costs Barnum to take this huge show about the states? But it doesn't matter because Barnum knows he'll get it back, and more. He spends money on seeing to it that his show is always the best and he also spends on publicising the name of Barnum. Investing and advertising, that's Barnum's trick.'

'I got charge of that,' said Wilkes, 'I post the bills, get the puffs in the newspapers, spread the word, hang the bunting, maybe rustle up a band to play Barnum into town. That way, when the caravan turns up, there's a crowd of customers there already, just begging him to take their dollars. Oh, I think I can say that Barnum knows my worth.'

'Indeed he does,' said Mr D'Orleans.

Merriweather regarded the bigger man with fascination.

'Mind if I inquire what is your function, precisely?' he said.

'I call it attending to details,' said D'Orleans. 'Mr Barnum is accustomed to the best of everything. He can't take his circus just anywhere. Everything has to be suitable. He can as easily set the show some place else. It's not just a matter of a likely spot to pitch the tents and corral the animals. Mr Barnum and his performers need their rest, away from the hurly-burly and quality accommodation is not always easily found.'

'Very true,' said Merriweather.

Mr D'Orleans adopted a confidential tone. 'Mr Merriweather, I take you for a smart businessman. A man doesn't come to have an establishment as fine as this without being sharp.'

Merriweather nodded complacently.

'So I hardly need to explain to you the opportunity this will afford?'

'No, no, I can see that. I heard what it's done for other places. Why only this morning, I was saying to Silas Amory that what this town needs is some big attraction. I guess the Barnum show would do it.'

'And you would be agreeable that Mr Barnum and his party lodge here? I did notice another establishment by the railroad . . .'

'That plague-hole ain't fit for Mr Barnum,' said Merriweather. 'No, you must have him come here. He'll get the best of everything.'

'That's well because, of course, that's what he is used to. Now, it's a tedious business but there are certain small matters that will need attending to before I telegraph Mr Barnum with confirmation that both town and accommodation will suit.'

Telegraph Mr Barnum! That was a good 'un, I thought, as I refilled the glasses.

In the event the business seemed anything but tedious to Mr D'Orleans as he listed the requirements of P.T. Barnum and Merriweather copied them down. D'Orleans was evidently a man who delighted in making the most thorough of preparations. He rocked back in his chair, put his shiny boots upon the table and invited me to light his cigar.

'Mr Barnum is partial to a good smoke,' he began. 'These will never do. But you can procure more?'

'Oh, cigars? I don't think that'll be no problem,' said Merriweather.

'And while this sort of thing,' he indicated the bones of the fowl on his plate, 'is quite adequate for Wilkes and I, when it comes to Mr Barnum, it simply won't do. I'm sure you understand.'

' 'Course I do,' said Merriweather. 'You just tell me what he wants and I'll see he gets it.'

'I should have your cellar replenished.' He tossed off a bumper of Merriweather's premium claret as if it were sarsaparilla. 'I can recommend some vintages, if you like.'

Merriweather frowned at the stranger and said: 'Pardon me, but I thought he was a teetotaller?'

'Mr Barnum is, certainly,' said D'Orleans. 'It keeps the temperance folk sweet, but,' and he touched his nose, 'there are those of his party who are partial to a good Bordeaux. With the time they have spent in France, how could it be otherwise? I shall need to inspect your cellar.'

'Well, there ain't much to inspect but I guess I can get more supplied,' said Merriweather.

'Then there's the matter of accommodation. He'll take your best apartment.'

'Nothing wrong with the one you've got, is there?'

'Mr Barnum will want something more spacious. And, of course, rooms for his closer associates.'

'Of course, of course. How many?'

'All of them, at least,' said D'Orleans.

'But I have gentlemen occupying half of them,' the hotelier demurred.

'That's your affair, of course. However, if I were you . . .'

'They'll be gone tomorrow,' said Merriweather. 'I'll pack 'em off to the Central Pacific Hotel.' Merriweather had begun to look uneasy. He loosened his collar, about which he appeared to be feeling some warmth.

'There will be no problem?' asked D'Orleans. 'Because if there is, you should say so now and we will decamp to the Pacific.'

'There's no problem. It's just going to be a big outlay. And what about my guests? They may never come back.'

'Spend money to make money,' smiled D'Orleans. 'Barnum under this roof should be advertising sufficient to put this place on the map. A moderate outlay now will certainly return itself and more later. There was a fellow in St Louis, had a small but decent enough hotel. Barnum stayed and now he's got the biggest place in town.'

'He's rich as creases,' said Wilkes.

Merriweather smiled uncertainly. 'Let me help you to another glass,' said D'Orleans. 'I think we understand each other. Now we come to those details peculiar to entertaining Mr Barnum's party.'

Merriweather sat stiffly, like a rod in a lightning storm.

'The General will expect special accommodation.'

'The General?' said Merriweather.

'Gen'ral Tom Thumb, o' course,' said Wilkes.

'You'll know that General Thumb is travelling with Barnum?' said D'Orleans.

'I suppose he is,' said Merriweather. 'What of it?'

'It's your beds,' said D'Orleans, 'I measured them at three feet . . .'

'And six inches,' said Wilkes, consulting his notebook.

'From floorboard to quilt,' said Mr D'Orleans. 'They will never do for the General. He will expect a bed of an appropriate size.'

'Well, where can I get one of those? A child's crib?'

'A child's crib? That would be far beneath his dignity, a gross insult to one of his high standing. Remember that the General has been exhibited at the royal courts of London and Paris . . .'

'Then mightn't he use a set of steps?'

'That would hardly do! The General is Mr Barnum's most prized exhibit and personal friend. If all is not acceptable to him, it will be no less so to Mr Barnum himself.'

'Then what shall I do?'

'Get a bed made,' said D'Orleans. 'And while you're about it, have the carpenter fashion a wash-stand and chair. And an escritoire, so he may attend to his correspondence.'

'This is outrageous,' said Merriweather.

'And have any regular-sized furniture removed from his room.'

'Is that everything?' said Merriweather, weakly.

'Yes. Excepting the matter of the Indians,' said D'Orleans.

'Indians?' said Merriweather.

'Just a few Cheyenne, some Apache and a bloodthirsty Kiowa called Yellow Bear who have consented to attach themselves to the circus. They're perfect gentlemen and won't give you any problems. So long as you don't inflame them, of course.'

'How?'

'Well,' said D'Orleans, winking at me, 'Be sure you don't put a Commanche in the same bed as an Apache, for one thing. Although I'm given to understand that a Kiowa with a Commanche might be quite safe.'

Merriweather's eyes were too clouded with the visions of ghostly dollars to see what was afoot but it was now clear to me that Mr D'Orleans or Barnum as we supposed, was having a rare game at Merriweather's expense. He and Wilkes were enjoying it mightily but no one relished the spectacle as much as myself. In fact, now I remembered how D'Orleans had looked when Merriweather had struck me, I fancied that it might even be for my benefit.

My enjoyment was short-lived. Merriweather invited his guests to take a glass of whisky with him in the saloon, no doubt intending to show them off to his other customers. Wilkes bent over the table and whispered in his ear. Merriweather, his head crooked in my direction, seemed to notice my presence for the first time and snapped, 'Don't stand there gawking, Billy. Ain't you got no work to do?'

IV

I had promised my mother that I would visit her later and was surprised and annoyed when I didn't find her in her room waiting for me. She wasn't in the kitchen and didn't answer when I called up the stairs. I asked Mary Ann if Merriweather had sent her upon an errand, but Mary Ann was too busy scrubbing the pile of dirty dishes our new guests had caused to bother answering questions from me.

35

I was about to walk over to the livery stables, where she sometimes went to talk to Old Henry, when I heard Elijah's bell. Wilkes's high-pitched laughter rang from the saloon accompanied by a low and silken chuckle that I guessed must belong to D'Orleans. Everyone was having a bully time and I longed to hear what was going on. But Elijah had summoned me and I must go. I could have taken the back stairs but instead, I fished my book from my coat pocket and hastened into the saloon, heading for the main staircase. Mr D'Orleans arrested my progress. 'And where might you be going in such an all-fired hurry? Won't you sit with us awhile?'

'Sit down, boy, you might learn something of the world,' said Wilkes.

'I have to attend on Mr Putnam,' I said to Merriweather, showing him the book.

Merriweather exploded. 'Putnam be damned!' he said. 'Our guests have requested your presence. You'll stay here.' Elijah's bell rang once more and so used was I to obeying its call that sitting there while it jangled seemed next to unnatural.

But how mightily pleased I was to join the company and hear Wilkes and Mr D'Orleans entertaining the entire saloon with astounding accounts of Mr Barnum's Travelling World's Fair. Mr Barnum was truly an amazing man. He had built himself a palace and called it Iranistan. He took to farming at Iranistan but he didn't use horses, not he. Mr Barnum's ploughs were pulled by elephants! He had built his own city. He had the greatest show on earth – a circus, menagerie and marvellous museum all rolled into one – and when it came here, which it would, as soon as Mr D'Orleans sent word that all was satisfactory, we'd see the miracles wrought by P.T. Barnum for ourselves.

Mr D'Orleans said that he'd taken a liking to me and would escort me personally through the menagerie where I'd see wolves and bears and leopards and tigers. And he would take me to the *kraal*, where we could watch the bareback riders and sharpshooters practising. There'd be dwarves and giants, wire-walkers and acrobats, bear-tamers and lion-slayers. He told Merriweather that it befitted the dignity of the circus to have the best seats occupied by the dignitaries of the town and he would be honoured if the hotel owner would accept the first two complimentary tickets for such seats. Merriweather took the proffered red-coloured tickets while D'Orleans presented a handful of yellow ones to the assembled company. 'Tell your friends,' he told them.

'Don't let 'em miss the day P.T. Barnum came to town!'

While the crowd was taking up their tickets and talking up P.T. Barnum, Mr D'Orleans said to me, 'I have quite taken a shine to you, Billy. You'll help us pave the way for the circus, won't you? I need someone I can count on.'

'Oh, I sure will!' I exclaimed.

'I'm glad. You can show us a place we can erect the tents and pavilions? And put up signs advertising the coming?'

I could, for sure.

'And maybe you could also help us with the tickets. Mr Wilkes?'

Wilkes, who had been exchanging a quiet word with Merriweather, gave D'Orleans his ear.

'I had just been thinking of how matters might be expedited if we were to sell the tickets in advance of the show, as we have sometimes done before. It's really not too troublesome and it would save much time later.'

'Well, I suppose we could . . .'

'Good, then I shall arrange with Mr Merriweather how we may proceed with sales of the tickets on the morrow.'

I basked in the glow of his attention and had it not been for my mother's recalcitrance, I should surely have followed the dream that was born then, of slipping away with this circus and never seeing Merriweather nor the Particular again. Here was I, Billy Talbot, who had never been anything and had never looked like amounting to anything, called to assist the most famous showman on earth. What with all the excitement, the merriment and the two glasses of beer I'd just had, I couldn't help voicing the question that was on the minds of everyone present.

'Are you Mr Barnum?' I asked and there was a perceptible hush.

No one could have been surprised at my question, only at my presumption in asking it. In his velveteen suit and silver watch chain, with his chest thrown out and his head back, he had the poise and the stature we would have expected of a legend. But he only laughed loudly and said, 'Barnum indeed!'

The hotelier laughed with his favoured guest and clapped him on the back. 'Barnum indeed!' he echoed.

I was thinking I never had enjoyed a night at the Particular so much. It was an occasion I should remember for ever, I was sure of that. Our guests seemed to think I was capital company and even Merriweather was casting me approving looks. Mr D'Orleans excused himself – he was tired and would have a long day of it tomorrow. He left Wilkes to tell us of how they had to build great water tanks to hold the rhinoceroses, which they called rhinonosceri, on account of there being so many of them and of how he'd questioned his own wisdom in calling his shooting gallery the 'John Wilkes's Booth'. I was ready to be entertained but Merriweather was looking about for someone to be confidential with and could find only me.

'Now this is more like it,' he said, rubbing his palms.

'Ain't it, though?' I said, glowing with pleasure. 'I did right, didn't I?' I think by then I actually believed I had been instrumental in bringing Barnum to town, when all I had really done was to gallop on ahead, waving an arm and hollering 'Barnum's a-coming, Barnum's a-coming!'

He too left the room shortly after and I gorged myself on tales of far-off lands, of adventures beyond the scope of my imagination and I congratulated myself that such wonderful people would actually stoop to take an interest in my poor self. Maybe the world wasn't what I had taken it for, after all.

Then Merriweather reappeared in advance of something pink and shimmering. But for the drink inside me, I would have been more shocked. Even so, the vision of my mother, the drab, stained and work-worn hermit of the wash-house, transformed by a quality taffeta dress, with her hair washed and combed and piled up upon her head and cheeks modestly rouged and powdered, sent a tremor through my frame. She was suddenly beautiful. I tried to say something to her but either the words never escaped my lips or she didn't hear me.

The rouge on her cheeks seemed of a stronger colour as she stopped by my chair. Wilkes said, 'You'll have to excuse me, Billy,' and got up and took her hand and together they walked down the saloon and I cannot tell you how I felt when she hoisted the hem of her dress and mounted the stairs.

Chapter Three

I

I WAS NOT feeling special bright when I awoke, on account of having discovered a hitherto-unsuspected fondness for whisky. In the period between my mother's ghastly ascension to Wilkes's room and my own unsteady flight to my eyrie in the eves I made my first acquaintance with hard liquor. I tried to rise but encountered a problem. How and when I was overcome by the villain who had trussed me up tightly and who even now was perhaps returning to finish me off, I did not know but tied fast I was.

That I had put up a fight before being overpowered by the gang there could be no doubt. The room was much changed. The chair on which I was used to hang my clothes was upturned, as was the rough bookcase, whose contents lay spread and damaged about the attic floor. The crudely-executed portrait of the man in the bearskin coat, by Elijah's brother, was newly cracked and hanging askew upon the wall.

Then I noticed my left boot, which circumstantially must have been the instrument of the damage; it lay immediately below and it came to me that its brother had escaped at speed through the window, the culmination of a mortal struggle between he and me, over the right to stay in possession of my foot. Satisfied with that, it was the work of a minute to realise that I was bound by no conventional bonds but that I had, in the throes of troubled sleep, only wound myself up in my bedsheets. And could have wound myself tight as a halter as I recalled how my mother had brought humiliation upon my head with the stranger from out of town.

I could remember that much more clearly than I had any wish to. What was more opaque was the interval that followed, in which I believe I had gratefully accepted a glass of whisky from Irving, or Merriweather, or any one of the gentlemen then in high spirits in the Particular's saloon. I had affected to pass off the incident lightly as if it were the custom or that I cared nothing that my mother had behaved as she had. With Wilkes and D'Orleans turned in, Merriweather and myself had become of augmented interest, being the only party present with any extra knowledge of P.T. Barnum and his imminent arrival in our town. Merriweather talked up the circus in a manner I believed might be worthy of Barnum himself and then became intimate with Mr Curry, who had recently been famously successful with a silver-mining speculation.

The faces about my table were still fired up with Barnum fever and plied me with whisky and hung upon my every word as I employed the little I knew to paint a gaudy picture of the amazing entertainment they had in store. I used the strongest colours to depict a scene in which elephants were as common as horses and giraffes left no one's bedroom a place of certain privacy.

Why yes, I said, matter of fact, it was *I* who had persuaded the strangers that this was the perfect place for Barnum. I had charge of many of the necessary arrangements and it was in my power to ensure that the top folk were given the proper seats and maybe introduced personally to Phineas himself. Another whisky? Mighty kind. My mother? Not mine, sir. Mine had been an industrious wife and religious mother, raised on a small holding in the distant Shenandoah Valley, whose husband had been killed upholding the Union cause and who had herself died, cruelly, resisting a fate far worse than death, at the merciless hands of the Confederate army. Had a halter been handy on that next morning, I am sure I would have availed myself of the perfect peace it seemed to offer.

But such is the indefatigable nature of the human spirit that not my mother's iniquity, nor my own admitted weaknesses, were proof against the clarion call of exciting and novel sounds that were wafted through my opened window to assail my ears on that bright summer's day. I had been half-aware of the music and that a band of musicians was blowing their best somewhere just below my window but when I heard the unmistakable sounds of loud acrimony and squabbling not even drowning waves of guilt and inadequacy could suffocate the stirrings of wild curiosity and prevent me from stuffing my blue woollen workshirt in my pants and hopping into my single boot – the twin would be discovered in the horse trough, I was certain – and escaping downstairs to the street.

It mattered not that I had risen late as the gentlemen whose breakfast I should have served had other matters to occupy them than ham and eggs as they clamoured in the lobby, protesting their sudden evictions. I might have had sympathy for Merriweather as he quailed under a barrage of robust abuse had I not known that it was only another quandary born of his own greed. I snuck past these rioters, leaving Merriweather to untangle his own knots and caught a ride on a wagon that was heading for town.

II

There was no question that word of the great event had already spread. We passed trails of people upon the road and were passed ourselves by a number of faster vehicles. At the town limits, we crossed the wide plaza, where teamsters camped and horse auctions were held. This day it was swarming with people. I jumped down and threaded my way through men who were pacing off and pegging out the area

43

of intended encampment and others who had gotten hold of the bunting and flags we used at election times and were stringing them between the grain store, the lightning tree and the liberty pole. Most folk who wandered about the plaza confined themselves to commenting on the operations and speculating upon the likely nature of the extravaganza itself. Overseeing the work was John Wilkes and my mouth dried and my heart missed a beat as he saw me and approached with outstretched hand. I had grasped it before I had thought to refuse.

'I have to talk to you about last night,' I began.

'Billy, I just larned that the lady I entertained is your mother. Well, I was real shocked but I congratulate you upon having such a paragon for your guide in life. She is the very model of modern womanhood and she did me an unspeakable honour.'

He put an arm about my shoulder and said: 'I'm sure you understand. Why, we're men of the world. These things happen, as we know. Life goes on and today life is looking very bright indeed. Can I count on you to help, Billy?'

Looking back, I think I might have acted in a way that would have better preserved the dignities of both my mother and myself. But even had I the necessary resolution, the revolver I had bought solely as an accessory of fashion wasn't over-choosy about its targets and I would most probably have hurt myself.

But it was hard not to be caught up in the excitement; impossible not to acknowledge the curiously friendly folk who had already accosted me with all manner of inquiry and entreaties for tickets. Rather than knocking him down or waving a gun in his direction I soon found myself up a ladder, with Wilkes up another as we tied a hastily-painted banner across a narrowing of the main street.

Then I was posting bills in shop windows, gossiping with traders and customers and relishing the celebrity and status my connection with Barnum had apparently brought me. To be the centre of anybody's attention was a profoundly novel sensation. As I swaggered along Main Street, it seemed that every eye was upon me and every tongue forming my name.

All morning more people arrived. Wilkes had seen to it that the telegrapher was kept busy informing surrounding towns and rail stops that Barnum was here tonight. Already buggies, coaches and wagons were streaming in, horses were tethered all along the streets and long lines of people stood before the makeshift ticket office that Wilkes had arranged outside the Mayor's office.

I watched as D'Orleans took their money and issued his tickets. When his customers had made their purchase they went back to milling about the town, wasting time looking at this and that, walking in and out of the stores and saloons, taking up good vantages on the plaza or just sitting on the sidewalk, shooting competing streams of tobacco juice into the dirt and reading the special issues of the *Bugle* that Amory had spent all night printing as soon as he knew what was afoot.

D'Orleans dealt his red and yellow tickets like cards from a deck but as fast as he could reduce one line, another had grown. From time to time he would stop and mount the table he had made from a couple of planks upon barrels, survey the crowd with concern and announce in a voice that carried to the ends of both lines, 'Mr Barnum appreciates your interest, folks, he surely does, but there is only a limited number of seats available for tonight's show. I must therefore prevail upon you to show forbearance and limit your purchases to six tickets per individual. Six tickets only, PLEASE!'

But that just got the crowd more agitated and more mothers with children attached, more farmers and merchants and drunkards and idlers pushed into the growing lines. When this was at its height, D'Orleans signalled me over to him and implored me to relieve him a while, while he attended to important business. It was maybe two hours before I saw him again, by which time I had significantly reduced the supply of tickets which were bundled in the carpet bag into which I put the takings. I had also had the enormous pleasure of being

45

able to hand four of the coveted red tickets to Cissy Bullock. What would she make of me now, I wondered, as she floated back to her carriage?

It was hot and uncomfortable work, unrelieved by the warm breeze that had got up and gained in strength, flapping the big banner and sending hats skittering about the street and causing wise commentators to remark that Barnum had better have brought strong stakes, if he wanted to keep his tents. There was some local superstition about this zephyr, that it only came when things were on the change or something awful was about to happen to the town. But when I had spoken of this to Elijah, he only snorted his contempt and said that was all a fallacy.

But just as the wind seemed ready to snatch the tickets from my hands and my eyes were red-raw from the grit that had blown in upon them, D'Orleans reappeared. He told the remaining crowd there would be plenty more for everyone the next day and me to get on back to the hotel, where I was wanted by Merriweather.

III

But it was Elijah, and not Merriweather who had been ringing my attendance and it was with some irritation that I mounted the stairs after a fruitless search for the book I had taken with me last night, into the saloon. I passed Merriweather in the lobby but he was busy instructing the carpenter, regarding the special arrangements for accommodating General Thumb.

I had only lately come to regard my daily visits to Elijah as blessed periods of respite from the mundane routines of hotel life and times at which I might exercise faculties that went untested anywhere else in this no-hope place. This afternoon was different and I was loathe to leave the scenes of so much unprecedented excitement and had half a mind to ignore the summons, borrow a horse and gallop back into town. The other half acknowledged that it had been a long morning and

46

that I had worked to exhaustion. Also, the effects of the whisky that so much novelty had distracted me from suffering, were now making themselves known. An hour or two with Elijah might be sufficient for me to recuperate before I returned in time to witness the arrival in town of the Greatest Show on Earth. Elijah recognised the condition I was in the second I began to make my apologies. I fumbled with the glass cover of the oil lamp and somehow caught it just before it hit the floorboards.

'This is too bad,' he said as he gazed vacantly through my presence. 'It's a poor enough show that you don't attend me because of some flimflam men and their circus and that I have sat here the livelong day with nothing to occupy me but my memories. But that you lost your *Great Expectations* whilst in your cups is beyond crediting. Well, Pip and Estella will have to remain at what they are about until we can get another copy.'

He sighed over the manifold follies of youth, mine in particular. His brow furrowed as he cogitated upon something before he leaned towards me, upon his stick and said: 'Billy, there is something I must talk to you about. It's a very important matter and I must be sure that I explain it and you understand it properly. I had thought to lay the matter before you today but it's clear that you're too tired from your gallivanting and addle-headed from whisky.'

And so I had been an instant before but now that Elijah had confirmed my suspicion of the other evening, that something of significance was to be revealed to me, I felt as alive as electricity and burned with curiosity.

'Pardon me, Mr Putnam, but you're mistaken. I never felt better,' I said. 'Please tell me all now.'

But Elijah was adamant. 'Tomorrow will be better,' he said. 'I shall expect you at sundown. We will take a walk. In the meantime and in lieu of our readings, perhaps you will be so good as to take down a little more of my memoir?'

I moved a lamp to a small table and opened the bound ledger in which was written already so much of Elijah's story, the place at which his angular hand was replaced by my own slapdash loops denoting that at which he had owned to himself that he was certainly going blind.

He said, 'Remind me of where we left off last time.'

'You had been in London some three months and had visited with the lawyer, from whom you collected your inheritance. The sum was much smaller than you had expected but Mr Bulstrode had been good enough to help you invest it in the hope of great return. We had just completed a passage in which Mr Bulstrode announced that he had secured an introduction to Mr Chalmondely-Palmer, agent for the Bombay Spice and Silk Company.'

'The Bombay Spice and Silk Company. Yes,' said Elijah and reclined in his deep leather chair and in so doing, sank back some twenty-five years.

I dipped my nib and began to scratch away as quickly as I could, my pen racing hard against Elijah's narrative.

'Bulstrode and I both thought it was a golden opportunity. We had heard of others who had made their fortunes by it. I let Bulstrode invest a small amount and it paid off handsomely. I ventured some more and this too made an excellent return. This continued for such a time that we came to regard the Bombay Spice and Silk Company as a convenient source of revenue. One had only to send in a little bronze for it to return as gold.

'Bulstrode visited me one day, greatly excited. He said the whisper in the city was that Bombay stock was about to soar and that he had mortgaged his home and staked all he had upon it. It was a sure thing and if I followed suit, I would undoubtedly return to America a very rich man indeed.

'I hesitated. I had never been a gambling man and a venture of this magnitude had my heart pounding and head reeling. This was too big for me. I would quit while I was ahead of the game. I told Bulstrode, who shook his head and looked at me as if to say well, that was my funeral. He left, whistling at my rashness.

'Doubt nagged me throughout the night. Supposing he was

vindicated? Would I see Bulstrode in a golden coach on the morrow? If he was right – and respected City capitalists were certain of the Bombay's future – then I would regret it for ever, I knew that.

'That I had acted wisely was poor consolation and when I rose, tired and haggard the next day, I had changed my mind and prayed I could find Bulstrode in time for him to make the necessary arrangements before all the world knew about the Bombay. I found him in his office with another, grandly-dressed gentleman. He betrayed no surprise at my sudden entrance.

' "I'm glad you've dropped by, Putnam," he said, "for this is Mr Chalmondely-Palmer, agent for the Bombay Spice and Silk Company. It's high time you made the acquaintance of the man who has made your fortune."

'I shook his hand and for a second or two I could say nothing, overawed as I was by the fine appearance of this gentleman. His suit, his hat, his rings and his manner all bespoke great wealth. Then I composed myself, said how honoured I was and asked Bulstrode if there was still time for me to fall in with him and invest my all. Mr Chalmondely-Palmer said it was all most irregular and Bulstrode was commiserating with me when the gentleman in the powder-blue suit appeared suddenly possessed of an idea. "Wait," he said, "I think I see how it might be done."

'It is unnecessary to go into the details of how my wealth was converted into stocks and bonds of the Bombay Spice and Silk Company but transformed it was and I shook hands with both gentlemen and almost immediately, I took three of my closest friends to celebrate with dinner at the pleasure gardens. I could tell them nothing and how it must have perplexed them, to see me so gay and so lavish with my entertainment.

'The next day I took my newspaper to my breakfast table and read of a massive fraud involving the Bombay Spice and Silk Company. The scandal was all over the second page but I had barely read the half of it before I had grabbed my hat and was running pell-mell down Chancery Lane to where Bulstrode had his chambers. I took the steps five at a time and burst into his apartments, where I received my second shock of the day. They were empty. Not physically so: the desk, chairs and carpets remained but not so any sign of Bulstrode. His pictures, books and papers, his certificates, plaster bust of Thomas Chatterton, knick-knacks and ornaments were all gone. It was the same scene in the adjoining room.

'I left the door and bounded down to the basement, where the porter had his office. The man said that Bulstrode had paid up to today and vacated early that morning. I took a cab to the Stock Exchange, where my worst fears were confirmed. The Bombay Spice and Silk had crashed and I was newly penniless. How I cursed Bulstrode and the man who called himself Chalmondely-Palmer but how much more and how bitterly I cursed myself.

'I pass over the next two days as they did me no credit. Suffice it is to say that I lay upon my bed much of the time and bemoaned the unfairness of my fate. On the third day, I called on friends I had made during my stay in London but, as did those of the prodigal in the parable, mine had deserted me to a man. They were apologetic but their suggestions, that I find myself a good post somewhere, or go home to America were unhelpful and it was plain that they would rather I took myself and my ill-fortune somewhere else. I found myself alone in a strange city with barely a penny to my name.

'The education that I had thought to complete in London after I had collected my grandfather's bequest was useless to me now. I exhausted the introductions I had made without any success whatsoever. I moved from my comfortable and spacious lodgings off Green Park, to a hellish boarding-house in Seven Dials but my spirit revolted at the noxious conditions and I spent what money I had assigned to accommodation, on two months' rent of a single clean room near the river, in Bermondsey.

'I had precious little money and eked out what food I

allowed myself each day. My palate no longer revolted at thin, fatty soup and stale bread. I sought employment but my expectations were soon spiralling giddily downwards. After seeking positions in government offices, I tried to find reporting work on newspapers and in Doctors' Commons and then applied for a succession of posts as personal tutor and as schoolmaster. Perhaps my foreignness of manner or appearance – for I had pawned my suit and looked now much reduced in circumstances – counted against me. I tried for work as a lowly clerk and then, when calamity loomed and nothing was in prospect, I offered myself as a labourer – to builders and rag merchants before seeking work on the docks amidst which I lived. But still I was without success. I have not the build of a labourer and my hands, that are more used to the feel of a book's leathern cover than a pick's shaft, betrayed my unfitness for the work.

'When I had nothing left for food and only some days' rent of the room, I joined those people who glean a small living from picking over the ash heaps and do other unmentionable work in the fight for existence. I failed in my every endeavour; others more tried and used to these conditions faired better and took what I might have had.

'My poor diet, my hag-ridden mind and the foul places I was obliged to habituate affected my health, which soon deteriorated and I wandered about the docks, devoured by hunger and becoming weaker by the hour. When all hope had departed and I no longer had a roof above my head, fortune came to my aid in the form of a fellow countryman, John Andrews, of New Bedford, Massachusetts.

'To my shame I had been contemplating suicide and intended to offer myself to the embrace of the river and become only another of the frightful things that were daily washed ashore or discovered in the mud at the ebb of the tide. To this end, I had been making my way through bustling places where gangs of men were unloading ships, and great consignments of goods from across the oceans were being hoisted aloft into warehouses, where sailors came and went

51

between chandlers' shops, instrument-makers and pawn-brokers and spilled out from low taverns and brothels. There was nowhere here that suited my fatal purpose and I went on, down a narrow street between high warehouses, towards a quieter part of the waterfront.

'It was here that I fell against John Andrews, or he against me. I was weak and dizzy, he drunk. Whatever the origin of the accident, I collided with his massive bulk and the air was filled with his imprecations and I saw the blade of a knife glint in the waning sunlight. I don't know what I said. I know I asked for no mercy and may well have implored him to do his work swiftly. I expected the deadly blow and no more.

'I next found myself upon the cobbles and for a moment I thought myself cut and that my life blood must be seeping away towards the river. But I felt the fire of brandy in my throat and the face of the sailor was before me. "I'll be damned," he was saying. "A Yankee!"

'He had a good heart, this Andrews and when I told him of my plight, he helped me to a tavern and watched me like a mother as I devoured a plate of lamb cutlets and potatoes. When I was much improved by the meat and the port-wine he made me drink, he bid me tell my story, which I did in full. He said I had been a fool and I said I could hardly argue that point and that my only wish was to return home to America. I might sink or swim there but I would be among my own, which I thought must be an infinitely more hopeful situation. I owned, however, that there was small hope of that.

'Andrews only laughed, a big and booming laugh, that had the sailors and porters and prostitutes turning towards our table. "What a weak specimen of American manhood you are" he said, "to falter at such a low fence." He called to a man at the bar, who was entertaining not one, but two ladies of the London night. "Jack," he called, "I have an educated Yankee here, the very man for you."

'Later I would thank God for my fortune. Then, I only thanked John Andrews, for introducing me to Jack Fairchild, first mate of the passenger steam packet *Britannia*, due to set out from Liverpool for Halifax and Boston the next week and still in pressing need of a steward.'

Elijah paused and I wondered if he had finished for the day or had merely stopped to collect his thoughts. I was dead tired and my handwriting had become a record of my exhaustion. He took a breath and continued his story. There was a journey to Liverpool, a sea voyage and I thought I heard mention of Charles Dickens. But by then I must been dozing because the next thing I knew, Elijah was saying, 'Enough, boy, enough,' and lifting me upon the sofa, where I gave myself up to sleep.

IV

I was fairly blown along the road to town. The wind had gotten up while I slept and from the top of the hill I could see the fun that nature was having with man and his workings below. The big banners we had hung this morning were gone as was the bunting on the plaza. Small objects were chasing around in pockets of chaos and people were running about in the streets, for reasons I couldn't guess at that distance.

Elijah had been incensed that when I awoke I had made feeble excuses and gone quickly, anxious that I was missing the arrival of Barnum's show, but that was no matter; this was too big a deal to miss. There was no sign of any such event having occurred as yet. I crossed an empty plaza and was caught in a sudden blast that funnelled violently into Main Street, sweeping up a huge cloud of dust and straw, chaff and grit, hurling it against the offices of the *Bugle* and into the eyes of anyone who looked the wrong way.

Some part of the crowds of the morning could be seen through the windows of the saloon and in other places of refuge but hardier folk were on the street, appearing and disappearing in clouds of wind-born debris and mouthing words I couldn't hear, because of the dreadful ruckus created by the wind as it whistled through fissures, loosened tin roofs and went searching for anything that wasn't nailed down.

Women found their skirts turned sails and relinquished any choice of direction but the movements of a conspicuous party of men retained some purpose; they were darting this way and that and with bandannas and handkerchiefs covering their faces, they might have been a great gang of outlaws or a band of Confederate renegades, searching for a bank to rob.

One of their number separated from the pack and the dentist, Abe Oliver, was blown over my way. 'Nice weather we got for Barnum,' I hollered to him but he startled me by spinning me about and pinioning my arms behind my back. The cry went up, 'They've got one of them!' and many hands laid hold of me and hustled me along the sidewalk and into a sheltered alley. I was thrown to the ground and a crowd of townsfolk gathered about me, not one of them looking like he bore me any goodwill. I need hardly say that I was bewildered and not a little alarmed at this strange turn of events.

'What's the matter? Whatever's happened?'

'As if he don't know!' snapped Abe. 'Where's our money, you thief?'

Mrs Roop, the druggist's wife was shouting into my face, 'You'll pay, you will. Every penny, you'll pay!'

'Where's our money?' went up again.

Someone at the back said, 'Git a rope.'

'I don't know what's going on,' I cried. 'What are you about?' I must have looked white with fright, because someone else said, 'Let up on him, Abe. Maybe he wasn't in on this.'

'On what?' I cried and Judge Eckert, who had elbowed through the crowd and was now keeping the rougher elements from exacting their own justice on me, said: 'We'll find out the whys and wherefores in a proper place. Now, boy, let's have the truth. Have you been a part of this?'

'I don't know what you mean,' I said, 'I've been with Elijah Putnam all afternoon. What's happened?'

'I'll tell you what's happened, boy. The men you kindly brought to this town don't have nothing to do with P.T. Barnum. They're guinea-droppers and sharpers and they just lit out of here with all the ticket money.'

He must have known I was innocent from the look on my face.

'How do you know?' I stammered. 'Maybe they've gone to meet up with the circus.'

'We just had a wire from Syracuse. They pulled this trick there last month. Those boys are long gone and our money with them.'

What could I say? I had been taken in as they had. We had all believed these nattily-dressed and sweet-talking gentlemen and I was the bigger fool than they. But because I had swelled myself up like the cock of the yard and had talked myself blue about Mr D'Orleans and acted like I had the ear of Barnum himself, I had done half these swindlers' work for them.

Eckert could see that I was only a dupe and most of the faces I recognised were in agreement but many were by no means satisfied and I was shoved and kicked as I retreated before them out of the alley and into the windy street where I began to run, intent upon putting the shame of it all as far behind me as I could. But then someone coming out the hotel spotted me and hollered 'There's Billy Talbot making a run for it!' and the bar emptied and it looked like I had half the town hard upon my heels.

I ran the length of Main Street, making hard progress against the tearing wind and saw that some of my pursuers had already left off the chase and returned to the bar but a gang of young bucks, no doubt hot with whisky, were gaining upon me, calling like hounds on the trail of a runaway slave.

I turned down a side street and leapt a fence and then another, trampling flowers and vegetables, my heart bursting and my breath short. I fled through the open gate of the brewery, vaulted barrels and lost precious moments as I located the gap in its back fence and then found myself on open ground, nothing but the distant hills and a great dark cloud before me. Still I was pursued: dangerous marshlands lay off to the east and from the west came the cries of another pack of hunters and so I ran on, hopelessly, unbelieving that this was happening to me, yet certain that a dreadful fate would overtake me at any moment.

'We got him,' someone shouted and finding myself on a road once more, I stumbled on, slowed by the wind that shot through my shirt and found ways through my ribs, and bowed my head down against the buckshot of wind-blown dust. I forced my way against the gale, my steps becoming leaden with fatigue and I knew that the end was near. I could go on no longer.

And then I was aware of being a part of a rampant confusion of noise and thought that my exertions had brought me to the edge of madness and that I had begun to hallucinate, for amongst the apocalyptic din of the wind I thought I heard music.

I looked up and shading my brow, perceived that I was in the midst of a massive cloud of wind-driven garbage. The weird sounds were still audible but I could hear nothing of the men behind. I stopped and sank to my knees, finished.

Out of the darkest part of the storm, vague and shadowy forms materialised and took shape and I doubted my raw and streaming eyes, which now beheld the strangest, the most extraordinary of sights. A great giant of a man, taller by far than anyone I had seen before, mounted upon a camel and at his side a tiny midget, upon an animal whose like I had not seen but which evidently recognised my kind, for it spat at me as it passed.

Chapter Four

I SHOULD BE at other work than this. In the lobby beyond my office door are probably a whole roomful of people, half of whom will be awaiting my pleasure only so they may press more money upon me. They would have me sponsor this or endorse that, or simply do nothing so that they may further their own schemes. I pray that my loyal secretary and guardian of my secrets, Miss Tummel, will protect me from such distractions a little while longer.

But even she can impede my progress. She has reminded me that there is a speech I am to prepare and must give to the greatest of our great land. Its acceptance will inevitably result in the filling of the coffers of my associates and of my own purse too. However, compared with the tonguey rhetoric which was once my stock-in-trade and which might have earned me fifty or a couple of hundred dollars, or a few months in jail, it will be a poor affair. You who have the priceless leisure to read books for your own diversion may take me for a robber at least but if I commit robberies now, they are done in your name.

While we talk of robberies, I have one for you now. Readers of popular fiction may consider this a paltry affair: the theft

57

has already been committed and there has been no fancy-play with six-guns. I'm sorry for that – if you prefer something more racy, you must open a dime novel or a daily newspaper.

A discovery was made while I lay asleep in Elijah's room. D'Orleans had closed up the ticket office pretty sharpish; no one knew why. Then a couple of rounders had galloped through town, hollering about Barnum's caravan coming up the road from the east. Soon after, riders and folk in buggies and on foot were streaming out of town to meet him, no matter that a wild wind was all but blowing them back into town. The rest of the populace found shelter and waited for the zephyr to blow itself out. Sometime during this, D'Orleans and Wilkes took themselves and the money out of town, most likely on stolen horses.

And P.T. Barnum did come to Hayes, Missouri, though I doubt it's well-documented. The whole procession of gaily-painted covered wagons, teams of thoroughbred horses, great swaying stages packed with men and women inside and on top; freaks of nature on horseback and astride camels, Indians in the boots of coaches, huge carts piled high with cages of outlandish animals and ropes and tackle, canvas and abundance of mysterious contrivance, came quickly upon us and as quickly passed right on through.

We watched them rush headlong past, drivers whipping on the beasts with cries of 'Hi-yi!' and 'G'lang!' through crowds who had turned out to see Barnum arrive and you can imagine the kind of feelings that were abroad when it was realised that not only had the townspeople been swindled of their money but P.T. Barnum wasn't even going to stop in Hayes anyway. The Barnum circus, looking neither tuckered nor travel-stained, as the efficient machine had unloaded from hired freight cars just down the line, shoved for the next town, where they mounted a memorable show and those who could still afford to follow him and see it, said it was wondrous to behold.

I don't know that Barnum already had intelligence of something amiss in our town but he sure seemed in an uncommon hurry to put some dirt between him and Hayes. At least, that was the verdict of the informal inquiry held in the lobby of the Particular Hotel, the next morning. A deputation of citizens had arrived, headed by Judge Eckert and Sheriff McCulloch.

'Maybe we was swindled by Barnum,' someone said. 'And it was all like we thought. The smooth-talking feller was Barnum himself.'

'Don't be so foolish,' said McCulloch, 'Barnum ain't the man to do nothing of that sort. Fact of the matter is, he never planned to stop in Hayes and was only makin' for the next place. We was a passel o' fools to get taken in like we did, but it wan't Barnum's fault.'

'They must have been considerable smart fellers to get the drop on us,' said Old Henry.

'Smart?' said a deputy. 'I'll say they were. Why, those two boys were probably the slickest, sharpest operators as ever palmed a silver dollar. Didn't you hear they did the exact same as this in Syracuse? And they're double-smart people, in Syracuse.'

Others nodded and murmured their agreement, consoled in part, that they had been some taken in by the best. As we had appeared closely connected with the swindlers, Merriweather and I were keenly questioned. I told my story a number of times, repeating and enlarging on details I had given before and was believed in the end, in a grudging sort of a way, but not before I had been accused, sniped at and generally made to feel like the biggest fool in a ship of the same. That I might have easily borne for I felt as much myself but what had unnerved me during the ordeal was the entrance of Mrs Bullock and her daughter, Cissy, who swept past me and took seats at the back of the crowd. When I had been interrogated, derided and sent about my work, the crowd listened to Merriweather as he protested his innocence and neatly attached any remaining blame and suspicion to my coat-tails.

I hung about the doorway, waiting for the crowd to

disperse, that I might exchange a word with Cissy: her mother was a placid woman, generally amiable and not as decided in her opinions of me as was her husband. I had every hope of being able to wish her and Cissy a good day, a brief exchange which would have cheered me immensely and gone a long way towards compensating for the blight I had felt that morning.

They were last to leave the lobby and I followed them down the steps to their buggy. I walked over to the fly and opened the door and let down the step, intending to hand in first Dame Bullock and then Cissy herself. I longed for the soft touch of her hand in mine. But first I offered Mrs Bullock my hand and she astounded me by brushing it away with her parasol, snapping, 'Unhand me, you ruffian,' before boarding under her own steam. I looked to Cissy but she only glowered and avoided my gaze. When I asked what was up, she said, 'You leave us be. Poppa was right. I was blind. You're nothing but a low-down swamp-rat and I don't want nothing to do with you, ever again!'

'But, Cissy,' I said, quite thunderstruck. 'I just told the inquiry, I had nothing to do with the swindle. I'll pay you back your money myself.'

'I ain't talking about the swindle,' Cissy said. 'I was referring to the shame your family brings to this town. I heard,' she said, with a look of sour repugnance, 'all about your mother, Billy.'

She cracked her whip and the buggy moved off, leaving me such a sorry individual that had I been a horse, or a dog, I would most likely have been shot.

II

Merriweather was looking for me but I couldn't face his certain wrath. He had been made to look a bigger fool than he was and would be seeking to vent his ire upon me. In other circumstances, I might have gone to my mother but now that was out of the question: because of her, my Cissy had spurned me. I climbed the old tree I had spent whole days in as a kid and mused upon my relation, whom I occasionally glimpsed through a veil of yellow leaves as she took linen to and from the wash-house.

The memory of the night she had wafted past me in a fantasy of taffeta and scent made me nauseous. But it also set me thinking. I had seen my mother dressed up before but never so perfectly as that night. I had an imperfect memory that Merriweather had once bought her dresses and that at some time in the distant past there had been something between them and only now understood that he must have used her and discarded her. At the time, I only saw the dresses and noticed that for a while she didn't live in the lean-to behind the wash-house. Then I brought to mind other occasions when she had dressed fine but I didn't recall them well as these were nights on which I had generally been sent early to bed.

I was sickened by an abrupt realisation. Parts of a puzzle I should have completed years ago fell into place. Bullock's estimation of the Particular and of its inmates suddenly made sense. I had taken the bad name of the hotel to have some reference to its boorish and drunken owner and perhaps to the edifice itself, which had once been quite grand but was now broken-roofed and in need of a multitude of repairs. In truth, the establishment was a sham: a worn-out suit with brand-new pockets and everyone knew it.

Now I perceived that we took in any ragtag and bobtail at cut rates; that Irving was whispered to be wanted in Wyoming; that mystery surrounded the blind schoolteacher Putnam. Our poor name might have been born out of any of these facts. But that the reason some folk drove out of Hayes to stay in the Particular at the failed hamlet of Rodericksburg was because of the particular services that Merriweather could arrange, at a price, might never have occurred to me had not a snub from Cissy Bullock awoken my slumbering senses. I thought at first that I must have been blind, or he too discreet, for me not to have seen what was going on. But I

61

searched my mind, and later the diaries I had kept as a child, connecting dates, impressions and memories and arrived at a conclusion that was as inevitable as it was terrifying. Unless there was something I had overlooked, it was awfully clear that my mother had been not only the gewgaw of Merriweather but had most likely been pimped by him to a succession of our honoured guests.

I thought of Cissy and how she now appeared as impossibly remote. Did she know what I knew now? That seemed impossible. Her father would slander my name yet never tell her that. But recent events were being talked up all over town and the customers who had been in the saloon that night had not omitted to include in their accounts of the evening, that Mrs Talbot had finished the night with the Wilkes man. If Cissy didn't know the extent of what was going on now, it couldn't be long before some gossip poured it into her ear like so much mercury.

III

In the afternoon, I knocked upon Elijah's door. I had nowhere else to go and longed for the blanket of routine.

'You're early,' he remarked.

He said that Mr Merriweather had lately been with him and had acquainted him with the fact that my name was presently not good currency. 'He said it smelt to high heaven, in fact,' said Elijah. 'Well, never mind that now; we shall work on my memoir and when it is dark we will take a walk. It will be safer to talk without these walls. I have that to relate to you that will make you think differently of yourself and perhaps you will then not give a hang about the opinion of these small-town prattlers.'

Though electrified with curiosity, I knew it was no good pushing him and resigned myself to the ledger and pen. Elijah settled himself in a rocking-chair and took up his story.

'I had embarked upon the ocean crossing, had I not?' he asked.

'Not so far as that,' I said, for I had dozed through the last part of the narrative and this had gone unrecorded in the ledger.

'We won't mind the details. It's sufficient to say that I got myself to Liverpool in time to join the steamer *Britannia*, bound for Halifax and Boston.'

His pale blue eyes fixed me with their sightless gaze.

'I was barely aboard before I had been told that among the eighty-six passengers I would be attending were Mr and Mrs Charles Dickens. What do you think of that, then?'

'Dickens? You met him?' I asked, astounded that the man whose life and works had formed such a disproportionately large part of our studies, might be personally known to my tutor himself.

'Not so fast,' said Elijah. 'All in good time.'

'I'm listening,' I said.

'Don't just listen, boy, take it down. Now, I would hardly have taken my fellow stewards for bookish men but both they and the crew were much exercised by this news. Such was, and remains, the celebrity of Charles Dickens. I was surprised that not a few knew him from his works themselves but many more knew him as the popular figure. They had seen his name time and again in newspapers and the likenesses of him and his creations decorating all kinds of products and advertising. Why, if you had asked them whom they considered the most famous man on earth, I guess that some might have answered President Tyler and others Queen Victoria but I would place a hefty wager that many more would have promptly replied, "Charles Dickens."

'So you may imagine there was not a little competition among we stewards for the honour of attending on the great man and we were sorely disappointed when he elected to ensconce himself in the ladies' saloon where he would be served by a Scottish stewardess.

'I caught sight of him the first night out. He was taking the air on deck before turning in. Against the weather, he was wearing a great pea-coat and a pair of cork-soled boots. At about thirty years of age, he was not much older than myself but what a gulf separated us! There was Boz, sipping his brandy, long hair blowing in the sea breeze, apparently without a care in the world, cutting through black waters towards a country that already loved him as its own fortunate son. And there was I, risking the fury of the chief steward by standing out upon the companionway, the better to catch a glimpse of the man who had come from nothing and made himself what he was, with no better weapon than the tip of his nib.

'I longed to drop down the ladder and strike up a conversation with the immortal who had given life to Pickwick and Sam Weller, Fagin and Sykes, Squeers and Quilp. For unlike my colleagues and, I suspected, most of the passengers, I had read these books and his sketches of London life attentively and had long been fascinated by their author. But he finished his drink and ducked back inside before I had summoned the resolution to ask if he would like a second and that was the last I saw of him for perhaps five days.

'When my labours were over, I lay upon my bunk, my mind churning with possibilities. This Dickens was not only the talk and toast of London. In America too, his admirers were multitudinous and eagerly awaited the arrival of each new part of his latest work. These no sooner arrived than they were hurried to booksellers and to newspapers and printers and copied until there were sufficient to satisfy even the furthest flung territories. We loved him as one of our own. His democratic concern for every stratum of society, his advocacy of reform and stout refusal to pander to a single class of reader had us adjudge him an American in everything but birth.

'And here he was, sleeping peacefully, perhaps only a few feet above my head. I was excited by his proximity and yet recognised that I had no better chance of conversing properly with him than had one of the stokers. This seemed terribly unfair: because of my close study of his books I felt that some strange bond existed between us that he would acknowledge warmly were I only to broach the subject.

'I might mention here that I had not only read everything

he had produced, but, coveting his colossal success almost as much as I admired his genius, had already begun something of my own, in emulation. I had perhaps four chapters written, with which I was immoderately pleased. They were about me now and I became consumed with the notion of encountering Dickens and showing him the leaves and giving him the satisfaction of knowing that it was he that had stirred my dormant talent. But the next day saw a livelier sea and anyone without his full complement of sea legs betook himself to his bed and stayed there, Mr and Mrs Charles Dickens among them.

'My own crossing to England had been a smooth one and the experience had persuaded me that constitutionally, I was a good sailor. This delusion sustained me for the first days of the return voyage and I was irked that I had never a sighting of his inimitable person. I expected to see him scribbling at a saloon table, at any moment. Conditions worsened on the third day and no one had any thoughts of anything but their own well-being while we were tossed from one giant wave to the next, for the idle amusement of the elements.

'The passengers kept to their cabins but we attendants worked on, our nausea made subservient to the terrifying temper of the chief steward, though few of our charges welcomed our attentions, preferring to keep to their cabins and survive on diets of brandy and water and hard biscuit. And yet there was sufficient opportunity for accident and catastrophe. A steward blinded a passenger with spilt lobster sauce and, descending a companionway, another, delivering to table a huge round of red beef (optimistically, in my opinion), fell hard and broke his foot. Following behind, I received a deep cut to my eye.

'Inanimate objects achieved lives of their own in this floating revolution. Cups and saucers performed acrobatics. Crockery smashed with almost rhythmic regularity. Objects on one table were found a moment later on the next. A gross of porter bottles broke free and could be heard rolling about the deck like drunken revellers, needlessly providing another

65

hazard for those foolhardy enough to attempt a promenade from stem to stern. Seeming to sense that normal bounds of propriety had been cast asunder or might be suspended without impropriety for the duration of this hellish crossing, humankind behaved with as much irregularity as anything else aboard this crazy vessel. Of the passengers, one perceived that his worldly wealth would be useless to him in the next and proceeded to lose everything at *vingt-et-un*. A supposedly poor clerk was of a similar opinion and kept us busy fetching bottles of champagne. Among the crew, the cook salvaged some sea-damaged whisky and was discovered drunk by the captain who ordered him hosed sober and sent upon the next four watches without his coat. Worse for me was that the pastry chef succumbed entirely and I, though protesting I was no better than he, was ordered by the captain to take his place in a tiny cabin on deck. Propped between two barrels I was made to roll out dough and prepare sweet fancies, the sight of every one of which magnified my anguish and caused my stomach to revolt in paroxysms of agony. As a result I cared not a jot then that I was unable to see Dickens who had found his feet and was reported entertaining fellow passengers with a borrowed accordion.

'But worse was in store. On the tenth day out from Liverpool, we were caught in a terrific storm that threatened to blow down the smoke-stack and offer us a fiery alternative to the watery end we expected at any minute. When it subsided sufficiently to make a walk along deck less than a method of certain suicide, we found that a lifeboat had been smashed to fragments and that the wooden paddle-housings were likewise destroyed, so that now water was scooped up and thrown on the decks, or over anyone condemned by duty to brave the elements.

'At last, when calm returned and I could face my cakes with an equanimity unimaginable the day before, my thoughts turned again to our illustrious passenger and I pondered the problem of how I might meet with Dickens. The initial excitement passed, it came to me that encountering him now might actually harm my cause. How seriously could he take the babblings of a steward about some unlikely book? I was cast low for a full day but was then inspired by what appeared as a brilliant idea: once arrived in America, this hero of the people would surely be in need of an aide, a secretary perhaps, for the duration of his stay. It was impossible that he should deal personally with the deluge of correspondence that would inevitably follow in the wake of such an august event. I decided upon approaching him on land, in the guise of a free citizen of the United States.

'The difficulty would lie in securing an introduction to the great man. I turned over innumerable schemes that I thought might achieve this end but rejected them all and was in low spirits during our brief stop at Halifax. My optimism was fully restored when we finally berthed at the busy port of Boston. No sooner had the painter been tossed upon the quay and the planks let down than the ship was boarded by piratical members of the Eastern press, some local dignitaries and by a certain luminary whose face I was startled to recognise. This was the artist, Francis Alexander, in whose employ my brother George now was and whom I had espied as he left his house, the morning I had paid a visit to his pupil, before taking ship for England.

'The commotion on the forward deck was immense. Reporters were swarming like so many bees, the crew were tying off gangplanks and crowds on the quay were cheering anyone who made use of them. In this confusion, I was able to approach quite close to the bearskin-coated young writer and hear him receive Alexander's introductions and note that Dickens had agreed to sit for his portrait during his stay in Boston.

'I hugged myself in joy. To further my design now, I had only to make my way to Alexander's studio and confide my plans to George and then to take up my position as secretary to Charles Dickens. And then, when Dickens realised what a protégé he had, what a world might be mine!'

'And did it work out?' I asked, forgetting my role as

secretary yet knowing something of Elijah's more recent history I felt I could answer this myself.

Before he could form his answer, I heard a commotion upon the stairs and then the door flew open and Merriweather burst in, with Silas Amory on his heels.

'Is that you, Merriweather?' said Elijah, angered by the unprecedented interruption. 'You had better have good reason for this.'

'Damn right I have, you old fool,' Merriweather cried. 'We've been robbed. Somebody cleared out the safe!'

I looked at Merriweather, his face crimson with emotion, his small black eyes fixed on me like the sights of twin rifles. Amory regarded us both, coolly and dispassionately and then Merriweather too, with equal impartiality.

'Does something go forth here, is something afoot, gentlemen?' he breathed, with the sibilance of snakes. Elijah rocked in his chair and continued to stare at a vacancy somewhere between us all.

Chapter Five

I

ELIJAH BROKE A moment's silence.

'So you have been robbed of a few days' takings. What of it? I don't suppose it amounted to much,' he said.

'I'm smashed, you fool,' said Merriweather. 'And by heaven if you had anything to do with this, I'll break you too.'

'Keep a tongue, Merriweather. Everyone gets robbed sooner or later, one way or another.'

I had seen Merriweather out of sorts before, enraged and in a drunken fury more often than I would ever want to remember but this was something different. He was frightened, abstracted, his eyes publishing the turmoil of his mind as he circled Elijah's chair like a coyote about a big fire. Elijah followed the sound of his boot heels and said: 'How can you be smashed?'

'I ain't about to explain my business,' Merriweather snapped, fixing us both with his squinty gaze. 'You tell me what you know now 'fore the trail goes cold.'

'You're being foolish, Merriweather. What can a blind man know about any of this?'

'Must have happened late afternoon, yesterday,' said Merriweather, turning to Putnam, ' 'bout the time you and the boy were supposedly closeted here, together.'

'We heard nothing,' said Elijah.

'Of course you heard nothing,' said Merriweather. 'The safe was opened with a key. Now, how in tarnation could they have got a key? 'Less someone here gave 'em one.'

'They? Your recent esteemed guests, I suppose?'

'Them two cheating, lying, fraudsters, yes. And somebody gave 'em a key!'

'There is only one key,' I said in answer to Merriweather's menacing glance. 'An' you got that.'

'Someone knew where to find it,' he said. 'Now who d'you suppose that was? Maybe someone who had been tight with those two all the time they was here. I'm telling you, boy, if I find you had any part in this, I'll kill you myself.'

'What are you about?' said Elijah. 'I won't have the boy threatened. All this over a few dollars.'

'Don't you listen?' roared Merriweather. 'Didn't you just hear me say I was smashed?'

'How can you be ruined?' said Elijah. 'You had better explain.'

But Elijah was answered by Amory, who had folded his lean frame upon the arm of a chair and had remained there, smoking a cigar and observing all.

'There was more in the safe than money,' said Amory.

'I don't want my business broadcast about town, Silas,' said Merriweather.

'Our business, Merriweather. You recall that I was staked in this affair too,' said Amory. 'The stock and deeds were in your keeping.'

'What deeds?' asked Elijah.

'You know nothing of this?'

'Of course not. Get on with it.'

'A couple of days ago, we decided to go ahead with a deal we had been negotiating with Mr Curry, the silver speculator. We bought sixteen thousand feet of the Blue Beyond Mine in Washoe Territory and the deeds to Little Irma, a mine with very good prospects. Both speculations are part of the

70

Humboldt, of which I guess you must have heard something.'

Of course we had. Humboldt county was the richest in all Nevada.

'The Blue Beyond is a sure-fire thing and anyone in mining circles knows they'll hit pay-dirt any day now. Curry was stopping over on his way to New York to see his partners about floating another mine on the Stock Exchange. Meeting Curry seemed like a lucky break.'

'Sure was,' said Merriweather. 'At first I couldn't make any headway with Curry and he wouldn't let me have anything. But I talked him round and we got what we wanted. But that stock and those deeds were stolen from the safe. If I don't get them back and soon, I'm ruined.'

'How so?' asked Elijah.

'Because I put up the hotel. It was the only way. That stock'll value at ten times this hotel any day now.'

'And you,' Elijah asked Amory. 'Have you lost the *Bugle*?'

'I wasn't in so deep,' said Amory. 'But there was shareholders' money involved.'

He turned to Merriweather who had seated himself on the end of the sofa and was holding his head in his hands. 'As your friend, I commiserate with you but as a businessman, I must hold you responsible. The shareholders will expect redress, Merriweather, and in full.'

'What am I to do?'

'Go to the Sheriff,' I suggested.

'Haw! When I'm in need of a fat carcass to hold down my cushions and drink my whisky I'll send for McCulloch. Not before.' He eyed me again. 'Don't you know nothing about this? At all?'

'Billy was with me,' said Elijah. 'It ain't in his nature to do a thing like that.'

'It's in anybody's nature, you cuss'd fool,' said Merriweather.

Elijah rounded upon him. 'Don't speak to me like that! I've had sufficient of your accusations and insults. Get out, Merriweather. It'll do you no good to land on the wrong side of me.'

71

'Not today, Putnam. I've jumped through enough hoops for you. I've paid you well for your discretion, I reckon, and who knows but what I'll realise, soon as I recover what's gone from the safe, may be worth a whole lot more than anything I might expect from you.'

'You have expectations of me?' said Elijah, with mock astonishment. 'I'm astonished. What expectations are they? I never led you to expect anything from me.'

'You're lying!' exploded Merriweather. 'What of your *great investment*? Wasn't it only last week you said you expected it to pay off very soon?'

'Well, so it may, so it may,' said Elijah, mysteriously.

'And didn't you as good as say it'd be mine, if anything were to happen to you?'

'I may have voiced my concern apropos its fate after my death.'

'And I said I was the man. After all I've put up with, you owe it to me. Look at the years I've kept Billy and his mamma. Now you tell me you're dying, Elijah, you ain't thinking of cheating on me, are you? I've a right to know what you arranged with that lawyer.'

'The hell you two crooks talking about?' said Amory.

'This is a private matter which should not have been touched on here,' said Elijah. 'We will pursue it at another time.'

'First thing is to catch them two fellers,' said Merriweather, realising his indiscretion.

'We'll have to do that ourselves,' said Amory. 'I agree that the law is unlikely to serve us here and besides, the fewer who know about the Blue Beyond the better. It's also possible they've lit out for places West where there *is* no law.'

'How about wiring Pinkerton's?' I suggested.

'Costs money we just lost. 'Sides, I'm in no mood to sit on my hands waiting for news from some paid-by-the-day agent who mightn't appreciate the urgency of our predicament. No,' he said, as he stood and picked up his gloves, 'I'm going to track these boys down myself.'

'Well, I'm glad something is decided,' said Elijah. 'Billy, show our guests to the door. We have work to do.'

'Robbed! In daylight, from my own parlour!' exclaimed Merriweather as he left the room.

'The world's coming to something, ain't it?' said Amory coolly, winking at me as he lit a cigar and followed the hotelier down the stairs.

When the sun had gone down I led Elijah out of the hotel by the back door. He was keen that we should slip out unnoticed. He waited until we had passed the outlying houses of Rodericksburg and were upon a track that wandered through tangly copses and around fields planted with corn and cotton. Although the sky was peppered with stars, once among trees I could barely discern the way. Elijah was more certain of his footing and walked with purpose, swinging his stick and sucking in the night air. The illness he complained of indoors seemed palliated, even vanquished and with darkness making us all but equals in senses, I wondered if Elijah were not the haler of we two.

I strongly suspected that some large part of Elijah's illness could be ascribed to the impotence he felt at being deprived of his sight and that only pride and fear kept him a prisoner of his own apartments. I reckoned that the feebleness, fussiness and ill-temper that made him appear so much older than he was were all attributable to the sightless condition against which he raged. I remembered the active man, striding down the aisles between our school desks loudly declaiming from Shakespeare while swiping with his stick at miscreants. It was a pitiful sight to see him now consumed by fear and frustration, hating himself for his own inadequacies and apprehensive of his new vulnerable relation towards others.

'Will Merriweather lose the hotel?' I asked.

'It's of little consequence to me whether he keeps it, loses it or sends it to perdition. My purpose there is almost finished.

73

I can end my days in one bed as well as another.'

'What purpose?' I asked.

'Are we alone, Billy?' he said and we stopped. I looked and we listened.

'Who else would be out here at this time?' I said.

But he listened a moment longer before he was satisfied.

'Then it is time I spoke to you as I have promised,' he said and we walked on. 'If you are to understand my purpose, you must understand also something of me. You know a little of my history already, having become of sad necessity my amanuensis. No doubt you have wondered why I have always forbidden you to read more of my memoir than you have written up?'

I agreed. My curiosity about Elijah's early record was burning but he never permitted me time alone with his ledger, that I might gratify it.

'Had I allowed you to do so, you should have learned prematurely what I shall reveal to you now and that would never have done. Everything depends upon you being ready.'

'Ready for what?' I asked and Elijah lashed out with his stick, missing my head by inches.

'If I am to be interrupted every minute I shall never finish,' he said. 'Your infernal curiosity will be the death of you!'

He composed himself and took up his story once more.

'I have told you something of my childhood and of how my brother George and I were raised in anticipation of great wealth. My great-uncle in England had allowed us to believe that he was immensely rich and that, *post mortem*, his assets would pass to his only surviving family. In a word, us. He had gone off to England as a young man and his letters always crowed of new and great successes in various endeavours. If you believed him and we did, he was the toast of London, a brilliant success and the possessor of a great fortune.

'Because of this, my father never applied himself to the family paint business which began to fail and was on its last legs when I left for England. My mother spent an inordinate amount of time ordering the dresses she would wear when

74

the time came and perfecting her social graces. Both borrowed considerable amounts of money against their future expectations. I took my lead from them, leaving off studies that seemed pointless in view of the life I would have later and gave myself up to idleness, spending my days reading novels, bettering my mind and acquiring the skills of a dilettante.

'My brother George dabbled too, mostly with paint. But he had never been as impressed by our imminent wealth and was interested only in painting pictures which seemed to me gaudy and crude but in which others detected signs of a growing talent. While I flitted from one interest to another, he applied himself to his brushes and his canvas. I was surprised when he cast about for a position and more so when he was taken on as apprentice to Francis Alexander, a portrait painter of no inconsiderable reputation at the time.

'It was of little consequence to me that he chose this course. The news from England was that our great-uncle lay upon his deathbed and might have expired by the time we had gotten the letter. Then a message arrived from our attorney in London informing us that our relation had indeed died. Mr Bulstrode offered to wind up his affairs in London for us. My father said it would be best if one of us sailed to England and made sure everything was done right and that we weren't cheated by no thieving lawyer.

'My father was unwilling to travel himself and suggested that George or I went in his stead. I had long been captivated by the idea of London, a fascination borne in part of my readings of novels and I implored him to let me go. George, who had only lately begun his pupillage under Alexander, readily agreed.

'When I arrived in London I discovered that our great-uncle had also been a great liar and had hugely exaggerated his wealth. If I was disappointed, I knew how much harder my parents would take the news. I took charge of what there was but wasted some part of it debauching myself in a city only too well-equipped for that purpose. The money began to dwindle but Bulstrode stepped in, with offers of doubling and trebling what was left in the Bombay Spice and Silk Company.

'You know the rest. Of how I was bilked of the money and condemned to immediate poverty and returned to America not as a glittering passenger but as a lowly steward.

'Buoyed up by a single, great idea, I invested that voyage with every grain of hope I had left in my soul.

'Arriving finally in New York, I had a small mishap as I disembarked the ship. In the excitement of the moment, when reporters and crew and visitors and hordes of the simply curious were pushing about the deck to get a sight of Dickens, I slipped from the gangplank and into the water, betwixt ship and quay. Such was my relief at returning safely to the land of my birth, I was unshaken by the accident and even felt I was being washed clean of Europe and all the ill luck that had dogged me while I was there.'

III

We had left the trees and were mounting a hill on which were dark amorphous shapes that might equally be bushes or cattle, so weak was the light. 'There is no one about here?' asked Elijah.

'Of course not,' I said.

'Then let us sit,' he said and we made ourselves comfortable upon the grass. 'I remember this view,' said Elijah. 'Can you see Rodericksburg?'

I could: only two or three lights were showing there.

'And Hayes?'

Hayes was a bright speckle in the distance.

'And beyond, the Mississippi?'

I followed his pointing finger and discerned a faint broad streak of silver-grey. We had walked that route before but I had never noticed that the river could be seen from that vantage. It took a blind man to show me that. 'You shall be upon that river soon,' Elijah told me but he hushed my inquiry and continued his story.

'George was overjoyed to see me, though saddened for my

parents' sake to hear of the loss of our fortune. I assured him that this was but a temporary state of affairs; that I had plans afoot with which to make something of myself. George found me a palliasse at his humble apartment and I began by informing him that Dickens would sit for Alexander shortly. I said that I would have him ask Alexander, whom George said liked him well enough, to propose his brother as aide, whilst Dickens was in America.

' "But where will that get you?" George had asked. "What will be the good of it? You can be a secretary to a man of business and earn more, I'll be bound."

' "George, you are a painter and will have Alexander as your patron. I am a writer and would have Charles Dickens as mine. Imagine the start that will give me in the world of letters."

' "You? A writer?" George had said, but I forgave him, as he had rarely seen me about my work and much of my novel had been completed whilst I sailed towards England. He appeared doubtful but in the end he agreed to ask Alexander if he would make the proposition to Dickens.

'I found employment as schoolteacher and after teaching all day, worked hard upon my novel at night. I moved my few possessions into a cool and clean room close to the school house. In this way, time passed and I let a week slip by without calling upon George, so taken was I with the novelty of my new job and the progress I was making with my story. Another week went by, during which I sent George a message, asking him to visit me but when he failed to appear, I called and asked for him at Alexander's studio. There I received a jolt. I was told that Mr Putnam was not presently at the studio as he was travelling with Mr Charles Dickens, the writer, as his personal secretary.

'I returned to my room, raging at George's perfidy. I didn't know then that Alexander had misunderstood George's suggestion and George had been dismayed for me, to hear that his services had been offered and accepted by Dickens. I thought there was nothing to be done and I went back to my teaching and wrote a little more of my story. But the notion of meeting with Dickens would not leave me alone. It became an obsession. I was certain that some strange bond existed between us. And I might tell you that even now, that this impression remains with me.

'I procrastinated, but in the end I decided to follow Dickens and speak to him directly. A month later saw me up the Mississippi, chasing sightings of Charles Dickens. He was seen here, had stayed there or set off from that place to see the prairie. I was here in Hayes when I received firm news that Dickens was heading for Canada and would shortly return to England. I had missed my chance.

'What to do? I couldn't bear the thought of returning home with the news that I had gambled and lost our inheritance, reduced though it had been. I doubted my father would forgive me, such was the reputation he had built for himself upon its back.

'I had not the fare to return to Boston but took a job tending bar at Merriweather's Particular Hotel. I saw small reason to move on. I had food and shelter and there were hours in which I could attend to the business of novel-writing, should I so desire. It was known that I had taught school at Boston and, on the death of the ancient spinster who had educated the Hayes young, I was offered the post of school-teacher.

'An incident that occurred shortly after I took up the position has some bearing on this story. I had returned to the hotel one afternoon to collect the final day's pay that was owing to me. I found the saloon empty and thought I heard noises from Merriweather's parlour. I walked straight in and was confronted with a scene that haunts me still. It is too grotesque to contemplate and I cannot bring myself to describe it. But I can tell you that it involved that man and one of my young students. I was aghast, appalled and fled the hotel, regardless of the plight of the boy.

'Merriweather came to me soon after, begging for my silence. The boy was son to a prominent Hayes family who

78

would surely have had his blood if ever this frightful matter came to light. I had scorned Merriweather from the first moment; had found him bigoted, intolerant, avaricious and drunken and he had made my life a hell. You, of all people, will understand. But now I had him at my mercy. He implored me to accept a certain monthly sum. I suggested a larger one to which he agreed and with an augmented income I was able to marry the widow of the bookseller and live uncommonly well, for a schoolteacher.

'I had been in Hayes nearly a year, when I received a letter from my brother George. I had written to him, angrily demanding that he explain his recent behaviour. He had replied and apologised profusely and begged me to understand that the matter had been decided by Alexander and it was not his place to question his patron. Tactfully, he omitted to retail to me his experiences with Dickens. He spoke of visiting our parents, to whom he had broken the news of our misfortune, which had come as a terrible blow to them. George had done his best to make light my part in this mischance but the facts weighed heavily against me. It was clear that no merciful welcome awaited this prodigal.

'Then George asked me something quite extraordinary. He asked if I would take charge of a baby and its mother. You may imagine my astonishment. I read on and discovered that while travelling with Dickens, George had found opportunity to father a bastard child. He said that the woman had appeared in Boston, seeking restitution but at that time he was engaged to be married to the sweetest girl in Massachusetts and his mistake now threatened his future happiness. He contrived to avoid seeing the woman himself but mailed her money and sent her back to Cairo, promising that he would make such arrangements as would be suitable to all.

'George beseeched me to help him. He said that he knew the enormity of what he asked but he had nowhere else to turn. It lay in my power to save or ruin his life. George was fortunate in that my wife Rosalie had discovered, during her first marriage, that she was unable to have children and adoption was now a common theme of her conversation. Up to then I had side-stepped the subject, feeling that a child would only be a draw upon my capital and on the precious time I needed to write my novel. However, the novel had become wearisome and I was loathe to seat myself before another sheet of white paper. I was even beginning to admit that I might have overestimated my gift and that perhaps my talents lay in a different direction after all. That was a painful realisation I deferred by writing a very little more, each day.

'I put the matter to Rosalie as a purely hypothetical circumstance. I told her, in fact, that it was the foundation for another story I was planning. She said that, were she in the hero's position, she would certainly do all she could to raise the boy well and find some respectable occupation for the woman. But I demurred and wrote to George that I regretted that I was not then able to help him. George wrote again and his tone was pitiful. This was no Merriweather who was begging for my grace but my brother George, the painter and clown, who acted the goat but never meant anyone any harm. I relented.

'I fetched the woman and a baby boy from Cairo and used my influence with Merriweather to secure her a job and accommodation at the hotel. I allowed her to wet-nurse the child for a short time but we deemed it right that as soon as was possible, he should be removed from his mother and placed in our home where he might be raised with more propriety.

'George sent regular payments to help with the child's upkeep. Being little interested in children, I felt I had fulfilled my obligation to my brother and left him entirely to the care of my wife. At first the boy made little difference to our lives, if you discount the sleep we lost and the time that now had to be devoted to satisfying his various and always pressing needs. But Rosalie began to spend longer with him. Her conversation solely comprised him and I understood that she was lavishing upon him the love she had once bestowed on me.

'However, we struggled along in this way a few years until

the child had become the cause of fierce acrimony between us and our very union was endangered. I wrote to George, who was now married with a child of his own and told him that something else must be done with the boy. He offered to increase the amount of upkeep he sent and trusted that would settle everything. Dismayed by his complacent attitude, I told him plainly, that if he didn't do something about the matter and quickly too, I should pack the child off in a coach, bound for Boston, Massachusetts and addressed to George W. Putnam, Esq.

'That brought George himself to Hayes. I met him one afternoon after school, straight off the coach. He said that he had something of immense significance to reveal to me. It was a secret he would have taken with him to his grave had not I forced his hand. He trusted that I would be as discreet. And then he told me something which changed my mind about being rid of the child.'

Elijah turned to me, as if he could penetrate the blackness of the night and his condition. He asked me if I recalled him once arriving home later than expected and taking a sudden new interest in me. 'I remember it,' I said. 'You picked me up and looked at me strangely. And then you said "This changes everything." '

'Changes everything? Well so it did and so it shall yet, boy. Because I had within the hour been with my brother who had travelled from Boston to tell me personally that the child, by which I mean you, of course, was not his own, as he had been obliged to pretend but was in fact the illegitimate siring of his famous employer.'

'Can I have understood you right?' I breathed. 'Can you really mean that I am the son of Charles Dickens?'

IV

Forgive me a cigar, an interlude and a low flight of poesy – the comet of my elegant years has brought affectation in its tail. It has also brought me wealth and considerable

81

influence. I am welcomed in inner circles and have become well-schooled in the ways of the world. If I have not had the ear of kings, I have been confidante to powerful men whose appetites have decided the fates of nations and these have to me whispered in spittle their secrets and cold hearts' desires.

And now, after being so long and so high in this complicated city, neither shock nor surprise nor the thrill of novelty are part of my experience. Sophistication may ultimately bring ennui and we who may now do as we dreamed can become inured to excitement and new things.

It was not always so. There was a time when I lived in a seemingly perpetual state of surprise and amazement. But age and experience changes all and now controversy and scandal merely occasion an arched eyebrow. And I know that not once in all the years since have I been as completely dumbfounded as I was when Elijah Putnam revealed that my father was Charles Dickens.

V

If that didn't beat everything. Billy Talbot, natural son of Charles Dickens, the most famous writer on earth. I wished I could believe it.

'You're kidding me, ain't you?' I said.

Elijah put a thin hand on my shoulder and helped me stand. We walked back down the hill and into the woods once more.

'Think upon your past,' he said. 'Bring to mind our years of schooling together and what its nature has principally been. Well? Has not Charles Dickens been our special study for as long as you can remember?'

I couldn't argue that. Why, I probably knew more about Charles Dickens' writings than Dickens himself. Not that I ever complained. I had liked him and had maybe spent more time amongst his Swivellers, Sawyers and Allens than I had shooting spit with the boys in town.

'And why was it, do you think, that we paid so much

attention to the history, the geography, the morals and the manners of England and the English?'

'You just said it would be useful to me one day.'

'So it will. Billy, I have known of your parentage for many years and have made it my purpose to prepare you that you might be worthy of it.'

His grip tightened. 'What was that? I thought I heard something.'

I peered into the bushes but could discern nothing.

'Wild animal, most likely,' I said. 'Ain't no one going to be out here at this time.'

'I hope you're right,' he said. 'But do let us be out of these trees before anything else is said.'

We walked through groping undergrowth and I cleared the way for Elijah, lifting branches, guiding him about obstacles and all the time, my mind frisking and fooling itself and echoing with my voice and those of folk I knew or had known. 'I am the son of Charles Dickens!' I repeated, 'Charles Dickens, my father!' I tried out 'Billy Dickens' and heard members of a town chorus chanting, 'There goes Billy Talbot. Charles Dickens' son, you know,' and, 'We always thought he was kinda different.'

The wood that Elijah imagined capable of concealing a hundred pairs of ears, all desirous of establishing Billy Talbot's parentage, was left behind as we made our way carefully back down the grassy slope, Elijah holding my arm tightly.

'Well, that's the cat out of the bag at last,' he said.

'Tell me what you think.'

'I don't know what to think yet,' I said. 'If I'm Dickens' son, why wasn't I told years ago?'

'That would have done no one any good, you the least. The way I have arranged things is one by which we may both profit.'

'I don't understand how this is possible. How can I be Dickens' son?'

'If you will contain your interruptions, I will explain.'

He began by reminding me of the day on which he had

held me 'as if for the first time'. I tried to compare my memory of Dickens' physiognomy with your own unformed visage. There were similarities. Your bones are not dissimilar. There is a lot of your mother in you but also the fine features of the Dickens line. Believe me, I was as dumbfounded to discover your lineage as you are now. I had sought a connection to this great man and what a connection had now found me. It was as though fate had ordered it.

'George told me that this story had its beginning in a small settlement at the confluence of the Ohio and Mississippi Rivers where the Dickens party made an ill-advised stop. It was a depressing place and Dickens had been in a mood to be diverted. My brother George, Charles and Kate Dickens were lodged in two log houses that served as a rudimentary hotel. Kate Dickens, whom my brother said he respected but rather, I believe, worshipped, retired early to her cabin with some ailment of a womanish kind. This left Dickens and George with the oafish landlord and his daughter. They were rough, simple folk and I'm sure they never knew what celestial company they kept that night. George said that to their poor host, Mr Dickens and his companions were only rich city folks from whom money must be extracted some way or another.

'The daughter was no great beauty but some might have discovered in her a certain attraction. They made what entertainment they could. The father produced a fiddle and Dickens partnered his daughter in a reel. The whisky jar was uncorked and Dickens gave them a song. George offered them something from *Hamlet* which, he said, delighted Dickens but which, I suspect, must have perplexed everyone else.

'George would have quite been in his element for he loves to act the fool and I expect he was disappointed when his employer made unmistakable intimations that he would be alone with the girl. The father had bid everyone good night an hour before, after instructing his daughter to ensure his guests were made comfortable. The next morning, George settled their account but shortly afterwards, he witnessed Dickens pressing an additional sum upon the girl's father.

'Certainly it appears that Dickens had been weak. Who has not been at some time or other? But George has Boston for blood and he was sick with disapproval and disappointment. "My opinion of Dickens the artist remains constant," he told me, "but as for Dickens the man!"

'You are proof that the night was not without its consequences. Once the girl was found to be with child, attempts were made to discover the well-heeled traveller who had made her so and from whom something more than a few dollars must now surely be due. The girl's father levelled a loaded gun at the shipping agent and was able to discover that the Dickens party was "of London, England", whilst his companion, Mr Putnam, had given his full Boston address.

'This was the address to which the father made application, not through any gentle intention of being discreet regarding Mrs Dickens but rather that it would surely be easier dealing through an American of an established address than with the malefactor himself, now God knew where in an impossibly distant country.

'The result was that my brother George received a message, whose meaningful import it took him some time to discover amongst the scrawlings of a barely literate man. George wrote a careful letter to Dickens, to whom the news came as a lightning bolt. His good name, his celebrity and his moral reputation were now gravely imperilled. Dickens entrusted the entire affair to George. Had he known how then he stood in George's opinion, I guess he might have sailed another course. George himself wavered and he told me that he only took this great commission for Kate's sake. George had fallen under her spell the minute he met her and he would venture much to protect her from the ill-effects of this sorry business.

'My brother told me that it was only in desperation that he revealed to me the identity of the child I had been raising. He said he could scarcely now take it himself without expecting some hard questions from his new wife. I was, as I said, dumbfounded. I looked you over. I held you and I caressed you. You, the son of Charles Dickens. I knew not how but felt that this knowledge would change my life, could change everything.

'I agreed to keep you and George, much relieved, returned to Boston. For some months I was exhilarated by the great secret I now possessed and small wonder you marked some change in my bearing towards you! But this could not last for ever and before long, it became a source of gnawing frustration. What was the good of the child being the progeny of Dickens if I could tell no one? This was a question that began to consume me. And yet I could see the sense of it. If I revealed all, most likely I would not be believed. Even if I was, what then? I had not a real child of his, born in wedlock, but only a bastard. I held my tongue, simmered some and thought hard upon the matter.

'And then it came to me, the indistinct glimmerings of an idea. At first, I thought I could discover some way in which I might enjoy the fortune and renown my attachment with you must bring. But I was wrong: no other scheme offered itself; the idea would not go away. Eventually I admitted that no other course was possible. It might cost years and even then, I could hardly be sure of success. But what choice had I? To remain as a humble and anonymous schoolmaster for the rest of my life? My upbringing had fitted me for better things. At least this offered the hope that one day the world might know me. I decided to take sole charge of you and raise you as the sort of boy Dickens would have, one day, to own as his son. I intended that such should be your knowledge of and devotion to your father that when at last you were revealed to him, he should love you as well as any of his sirings born on the right side of the sheets.'

'He could never admit me,' I said. 'Not in England, nor here.'

'I have been nourished by the conviction that he will. He has proved he has the independence of spirit to speak out. Look how he withstood the fire of the American press for having the audacity to suggest we robbed him of his copyright; how he has ever had the courage to vilify those institutions rotten with ineptitude, unevenness and corruption. I judged that were you made known to him and he had a chance to appreciate what a fine man I had made of you, then there lay the probability that he would defy all and claim you for his own.'

'Why would you do this?' I ventured. 'What would you gain?'

'Gain? Oh, I have no doubt there will be some recompense of a pecuniary kind. Dickens is bound to appreciate the expense I have incurred raising you on a schoolteacher's wage and afterwards, upon the little money that became mine upon the death of my wife.

'But it wasn't for that I bent myself to the great work of making you acceptable to him. It is true that I had once thought to use you as my introduction to Dickens. I thought that through you, my own poor efforts as a writer might be put before him and that he should recognise in them something of the spirit that had stirred his own genius and that he might be moved to guide me and even to offer me his patronage. Well, we all sustain ourselves with illusions and mine was that I could create anew what I had read in the great and revealing novels of others and take some share in the recognition and glory that were the dues of Dickens and those few like him. But what I gave birth to was mere pastiche and from the workings of others I had mined my own fool's gold. The hardest thing I have ever done is to shed that illusion and tell myself that I could no more complete my novel in such a way that it might slip unnoticed between others on my shelf than I could fly.

'Though it pained me to admit that I was no writer, I drew consolation from a new-found ability to teach. The boys I taught budded and blossomed under my care. My first charges are now successful men both in Hayes and in the cities. And you, my special avocation, have been my greatest triumph. You know your father's works as well as he: his novels and stories, his journalism and essays. You have had the liberal education of an English gentleman. You can even speak the Queen's English when I'm there to remind you. But your education came at a price.

'I knew not how long I had for my work, only that I had no time for wasting. So, while I had once accused my wife of spending too much time with you, now it was she who complained that I monopolised you as I took sole charge of you and spent every possible hour with you.

'That Rosalie was upset was natural. She had become mother to you but she made herself now an obstacle in our path. She grew noisy and quarrelsome and made demands that were quite incompatible with the great task we had set ourselves. She interrupted us, bothered us and wasted our time with argument. I knew not how the matter would resolve itself, but it did, in the most awful of ways. Do you remember the day Mrs Lowell, the teacher, took you to see the captured ships tethered on the river?'

I nodded. Elijah shifted uncomfortably. I thought his movements betrayed his agitation and that perhaps he was opening a box he would as soon remained closed.

'On that day I had some business in town and returned home alone. Before I had rounded the last corner I saw the people running, the bells ringing and the flames shooting high in the sky. My house was ablaze and when its raging power had at last been extinguished they found my poor Rosalie among its ruins. The fire had most likely started from a fallen ember and Rosalie had slept until she could not wake.

'Lately I had become concerned that she might, in one of her fits of hysterics, cause harm to herself or to you and Dr Coldbridge had prescribed tincture of laudanum. It's my guess that the dose she had taken that day had been overstrong and that she had been unable to rouse herself when the fire took hold.

'I could not wait to be transfixed by my grief. We needed immediate shelter and I moved us that night to the Particular. Melik Merriweather was not, of course, pleased at losing two rooms to me and said you must earn your board. I was not unhappy at this. The young Charles Dickens also had known drudgery. So I allowed him that, on condition I might have you at times I decided. We adjusted ourselves to our new lives and when my grief had subsided and I had found that the money my wife left allowed me to leave off schoolteaching, we worked on. I did not know when Dickens would return to America.

'The newspapers, edited by jealous men without a tenth of his talent, had raised an outcry about the speeches in which he insisted upon international copyright and as soon as they discovered that *American Notes* was only fair and not blindly laudatory of their country and later that *Chuzzlewit* lampooned them, they raised the cry again. I thought it unlikely that Dickens would return until it blew over, which it did quite soon and if his next books were received with any abatement of the enthusiasm that greeted his first it was only because the popular characters of his early stories had been supplanted by more complicated figures, that might be less accessible to a reading public more at home with Sam Weller and Mr Pickwick than with Mr Dombey and Carker.

'Still he did not come but my fascination with the man persisted. Though I wrote no stories, I began a memoir, fondly believing that those parts in which he figured would be of great interest to him, were he ever to read them. It occurred to me that I might begin to make an account of my rearing of you, Billy. It would make an unusual story and my regret is that we have not brought the memoir up to date speedily enough for this to be accomplished.'

'But we have time, don't we?'

'I had thought so until very recently. You are almost, but not quite, arrived at the state I had hoped for. There are rough edges to be smoothed, some corners of your mind to fill. But there is no time for that. Two weeks ago I received from friends in London the news I have awaited so many years.'

I was petrified with expectation.

'Charles Dickens is making plans to visit these shores once more.'

Some involuntary and inarticulate expression of surprise and consternation escaped my throat.

'Initially I doubted the information but his man Dolby has already been seen in New York and Boston, inspecting suitable venues at which Dickens might give readings. The word is that he will be here in a matter of weeks. It's too early to know his itinerary, which is why I would have you in New York as soon as possible, that you might ascertain his movements and assay the best place to make yourself known to him.'

'I can't do that!' I expostulated.

'You must. He may not come again and now that I am blind I cannot come with you.'

'But he would not want to recognise me, even now,' I said. 'There would be a scandal. He would never place himself in such jeopardy. He should be disgraced and I should be vilified as a bastard interloper. I can't do it, Mr Putnam.'

'You must, Billy. Just get word to him of who you are and the door will be open. He could risk as much by shutting it against you.'

'What do you mean?'

'George has kept it from Dickens that his child is now cognisant of his provenance. As soon as Dickens understands what you know, he will be forced to take one of two courses. He will either try to hush up the matter, in which sad case I should make known to him that I have a telling memoir to publish, or, and this I think he will do once he has seen you, he will arrange for the news to come out in the best possible light.

'I am certain that he will be grateful to me for caring for you and moulding you as I have done. Mr Dickens will want to make my acquaintance and it is meet that you bring him to me as soon as you can. After that, it is likely that he will wish you to return with him to England.'

I protested the folly of his scheme but there was no use. I told myself I went along with it because if I didn't, Elijah would see no further use for me and with my name as muddy as the Mississippi, I'd be forced to leave town and Cissy

Bullock for ever. That was partly the reason. The other was that I couldn't help wondering just what it would be like, what larks it might be, for me, Billy Talbot of Hayes, Missouri, to be recognised the whole world over as the American Son of Charles Dickens.

Chapter Six

I

BY THEN, MY tally of birthdays had long certified me a man
yet it is only from this time that I date the loss of my boyhood.
Its last traces were roughly stripped away with the revelation
of what kind of a woman was my mother and what an
extraordinary man was my father. My soul warred with itself.
I was overwhelmed in equal parts to discover I was both
offspring to eminence and the son of a whore. Though I might
be intoxicated by the one case, I had only to remember the
other to be brought low again. The scales barely balanced. I
was always the disgraced spawning of the town trollop and
such a ridiculous fool that I alone had been ignorant of this
fact, or I was the obscured love-child of the celebrated writer,
in whose reflected glory I expected to bask directly.

Out and about, I thought myself son to Charles Dickens.
Of course, I never told anyone my secret but I didn't think I
needed to. I figured it would be quite obvious in my gait, my
air and my conversation. I had the intention of purchasing a
bow tie. But alone in my attic, my garret as it was now, I
agonised that the very thing that made me his son might bar
me from ever claiming my place beside him. For I knew he
could never admit to relations with a whore, no matter how

regular a matter it might be in London. Despondent, I began to glean some idea of what Elijah's pain had been.

I barely had time to consider the implications of either condition nor to fully appreciate the ordeal I was sure I would undergo if I had the temerity to present myself to Dickens when my attention was seized by a small notice in the *Bugle*, which, because it didn't concern the price of cotton and grain and horses and wasn't about outlaws and crimes or commonplace murders, had filled a space in a column on the back page.

Lately arrived in Boston is the celebrated English writer, Mr Chas. Dickins. Mr Dickins is in America to commence a lecture tour. Tickets for Mr Dickins' first appearance on this continent in twenty-five years are expected to be at a premium and immediate application is strongly advised.

'He's earlier than I had been led to expect,' Elijah said. 'But it changes nothing. I had decided you must go at once in any case. Things are getting a little too warm about here. Merriweather paid me a visit this morning.'

The last couple of days had persuaded me that going anywhere was an attractive idea. I was no more comfortable in town where I attracted the vocal disapprobation of swindled citizens than I was at the hotel where I might run into my mother, whom I could not encounter without being overwhelmed by shame and repugnance. And now, since the robbery, there was Merriweather, whose behaviour was anything but predictable. The day before, there had been bedlam in the lobby as he evicted a banker and a lawyer sent by old Curry to make an inventory of his recent acquisition. They were expected to return with the sheriff at any time. Their visit had brought home to Merriweather just how serious his position was. Previously, he had seemed to retain some store of hope, as if it was all some little misunderstanding that might be ironed out. But now he was feeling the ground shifting beneath him and was as uncertain as a tall building in an earthquake.

This morning he had again accused Elijah of being some-how complicit in the robbery. Elijah reiterated that both he and I were completely blameless and asked why Merriweather had not been satisfied with what he had already been told.

'Because,' Merriweather had hissed, and I could see again his fat face up close as it always was when he was mad, with his jowls puffed out like twin sacs of venom, 'Amory seen the two of you out on the hill in the middle of the black night.' Elijah had borne his foul breath on his cheek as he paused to register any reaction his words might engender. Elijah said that where and when he chose to take his constitutionals was none of Merriweather's tarnation business but Merriweather refused to leave off, accusing us of having a secret rencounter with our confederates in the robbery or maybe having even dug up the proceeds. All of which wild surmises reassured Elijah that our secret was not already abroad. But we could take no chances, especially with that sly Amory forever snaking about the place and I must set off tonight. I was very nearly prepared for that and the prospect of immediate travel filled me with excitement until Elijah added:

'And, Billy, you must take your mother.'

'I can't do that,' I said, aghast at such an idea. 'I can't take her to see Dickens.'

'I'm not suggesting you do, Billy,' Elijah said. 'But she must be got out of the way. As far as I am aware, your mother has never discovered the true identity of your father. However, if anyone were to suspect some part of the truth, she would be a direct route to the whole story. And make no mistake, Billy, there are many who would capitalise on that knowledge, perhaps by demanding money from Dickens or by hawking the story to the press, who are ever hungry for such things. Either case would sink ours, Billy, and I would rather have her safe.'

'Where will she go?'

'Back to where she came from. The swamp. Cairo. Irving once gossiped to me that your mother was in the habit of spending time at Henry's livery and that she had been seeing a man there. I have made some enquiries and it seems that this is a gentleman from Cairo, who has taken a particular interest in her. Not a pecuniary one, I might add. I neither know nor care to know the exact nature of their relationship, only that he will make adequate arrangements for her discreet accommodation at Cairo. I will provide you with sufficient money to escort her there, from where you will make your way to New York.'

I protested but to no avail. I was to accept the matter as a *fait accompli* and turn my mind towards making preparations for a quiet departure that very night.

II

Standing at the ship's rail the next day with my stovepipe hat newly creased by a speeding bullet, I reflected that Elijah's timing was perilously fine.

We had slipped away in the early hours while the hotel was abed and had walked down the road to a place in the trees where Elijah had arranged for Henry to have a fly waiting for us, that way the wheels and hooves might be inaudible from the hotel. We boarded the chaise and rattled off towards Hayes but rather than drive through the town itself where we might be observed by Amory or any other burners of the late-night oil, we detoured along a rough track that occasioned us not a little discomfort but would at least take us safely to the landing stage where we might await the dawn arrival of the paddle steamer.

We soon caught a glimmer of silver water and as we surmounted a slope were suddenly overwhelmed by the broad majesty of the river itself. My mistake had been to allow myself to be distracted by the magnificence of the scene before me. I had stopped the gig, the better to appreciate the moonlit spectacle below. My mother too was similarly affected and was saying something about her girlhood that I wasn't much minded to heed, when I heard hooves. It was a little-used route and immediately apprehensive, I stood up and strained my eyes.

My hat was knocked clean from my head and landed in the floor of the fly. The report of a rifle ripped through the night air. My mother screamed and before I could even think to take cover, we were both thrown back as Henry's skittish colt took off. By the time I had got him under control, we had left the trees and were on open ground. I scanned the brightening scene but could discern nothing of any pursuer.

We boarded the boat with no further drama although we had spent the last hour threading nervously among stacks of cotton bales and keenly inspecting every new arrival on the quay. I could think of little else but of how narrowly I had escaped death and I was speculating wildly about whose finger might have been on the trigger. Merriweather's? Amory's? Or that of some other unknown party? It wasn't the cold morning air that had made me begin to shake. Forget anything you might have read. The sudden realisation that you are the target of someone with a gun is not something you will treat lightly.

By midday, the forward deck was a scene of lively activity. It being impossible to distinguish a would-be assassin amongst the throngs of merchants, salesmen, preachers and the hordes of folk whose occupations I couldn't guess, I was persuaded that we had not been followed aboard and allowed myself to be pleasantly diverted by the novel and grand scene of which we were a moving part. We churned past men in small cabins erected on vast rafts of floating timber, traversing ferry craft, the bloated corpse of a drowned pig, a myriad of small islands and the beached wreckage of some old and unlucky ship whose quarters, judging from the curtains on the pilot's window and the smoke that rose from a roughly-made chimney-stack, had been appropriated as someone's home. Along the densely wooded bank were clearings that some-times boasted small settlements of log dwellings, whose occupants could be marked sawing wood and tending fires and whose children and dogs chased us down the shore until their interest was arrested by some other exciting spectacle. I stood with my mother, by the rail and we neither said a word, until she said, 'I mind the first time I saw this place.'

I waited for more but she lapsed into silence again and I had already begun to think upon other things when she continued. 'We lived in the most hopeless, God-forsaken, fever-struck place on the river. There wasn't nothing but a handful of broken-down houses. My folks had gone there as settlers after hearing of great things, that this was a fine new city in the building and all they had to do to for a wonderful new life was pay the agent his money and buy a steamboat ticket. And that's what they did and my pa said that when they fetched up at this place and had asked folk the way to Little Phoenix, near Cairo and had been told they didn't need to find no road to Little Phoenix as they was already there, my ma sat and cried, just cried and cried, 'til the boat was up around the bend in the river and we were left sitting on the chairs we had carried with us, with our precious few belongings scattered on the mud. We had nothing. No ticket home, nor no reason to go back, neither.

'Pa said we might as well make a go of it and for years we tried. We fixed up the old cabin and Pa scratched a living on the river. Then the fever carried Ma off and Pa was awful changed after that. He drank and when he was drunk he was dangerous. He blasphemed until even the preacher gave up on him and his kin. He beat me badly and I was scared, Billy. I never knew what he would do next.

'When I could get away, I would go down to a quiet and private spot on the bank and sit in the hollow of a tree and watch the riverboats. We had come by river and it was in my mind that one day we would escape the same way. Exactly what I prayed for, I don't know. The boats came and went, full of fancy people living lives whole worlds away from mine. But the boats never stopped at Little Phoenix, nor hardly ever at Cairo, back then.

'And then, one day, a steamer did stop and a party of gentlemen was put ashore. First, I thought they were lawmen, chasing some fugitive. God knows, there were enough of 'em holed up at Little Phoenix. But they was just idle travellers with the time and the money to nose about wherever the fancy took 'em, though what they thought they could see at Little Phoenix, I sure don't know. Papa saw a chance to make a few dollars and took 'em from the boat to our cabins and told them ours was the only hotel in the neighbourhood. We weren't a hotel at all though we sometimes offered a bed to anyone fool enough to break his travels in our neighbourhood.

'There were some young men and one had brought along his wife. Their speech was strange and I guessed they were from the East where folk are rich and do everything different. Elijah told me that you know something of what happened that night and to my shame I do admit the truth of it. I only ask you to mind that I was a young and ignorant girl, fearful of disobeying her father and who trusted the promises made to her by a young man who was as thoughtless as she.

'When 'Lijah came and took me away, I thought he was an angel from Heaven and we were saved. But it was worse than before. Merriweather, he . . .' and here she faltered. Now that the river breeze had blown the hair from her eyes, I saw she was crying, the tears coursing down her cheeks. I couldn't bring myself to get any closer, to enfold her in my arms, to offer the comfort any decent son would. She gripped the rail with whitened knuckles and so girded, she went on.

'I don't want to talk about Merriweather. You know him. I didn't know what to do. We had nowhere else to go and at least you had food. I looked after you the only way I could. I guess you don't think a lot of me, do you, Billy?'

That moment was the nearest I had come to a reconciliation with my mother. All kinds of troubled emotions struggled within. I had tried and summarily convicted her, had been among the first to cast stones, the better to distance myself and this woman who had been forced, I was obliged to acknowledge, to a life that must already have brought her more pain than the mere knowledge of it would ever bring me. What form my foolish forgiveness might have taken I can't say because I never got the chance to offer any for we were interrupted then by the greetings of a fellow passenger

99

who was walking briskly down the deck, smiling away just like he knew the pair of us.

'Maggie,' he said, 'I thought to meet you at Cairo but having some little business in St Louis, I reckoned I'd get your boat and shove down river with you. I've had the very devil of a job finding you all in these crowds. And this fine fellow is Billy?' He extended a soft and pink hand.

I gave him my own.

'Dwight B. Howells,' he said, 'I knew your mammy when she was a little girl living up near Cairo. My, she has changed since then!'

'Mr Howells discovered I was at the Particular when he stayed there on business,' said my mother. 'He and I have kept company ever since, on the quiet.'

'Had to be quiet about it, Billy,' said Howells, 'while we made our plans. That Muddywater's a dangerous man and I wouldn't ha' made it worse for your mother, not for the world.'

'Made plans?' I asked, astounded that my mother might have been involved in anything so designing.

Mr Howells tapped his nose. 'I got big plans, Billy. But not here. We'll find a quiet booth in the saloon.'

My mother and I followed the small, dapper fellow down a companionway and into a saloon that was anything except quiet, as sharply-dressed men loudly advertised their money and business, their raillery punctuated by the shrieks of the boat's steam whistle. However, it all appeared to suit the taste of Mr Howells, who had us seated and served with drinks in a twinkling.

'First off, Billy, you gotta know that me and your mammy have an understanding.'

'About what?'

' 'Bout getting married, Billy. Why, I intend to be your mother's husband and your new pappy. Well, go ahead and gape – the fact is, I love your mother, Billy, and I'm going to make a better woman of her. I've delivered her from her bondage. I even got old Putnam to stump up some cash and

I'm gonna lead her to a land of milk and honey. I'm taking her to Beulah, Billy.'

'That in Missouri?' I asked.

'Fact is, Billy, we got the chance to get rich. To get very rich. You'll keep this under your hat?'

'I won't say a word,' I said.

He lowered his voice and said, 'Just give me a moment to find my documents.' He rummaged in a capacious leather bag and salvaged a sheaf of colourful papers. 'Let's see what we got here,' he said. 'Keep an eye on the folk hereabouts. Anyone pays us any mind, you let me know right away, you understand? There's too many people on to this as it is.'

He spread out a fold-worn paper map and stabbed at some particular vacancy. 'That's it,' he said, 'the promised land.'

'It's a wonderful place, Billy,' said my mother, 'Dwight has something to do in Cairo but directly he finishes up there, we're headed out to settle in the richest territory in America.'

'We sure are,' said Howells, 'and it'll be no surprise to me, sir, if we've already made our fortunes by the time you get there.'

This was a barrel of news to me. My mother, to whose shrinking timidness I was more accustomed, now took my arm and looked me straight in the eye. 'And it's my dream, Billy, that is, if you can see your way to feeling a little different 'bout me, that you come on out and share this new life with us. Once you done whatever it is you're doing for 'Lijah out East.'

'Where is this place? And how would you make money there?' I asked.

'It ain't anywheres you'd know of, Billy. It's west of the Dakotas and maybe north of Idaho but it ain't so much a place on a map as the best chance any of us has of leaving this world a whole lot richer than we came into it. This land has soil you could grow rocks in, clement seasons and no Indians, neither. There ain't hardly any folks out there now but those lucky few that have settled are making money like they can't help it. Your mother and I will start with just a few thousand acres and see how it pans out. I have the designs of the house we'll build right here.'

I looked over these drawings and some other literature that all agreed that this was a new-found land that would be swarming with newcomers at any day. 'What are these?' I asked, finding a thickness of brightly-printed papers.

'Well, a house like that costs money and I'm supplementing my capital by working for the government, selling off spreads to likely settlers and I tell you, they're tearing them out of my hands. Pretty soon this whole land's gonna be sewn up tight and them that got on board quick will be rich men, believe me. It's a great shame I didn't know you earlier, Billy, when the land was going for a song. I could have made your fortune.'

Old experience had prepared me for the news that I had missed another golden opportunity, so I was only mildly surprised to hear that this one had passed me by, too. 'I didn't have no capital anyway,' I said.

'You can't be going to New York without money,' said Howells.

'I h'aint got nothing,' I said, ' 'ceptin' what Elijah Putnam gave me for use in New York.'

'And how much is that?' inquired the inquisitive Howells.

'Elijah gave me two hundred and five dollars. His savings.'

'Well, I don't know what your business is there but it seems to me that if a gent is going to trust you with all he has, looks like he's expecting to make a good profit. Some investment, is it? The stock market?'

I didn't like the turn the conversation was taking. I wouldn't have wanted to tell my tale of hubris and presumption to anyone, let alone in the company of my mother, who was still ignorant of her leading part in this sorry tale. So I said that it was indeed an investment opportunity and that Elijah was counting on a reasonable return on his outlay.

'Don't we all? Ain't it only natural?' Howells asked. 'But I must say it kind of saddens me to see him sending a young man all the way to New York to do his bidding. And let me ask you this, Billy. Putnam gets his ten or twenty per cent, if he's lucky. But what do you get out of it?'

This was difficult. I said that I owed Elijah, which I did, I thought.

Howells shook his head and said, 'I love your mother, Billy and I must say I'm distressed to see her child being used in this way. Altruism is a fine thing in its place but effort demands reward and I can't see how you're getting yours here. He's using you, boy, and it makes me mad. Damnit, here am I with pockets stuffed with gold and it tears me up inside that I can't find some way of helping you out. Heck, I ought to – we're almost kin.'

'I have to go to New York,' I said. 'I appreciate your concern, Mr Howells.'

'Concern, be damned! This is family business! I will not see no son of mine exploited like this. I should like you to finish your business, Billy: a man should never give up on a job half-done. But it would warm my heart and your mother's if you were to return to Elijah Putnam a richer man than he.'

I laughed at his optimism. I would have renounced my shaky claim to the kinship of Charles Dickens any day for the prospect of easy riches but that notion seemed as impossible to me as the fool's errand on which I had been sent. 'I guess some things just weren't meant to be,' I said, simply.

'You said you'd help Billy, didn't you, Dwight?' said my mother, whom the lustre of prospective wealth had already begun to change before my eyes. She hung upon his arm like a gaudy bauble, her eyes bright and imploring, her general turnout still unkempt and disordered yet still attracting the sidelong glances of men. These men perhaps saw in her shroud of tangled locks something of the mystery and promise of a coquette's curls.

'I wish I could help, sincerely I do,' said Howells, his brow furrowed and his face looking sorrier for me than I felt myself.

'It's a crying shame,' he said, 'that I have to enrich perfect strangers when I should be looking out for my own kin. There's folk out there I'm going to raise from the mud and who today have their homes on wheels but tomorrow will live in houses that look like they had grown up with the hills. How'd you think that makes me feel?'

'He's my only son, Dwight,' said my mother.

'I know that, Maggie, and believe me I'm as saddened as you are.' He rested her head upon his shoulder and said that was the way of this cruel world. I looked into my empty whisky glass and only thought that I was no worse off than I had been and might as well see my commission through, come what may, when Howells seemed struck by some inspired notion and said, 'Well, I don't know, but maybe there is a way.'

'Oh, Dwight, I pray it may be so,' exclaimed my mother.

'There's a sale of this land taking place in Cairo tomorrow. I'm going to auction off some prime plots and quite frankly, I expect to make a killing. Suppose I was to let you buy a small acreage, right here and now, then you was to go along to that auction tomorrow and sell it, you'd more'n double your money.'

'Can you do that?' I asked, doubtfully.

'Officially, no, I can't. Anyone finds out 'bout this and I'll be in a whole heap of trouble.'

'But you'll do it for Billy, won't you, Dwight?' said my mother, who had moved up real close to Howells and was talking in his ear like he was hard of hearing.

Howells smiled. 'I'm doing this for you as much as Billy,' he said. 'And I do expect my reward before I go to Heaven.' He laughed as loudly as any man about us.

'It sure is nice of you to offer to help me,' I said, 'but I ain't got money to buy land and even if I had, how could I be sure your scheme would work?'

Howells smiled at my simplicity. 'Because I'm the agent in charge of the sales, Billy. I'll make sure you get a prime plot, of course. Something others would want. A strip bordering some big spread, maybe, so you'd have to be bought out before the farm could enlarge. Or by water. I could fix it so you got something that others would pay through the nose for.'

'But I can't afford that. Now the price of land there has risen, I'm sure,' I said.

'I'll fix that. You use Elijah's money and earn him a better return than he could ever have gotten in New York and get rich yourself into the bargain. Now how's that sound?'

It sounded strange to me, the whole thing. Here was someone I never saw before, wanting nothing better than to make me rich. But my mother encouraged me and I knew that I was being helped along purely for her sake. It seemed an easy and attractive way of pleasing her. I agreed readily to Howells' proposal and he pulled out some deeds and began to fill in my name.

'Because of the intimate nature of our connection, Billy, I'm prepared to advance you the remainder of the sum. It will inconvenience me, no doubt, but there again, I also expect to make a pile of money at the land auction tomorrow.'

He continued to write until he handed me his pen and said, 'Sign there. And there.'

He dried the ink and put one copy of the document into his bag. 'There just remains the matter of the money,' he said. 'Shall we say $200? I should not want to leave you without some cash to hand, even for a day. Besides, we'll all need to stay overnight in Cairo before the sale. Congratulations, young man. You are now, for however short the period, the lucky owner of some of the finest acres in the American North-West.'

'Well done, Billy,' said my mother, when I had emptied the money onto the table and Howells had quickly counted and scooped the lot into his bag.

'That's settled then,' said Howells. 'Tomorrow we'll all make some money. I expect to have enough to withdraw from the land-agenting line and start my own big spread. And how about you, Billy, after New York? Will you come on out and join us, like your mammy wants?'

I smiled foolishly. It was like Howells had just given me a three-fingered shot of one hundred-proof confidence. By this time the next day I would be rich. I could dress well and travel in style. If I wanted to continue my quest, just for the hell of it or for the sake of quenching a burning curiosity, I would. But it would be my decision. I would be a big shot and if I chose to go meet another big shot, then that was exactly what I should do.

Chapter Seven

I

I MIGHT HAVE found the venue with ease by myself. I would only have had to follow the general flow of foot traffic which was converging in ones and twos and family groups on the city's theatre. It appeared that the time for the entertainment was imminent. A great and voluble crowd had gathered before the doors, reducing to a line three deep that wound about the corner of the building. I stood at the end of this lively mob, unsure that I had arrived at the right place. I wondered that some of these rumbustious folk should have any interest at all in a writer from England, no matter what his fame. But it was soon impressed on me that Louisville's populace was well-versed in the stories of Charles Dickens. Farmers with wives and shopkeepers and clerks loudly proclaimed their familiarity with poor Oliver Twist and Little Nell and the ogre Squeers and I heard it agreed that the English were 'considerable cruel to their children'. This was a big event in a small town and it looked like Charles Dickens would be reading to a full house.

It was a chilly evening as we awaited the doors to open, our ten cents and quarters ready. Somewhere behind these cold bricks was my father, Charles Dickens. I had never before felt apprehension that bordered on sheer terror. Look how great this man was that the simplest folk of the town had all turned out to see him! How could I, with what seemed now the most tenuous and perhaps repulsive of claims upon him, present myself and expect him to accept me? Several times I thought of melting into the crowd and turning my back on the whole crazy scheme. But I had only a handful of loose change and nowhere to go. I was far from Hayes and who knew but by the time I made my way back there, I might find the Particular's new proprietor less complaisant about having me cluttering up the place than Merriweather had been obliged to be. My only hope seemed to lie with Dickens. I would pursue my plan, hopeless as it might be. The recent reversal in my fortunes had left me with little choice.

Exhausted by the exertions of a sleepless night, lulled by the rhythmic vibrations of beating pistons and warmly comforted by my mother's body, against which I was propped, it was no wonder that I fell soundly asleep in the steamboat's saloon. I suppose it should have surprised me as little to find, when I awoke, that my mother and Howells were gone and not to be found among the disembarking crowds at Cairo. I alighted there myself a little wiser than I had come aboard, even acquiescent of the new turn of events. What did I expect of a woman who had whored herself to half the town of Hayes and had no more self-respect than the goats that copulated by the Particular's kitchen door? I shouldn't even blame her. It was my fault for being such a fool. There were many such as Dwight D. Howells aboard that boat and I could have easily been gulled by any one of them. I was just the kind of mark they valued: someone to buy shares in a great company that existed only in the mind of its vendor or a home in a chimerical new city.

I searched Cairo and inquired in all the hotels but my mother and her new beau had covered their tracks well. I wondered if she had entered into a partnership with this man or whether they had already split the gains and gone their separate ways. It mattered not to me then. They and their kind could hang. My immediate concern was for my own well-being. Just a pocketful of small coins stood between me and starvation. I determined to head East and meet my fate, whatever that might be. With insufficient funds to buy a ticket for the railroad, I set out to walk to Independence where the wagon trains provisioned and new Americans from the world over headed out West, to start anew. I reasoned that with so much traffic heading West there must be some little going back East as well. I would hop a ride on an empty wagon.

As it turned out, I had no need to walk the dusty roads to Independence. I got picked up by a carrier driving to Louisville with a load of cotton goods and reasoned that Louisville was at least one step eastwards. I was able to make myself comfortable among the bolts of cloth while the wheels ground in the dirt and we rolled slowly across the state of Kentucky.

Just outside of Louisville, as I was thinking of making my farewells to the taciturn driver, a spry but skinny old man jumped upon our tailboard without so much as a by-your-leave but he immediately made free with a flask of whisky, so we didn't mind him overmuch. He was a talkative old fellow and said he was going into town for a second helping of some amusement that had been held there the night before. Having made known his own business, he said he felt entitled to ask what was my own. I puffed myself up, somewhat. Well, I was no hayseed hopping a ride to town but a transcontinental traveller upon important business. 'I'm going to New York,' I told him. 'On the East Coast.'

But the fellow was unimpressed: 'An' whatcha goin' there fer?'

'I intend to visit with the writer, Charles Dickens,' I said, not for one moment expecting this jackanapes to know of whom I spoke. But rather than silencing him with his own ignorance, this intelligence profoundly animated the fellow. I found his toothless face scrutinising me like I was the last fool in Christendom.

'I guess an edjucated man has his reasons,' he said, 'but a

jackass like me just can't see why you would be going all the way to New York when the feller you want is right here in Louisville.'

'That's quite impossible,' I told him. 'Dickens is in New York today and tomorrow will be Boston-bound. You are mistaken.'

'Boston be damned. He's here. I tell you, I saw him with my own two eyes just last night or my name ain't Java Joe. That's why I'm going to town tonight. To hear Charley read again. You all get along to New York if that's what you want to do but I'm for seeing Dickens tonight.'

That he was confused and his witless mind had linked some itinerant lecturer or preacher with the ubiquitous name of Charles Dickens, I had small doubt. However, thinking that his confusion might afford me some diversion, I said, 'And Dickens, what was he like?'

'Well, he was kinda important looking, like he thought he was as good as the mayor or something. I hadn't heard of the man, to tell the truth – I been in the South Seas these seven years or more and there's some things you miss out on. But he had collected a crowd and they was all excited, so naturally I was curious to see what kind of man this was. I didn't know whether to expect a juggler nor an acrobat. I paid the same money as everyone else and found a place in a hall and waited for the entertainment. I had paid twenty-five cents for a good seat and I expected my money's worth.

'I won't say I wasn't disappointed to find out that all this fella meant to do was to read to us. When I discovered that was his lay, I meant to shove to the saloon. But it was kinda hard. The way he read his story made you want to stay on just a little bit longer, just to find out a little bit more. It was like one of the tales we used to tell in the foc's'le of the ship on the high seas, only he told it a whole lot better than the bosun ever did. Like I said, I'd paid my money, so I stayed and heard the whole thing. Glad I did, too.'

I was far from being convinced, of course.

'What did he read?'

110

He rubbed his chin thoughtfully, and settled against the backboard, the better to concentrate his mind.

'Well, he said that this all occurred in New England, but the way he told it, this story might have happened anywhere. It began with a cart, just like this one, I'd say. Nothing fancy, just a big covered wagon, the kind you can't cross a road without running into, these days.'

He paused to eject the last of a plug of tobacco, drew in and hugged his bony legs and did his best to recall the story. 'The man who had this cart, I took a liking to him straight-away. You seen thousands like him. They travel all over the country, selling anything they can get their hands on: pots, kettles, rifles, whisky, bibles, stove enamel, cure-alls, you name it. And whatever it is, you can be sure they'll talk you into giving double the price for it, because they have the gift of the gab.

'This feller had a wife and a pretty little daughter, couldn't have been no more'n five year old, I'd say, but her mother used to beat her black and blue and you could tell it riled old Charley. He'd clutch his breast and tears would spring from his eyes with just the remembering of it. Well, the little girl got sick real bad but because the family had no food, the snake-oil man had to stand 'pon his wagon just as usual and talk up his goods though his daughter lay a'dying upon his shoulder. Then, one afternoon, when she had been particular poorly, the li'l gal said "Kiss me, Father", and died and all the time they was a'shouting at her and her pa like it was all a part of the show. I don't hardly mind telling you, I was snivelling like a booby when he told us that but so was everyone else. The mother took on bad after the child died and went and drownded herself in the Ohio. The man hisself lived a real lonesome kind of life and might have ended the same way. But then, in a little place just upriver from here, in fact, he rescued another little girl. She was a poor little deaf and dumb thing but he spent his saved-up money on having her edjucated so she could speak to him in her own way. Soon, she began to take the place of his little girl that was gone.

'Well, you start edjucating people and nothing turns out like you want, does it? The girl went off to California with a deef and dumb boy, leaving the snake-oil man all to himself. He just went on selling his medicines and bibles and never thought he'd see his girl agin and no more did I. After five years, he was sitting in the van he'd made nice for her, an old man with all his hopes and dreams used up, when he woke up sudden and who do you think was there? Why, it was the girl herself with her husband and a little boy of about four year old. He was the sweetest little boy the man had ever seen and knock me down if this little feller couldn't talk and hear as well as you or me.'

He sat silent and satisfied and we deduced that his story was ended. The driver, who had said nothing the whole journey, remarked that the story was 'mighty fine' and he would be obliged if Java Joe would tell it over again.

'I tell you,' he said, 'it was better 'n a religious meeting. I know I went out that hall feeling better nor I ever did after any church service.'

I was in two minds about his story. The newspaper had clearly said that Charles Dickens would today be in New York. But here was a man who had seen Dickens right here in Louisville, Kentucky. Well, although Java Joe decidedly lacked the gravitas of a New York newspaper and I had never heard a Dickens story quite like that one, I was more inclined to take the testament of one who had been convinced by the evidence of his own eyes. If it was indeed Dickens who had made an unscheduled stop in Louisville, I would have been a great fool not to have stopped and made sure for myself. And that was why I let the little old fellow pull me down from the cart and lead me through a maze of backstreets to the theatre, where he left me in the crush of folk without tickets.

II

I waited in the chill dusk and the inclination to be far away from that place was strong but further procrastination was made impossible when the doors were flung open and I was carried in by the surging crowd and, the seats being filled, I soon found myself in a position of uncomfortable prominence, standing hard by the side of the stage and almost under a table which was covered with a piece of maroon velvet and upon which had been placed a jug of water, a glass and a lamp. From this position I would be able to reach out and touch anyone standing at the table. I looked to see if I might find myself a less conspicuous vantage but the small auditorium was now tightly packed and movement was next to impossible. When no more could be accommodated in the theatre without injury, the doors were closed and bolted against those luckless persons without. The noise was deafening as the audience vented excited anticipation and individuals called to others in the crowd. What on earth would a refined and cultured man such as Charles Dickens make of this boisterous mob, I wondered?

I had no wait to find out, as my attention was compelled to the stage by a flash of yellow nankeen. A big man appeared from the wings and strode over to the table above me. There was a momentary pause while the audience took in the sudden appearance of the stranger and noted his buff coat and maroon vest, wispy beard, and unevenly greying hair that was in need of a cut. Bright light from the table lamp gleamed from his forehead and sparkled in his eyes. Then, satisfied that his identity was established, they cheered and stamped.

The object of their approbation surveyed them as an emperor his subjects. He allowed the clapping and calling to continue for some moments longer before he raised his hands and the room became so quiet that the only sound was that of flies about the lamp. He looked around him and when his eyes had lit upon everyone in the house, including the whey-faced young man just below him and he had assured himself that no one would offer the smallest further disturbance, he took out a large handkerchief and coughed into it before carefully folding and replacing the linen in his pocket, clearing his throat, pursing his lips, taking a breath and speaking in a voice that was loud and resonant and freighted with strange sounds that I presumed were my first experience of an English accent.

'*Great Expectations*,' he began and paused again, that any shuffling or coughing might be silenced. '"Chapter One. My father's family name being Pirrip, and my Christian name Philip, my infant tongue could make of both names nothing longer or more explicit than Pip. So I called myself Pip, and came to be called Pip."' He looked up from his page and satisfied that he had the attention of all he went on with his task. He held his text at arm's length and the other he used to make gestures eloquent of characters and their actions. His voice rose and dipped and amazingly, one moment he was terrifying women and children as he sprang upon them the desperate convict Magwitch and the next his timbre had changed and here was the bluff and genial Joe Gargery. We were as amused as Joe was baffled when Pip spirited away his bread and butter and when great guns signalled the escape of prisoners from the hulks, I'm sure that we all heard them as clearly as if they had been discharged just beyond the window. Dickens rocked upon the balls of his feet, loomed and cowered and thoroughly convinced me that I was watching not just one man but a whole company of talented actors, performing against the most brilliant of painted scenery. He held his audience fast but as the story unfolded it was clear that he was finding it a taxing business. He paused frequently to take sips of water and then refilled his glass and took longer draughts, complaining that this was 'thirsty work'.

And very likely it was. This was no mere book-reading but a dramatic performance worthy of Kean himself. A mere modulation of his voice ushered into the theatre the damp night air of the marshes and with as little demonstration we felt the heat of the furnace at the forge. He mopped his brow and when he succumbed to a severe fit of coughing, I am certain that many of our number mistook it for Uncle Pumblechook's discomfiture on discovering his brandy qualified with tar-water and also thought that it was he and not the reader, who sought relief from the water glass.

I looked out at the massed rows of the audience: rapt listeners reflected in their expressions the action on the stage; young ones gripped seat backs and stood bug-eyed as if they were witnessing their first steam locomotive or some grander spectacle than that of one man reading from a book upon a stage. As, perhaps, he warmed to his theme or felt he had taken the measure of his audience, his voice became louder, his gestures more expansive, even flamboyant. He quickened his pace and fairly galloped through Christmas lunch, brought on the soldiers, lit the furnace, repaired the handcuffs and had Magwitch arrested and rowed to the hulks before you could say ' "Chapter Six" '.

He now abandoned his text, the better to directly address the many faces of his crowd. He filled his lungs and announced, in a voice that might have scared a mute in the gods, that they could read that book as easily as he and at times of their own choosing but tonight they were worshippers at the altar of Dionysius and were entitled to something more.

'Let there be no slavish following of the printed word. My work is written on better stuff than paper. It is carved,' he boomed in a voice such as Elijah had used when he recalled hearing Mr Macready on stage in London, 'upon my heart.' And with that, he hurled the book across the stage and into the blackness of the wings.

'And let us not celebrate our communion with small beer,' he said, with his water glass raised to them all, 'but straightways uncork the good wine.'

I noted some signs of restlessness and even alarm rippling through the temperate members of the audience. I thought that Dickens must have been alerted to it too, because immediately, he said, 'I mean only that I have distilled the essence of this fine story and have bottled it, as I might a medicinal liquor or a patent medicine.'

He stampeded through pages like cattle through corn. Words thundered like chaotic hooves as he scattered before him Miss Havisham, her toadying relatives and the young pugilist Herbert Pocket. The headlong charge ended when

115

Pip was allowed to kiss the cold cheek of the beautiful Estella. I noted that this was a moment which evidently much moved his author as tears glistened and his hand lay upon his heart.

' "You may kiss me, if you like," ' he said, in a breathy tone that I thought might just pass for a woman with bronchial trouble. The audience – the female part at least – was less doubting and he stopped to gauge the effect and to refresh his glass. As he slowly raised the flask to his glass, a sob pinched the silence of the hall. He dabbed his eye, replaced his handkerchief and recommenced at his momentous pace. At this rate I estimated he might gallop through the book in a little over half an hour but a difficulty arose when Estella had Pip at the mercy of her moods and Miss Havisham was offering her charge advice in dealing with the opposite sex, based upon her own interesting experience.

' "Break their hearts," ' he said in a voice that would have sounded well on the blasted heath. ' "Break their hearts . . ." ' he repeated and paused, I took it, for the sake of dramatic effect. I awaited the familiar conclusion but the pause stretched and then stretched some more. I watched him gesturing to the air as if from it he might conjure something he wanted. A man in the front row whispered to his wife and I realised that the spell was loosening its hold and that Dickens was, in fact, searching for the words that I, *sotto voce*, supplied. I whispered, ' "My pride and hope, break their hearts and have no mercy!" '

' "Hope, break their hearts and have no mercy!" ' echoed Dickens and proceeded like a train after halting for fuel; slowly he moved off, got up steam and was soon taking us rattling down the rails with him, slowing for the junction at which Joe Gargery is abashed before Miss Havisham, which the audience received with a gale of laughter, before speeding on to the discovery of Mrs Joe savagely assailed in her own home. Here he paused but the moment's silence in Mrs Joe's memory was rudely broken by a short and excited farmer at my side who reacted to the grim news with a loud 'Hooroar!' It seemed that in no time at all that Pip was appraised by Mr Jaggers that he had 'great expectations'.

Then there arose a problem similar to the last. Mr Dickens' memory appeared to fail him and this time he glanced at me, made sense of the words I mouthed and off we went again, the locomotive Charles Dickens only stopping to take on water from the glass before steaming through chapter after chapter. But now there appeared to be another difficulty. His words had begun to compact, as if the train had hit the buffers and every car behind had gotten crunched into the next. His speech had become indistinct. Mr Pumblechook found himself possessed of the abbreviated appellation 'Pulshuk' and Miss Havisham must have shuddered to hear herself repeatedly addressed as 'Müzavshum'.

He had begun to depart from the story. Not making small departures as might be attributable to the need to compress chapters into a manageable length but to diverge entirely. I prayed that I might be the only one sufficiently knowledgeable to realise that Pip never bought bogus real estate on the Mississippi or that Estella never shot Bentley Drummle through the heart but when he said that Miss Havisham's groom finally showed up with a huge bunch of red roses and fulsome apologies for being so dilatory, I awaited the critical response with trepidation.

But no riot ensued. The audience, which had been a little restless during his pauses and the bouts of coughing that had punctuated previous passages, now sat transfixed, hanging upon his every word, some frowning hard, others as frozen as objects petrified. In contrast, Dickens himself seemed rather pleased with the extemporary changes that he had made in his novel and thus encouraged, he set to work further re-editing a text that had served him well enough unchanged for somewhere above five years. He began by severely and ingeniously trimming the cast of characters. Mr Jaggers succumbed to a scratch from a poison-tipped quill. After unexpectedly entering upon a parliamentary career, Mr Wemmick was caught up in some mighty scandal, took the Chiltern Hundreds and returned to his castle, a chastened man. Miss Havisham and her tardy spouse lived happily ever after, both promising not to mention again what had, after all, only been a silly misunderstanding. Pip and Estella were drowned in a boating accident, off Yarmouth.

No characters of importance remaining to drive the narrative further, we concluded that the reading was finished. He straightened his back, took a drink and beamed out at his audience as if he would say, 'Well! And what do you think of that?' and awaited the recognition he plainly felt was due.

But the audience had yet to make up its collective mind. No doubt they were weighing the savage bowdlerising of the story against the fact that as entertainment, the evening must have exceeded the expectations of many. To fill an uncomfortable void, I began to clap and a few others felt obliged to follow and while this reluctant applause was in faltering progress, I seized the moment to make myself known to him.

'Your pardon, sir,' I called, 'but I must speak with you.'

He looked down upon me, his eyes twinkling in the gaslight. 'And I with you. Follow me to the rear exit.'

He bowed to the audience and prepared to leave the stage. As he turned, a thin woman with a face like screwed-up paper jumped to her feet and shook her fist. 'I don't know what you're about,' she said, 'but I know that book like I know my Bible and that warn't it! You'll read it like you wrote it or I'll have my money back!'

'Me too,' called others, in the gloom.

'If that ain't the genuine article, I'll know the reason why.'

'We want what Boston got. Not some durned experimint!'

'He ain't 'speriminting. He's 'nebriated!'

'Drunk as a skunk, I'd say.'

And that was all it took for the temperance types – who I noticed thirsted after lectures and similar blameless entertainments like drunks after strong liquor – to give tongue. The crinkle-faced gal's neighbour got himself up and called 'For shame, sir!' and others cried worse. A tall man with mismatched eyes and a nose like a letter-opener was propelled from his seat by his wife and perhaps felt it incumbent upon him to make her effort worthwhile.

'What's the meaning of this?' he exploded. 'Did we get what we paid for or not?'

'Surely, sir, that's for you to decide. What were you expectin'?' asked Dickens.

'Well, he certainly wasn't expecting that!' shrilled his wife.

'Heck no,' said another. 'I read that book and this was nothing like it!'

'This man has been trying to fool the good people of Louisville.'

'Something fishy about a fellow who don't know his own books!'

'I'd think so. And that odd-lookin' feller standin' right by him? He was feedin' him his lines, half of the time.'

'Why, they're in this together!'

About that time, the rougher elements in the crowd scented something more exciting than literary debate and began to push towards the stage. I looked for a door and was about to plunge into another part of the crowd when a hand gripped my shoulder. Dickens said, 'Time we were gone,' and hoisted me upon the stage. In seconds we were battling through the velvet skirts of the curtains and passing into a small room which Dickens locked behind us, before leaping up upon some boxes of properties which were stacked beneath an open window. Dickens lost no time in heaving himself into the aperture, becoming a great yellow nankeen balloon from which stuck a pair of expensive-looking boots. 'Push, boy, push!' he said as someone rattled the handle of the door and someone else cried 'Quick! In here!'

Our pursuers were through the door. I launched myself from the window and found myself in a yard, in which was no sign of Dickens. As faces appeared at the window above and I heard a nearby street door burst open, I heard a whispered 'Over here, son!' and there he was, leading a horse out from behind a fence. He tipped his hat to the interested party at the window. 'Jump up behind,' he called to me. 'This ain't no time to be hanging about for the gratuities.'

119

III

Some ten miles outside Louisville, we left the road and found a secluded place on the bluffs above the Ohio where we made camp. I went to scare up some firewood and see to the horse while Mr Dickens surprised me by opening a gunny sack and pulling from it a chicken and assorted fixings. He fell to work on skinning the fowl like he was born to it. I had never guessed that this might be an accomplishment prized among English gentlemen. When I had made my fire and had set a Lucifer to the dry tinder and the crackling flames had begun to thaw some of the chill from our bones, Mr Dickens filled a coffee pot from his canteen and hung it over the fire to boil and I voiced the suspicion that had been gnawing away at me, these last few hours.

'You ain't Dickens, are you?'

'Well, I dare say you ain't Professor Longfellow, neither. But did you think I was? That's what matters – did you?'

'I don't know. Maybe, at first,' I said.

'That's good, then. It was only the gin that let me down. Next time I'll stick to water. First time I ever tried the Dickens was last night and it went great guns. Went down better than anything I ever did before and that includes preaching in Arkansas, when I could whup 'em into such a frenzy that I just had to send out the plate to hear the clatter of silver on brass. When I walked off that stage last night, with all the crowd cheering and my bag full of money, I knew I was on to something.

'Tonight was regrettable.' He became intent upon tending to the fire. 'You see, I have an affliction which don't seem to be improving any and it was beginning to give me trouble when I read last night, so much so that I wasn't sure if I could finish the reading. This night I had provided 'gainst that with a little gin. Only I got so thirsty and didn't have no water and strong liquor has a tendency to bring out the blamed devil in me. Well, I'll just have to put a few miles between me and Louisville before I start in on it again.'

He caught the dripping juices of the fowl in a tin can and ladled it upon the beast's back. 'Don't that smell good? I was going to walk into town tonight and have me the biggest steak money could buy. I got the cash. But ain't it something better, being out here, smelling this? Food never tastes as good in a fancy restaurant, does it?'

When the chicken was cooked through, we hacked off tender slices and toasted Charles Dickens with mugs of hot gin and water. The food disposed of, the fire was built up again and we made ourselves easy in the bole of a tree.

'So how come a young feller like you knows them Dickens books so good?'

'I like to read,' I said, carefully.

'Me too. I read one or two of his books when time was hanging heavy up in Albany. Well, young feller, you going to tell me who you are?'

After his deception, I felt the obligation rather lay with him but I gave him my name, told him I was from Missouri and that I was headed for New York.

'You got any money?' he inquired and then he asked me how in that case I hoped to get to New York.

'I'll hop rides,' I told him.

'Well, if you don't mind when you get there,' he said. 'And what you going to eat?'

'I'll get by,' I said, which is easy to say when you have chicken fat dripping off your chin and your blood is warmed by hot gin and water.

'I'm heading East myself,' he said. 'And if you want to travel with me and help me with one or two little matters of my own business, I'll see you get there no later than you might have anyway and with no less fat on your bones.'

'What kind of business would that be?' I asked him.

'Why, the Dickens lay, of course. It ain't all as professional as it might be. Not just yet, anyways. I need someone to appear as my manager, take the money, settle the crowd and maybe give me a little prompt sometimes.'

'I ain't sure I'd be comfortable doing anything like that,' I told him. ' 'Sides which, it's risky. You almost got us lynched tonight.'

'That's what I'm telling you. It all has to be just right. There's just a few details to be attended to and then you just watch the dollars coming home to roost.'

'Someone'll find you out,' I said.

'Why? I keep abreast of Dickens' itinerary as it's printed in the newspapers or I telegraph if there's any doubt. Then I just stay well clear of those places. And my Dickens is faithful to any accounts of the readings folk might have read in the papers. I tell you, there's so much money to be made it would be a crime not to do it.'

'S'posin' someone who had been to a genuine reading turned up at one of yours,' I said.

'That an't hardly likely, considerin' the places I'll be goin', but even if that were so, he might only know the difference if he had a seat close to my table.'

'But he'd know what Dickens sounded like and how he gave his performances.' But nothing I said could dampen his optimism.

'Well, I ain't given to being swell-headed but I reckon by the time I've got Dickens up properly, even someone as had seen him might not be able to tell the difference.'

'You sound very sure,' I said.

'And why not? I *have* seen Dickens,' he said. 'In Boston, couple of weeks ago. I was there at his first reading. Everyone was so all fired up about his coming that I had to see what all the fuss was about for myself. I had to get someone to stand in line all night for a ticket.'

'You saw him read? How was he?'

'He was as good as any snake-oil salesman or salvation-seller I ever saw. Read the first part in a kind of English that was hard to understand. London dialect, I believe. But I listened hard, watched his every move and made notes. It hit me right away that whatever he could do, Hope Scattergood could do the same and make as much money, maybe.'

'Is that your name?' I asked.

122

'Hope's me. Mother was hopin' for a girl. But I reckon a man, like a patent medicine, succeeds best if he provides himself with different labels for different circumstances.'

He took out a pocket-book from which he extracted a handful of cards. 'See here: Arthur Newman, Horse Dealer, Dodge City; Clement Sampson, Dry Goods, of Minneapolis; Dr Benjamin Looker of Cambridge, Mass.: that's good anywhere but in Cambridge, Mass.' He read out more cards as he flipped them onto my lap. It was like a roll-call on Judgement Day. 'Professor John Turner, of New York; Colonel Eugene A. Dashwood, United States Army; Lieutenant Benjamin Jackson, United States Navy; The Reverend Peter Bliss, of Tulsa, Oklahoma.'

'These are all you?'

'My names have been legion, I admit. Different names for different games. I was most successful, I think, in the religion line. I was a hell-fire preacher in Arkansas and got so good I could scare the pants off most anyone and people came just to have the fear of God put into 'em and they would pay through the nose for salvation. I tried faith-healing here in Kentucky until I got caught trying the laying on of hands with the daughter of the mayor. I ain't knocking spiritualism, don't think that. There's a lot of money to be made table-rapping.'

'So how come you ain't still in the Bible line?' I asked.

'Well, that was all well enough, I might well have made a career of the Church but along came the war and I had to change all my plans.'

'You enlisted? For which side?'

'Hell no, I didn't fight for anyone, only Hope Scattergood. If I'd been possessed of some capital when that war started, I could have been a very rich man by now.'

He took an ember from the fire and lit a cigar. 'A very rich man indeed. As it was, I barely escaped getting myself hanged. But life's like that and there's always something else to try, just around the corner.'

'Like the Dickens scheme?'

123

'Pre-cisely. You got to grab opportunities as they arise. When I saw lines over a half mile long, everyone crazy for a couple of tickets to see Dickens, I knew there was money to be made and some fun to be had.'

'Fun?' I asked.

'Why, sure! If I only wanted the money I'd get a proper job and maybe succeed in business. But where would be the fun in that? You take P.T. Barnum. Half the crazy stunts he's pulled haven't earned him money, though I grant he always attracted publicity and that's worth something. And how much money did the Devil make when he gulled Adam?'

'And what will you do when this is all over? You won't be able to pull this trick once folk know that Dickens is gone back to England.'

'I know that but I'll make a whole lot of hay while this sun shines. I intend to work this thing up and read as often as I can while he's here. I tell you I never relished anything so much as I did reading to that crowd last night. I had 'em right where I wanted 'em. When Dickens goes I'll see how much I got banked. If I have enough, I'm going to get me a cure for my affliction. There's a doctor in Switzerland. He's expensive but his treatment works, they say.'

Reminded of his frailty, he coughed into his handkerchief. Even in the firelight, I could see that the linen was flecked with dark spots and he saw that I had noticed that and changed the subject. 'Directly after that, I'll head for the South. Southrons are generous folk and they do say there's a heap of money to be made now the war's over. You get a chance, you should get yourself down there. The carpet-baggers are picking gold off the streets right now. There's powerful positions just for the asking. I hear.'

He picked up his cards. 'But Hope Scattergood, that's me,' he said, almost surprised. It was as if he had only just then decided.

'You sure?'

'Sure as I can be. Now you want in on this or not? I ain't in the habit of taking on a partner and when I do it's generally

124

regarded as something in the way of a small honour.'

'I wouldn't feel right about swindling anyone,' I said. 'I never did anything like that before in my life.'

'Did you not?' he said and the way he said it brought to mind just about every dishonest thing I ever did, from trading in the gossip of the drummers, to sneaking legs of chicken from the kitchen, to my appropriation of any articles left behind by our guests, to once stealing a whole silver dollar from behind the bar to buy Cissy Bullock a necklace, which she didn't like anyway.

I'm sure that Scattergood knew exactly where he had directed my thoughts because he began to detail and justify his own colourful career. He had been son to ambitious French immigrants in Louisiana and his name was an approximation of something that sounded a whole lot better in French. But his family were determined that he should succeed in the New World and they changed it. They got him what education they could and it was expected that he would work his way up in one of the import and export concerns on the Gulf Coast.

But Scattergood had more spirit in him than to live out his life behind a desk, he said, and one summer's day, he signed on a steamboat as ship's purser and spent several years plying the Mississippi between New Orleans and St Louis. It was aboard ship that he first saw the real confidence men in action and watched with fascination as they selected their victims and worked their swindles in a hundred different ways. It was a short step between watching the cons and beginning to work his own. He started in a small way with card tricks and hide-the-pea but moved to schemes requiring more artful skills. He frequently gleaned some small knowledge of a particular passenger from the ship's register and used that cunningly to appear before him as an old acquaintance, turning the mark's embarrassed confusion to his own advantage.

He could have worked the river profitably for years to come but he needed to spread his wings and after that someone looking very like him appeared in most of the states of the

125

Union and in the Confederacy too. Sitting comfortably, with his gin and water and warmed by the flames, he took pleasure in outlining the varied methods he had perfected of turning a dollar. He had been a mesmerist in Mississippi, a medium in Georgia. He became a fashionable phrenologist in Boston but his interest in the cranium was his downfall when he began to experiment with trepanning, 'which was a whole lot trickier than I had thought. Messy, too.'

He had sold temperance to wives and whisky to their husbands, which, he confided, was the major ingredient in his popular line of patent medicines. The recipe remained constant and sold well whether labelled Doctor Roberts' Regular Restorative, Culpepper's Positively Scientific Fix-You-Up or Allbright's Proven Cure-All. Some folk, he said, bought all three lines while others would only swear by Allbright's or Culpepper's.

'Don't you think this is all wrong?' I said, ' 'Bout being what you are, a confidence man?'

'There's worse things to be than that, you know. People, specially American people, like a good confidence man.'

'That just can't be right,' I said. 'It makes no sense.'

'It's a truth. You never seen a good confidence man at work, one of these smooth operators possessed of so much charm it's almost an honour to be taken in by 'em?'

I thought back to Mr D'Orleans and admitted that he and even his dismal compatriot Wilkes had exercised some enchantment.

'It's the same all over. People like to see something well done and the skills of a good confidence man can be as impressive as those of a great showman or acrobat or the legerdemain of a professional gambler. The confidence man is known as well among the mansions and shanties of the South as he is in the cities of the North. You'll find him in the wild new towns of the Western territories and in the corridors of Washington DC. He's as American as Uncle Sam and P.T. Barnum and just about as well liked.'

'How can he be well liked?' I snorted.

126

'The confidence man is an American hero,' said Scatter-good. 'He's a measure of this nation's integrity.'

I smiled uncertainly but Hope Scattergood spoke with conviction. 'It's like this. Without a lot of good and trusting people to hoodwink, fellers like me couldn't get a living. It's a fact that you can't kid a kidder. If the country is awash with con men, just think of how many trusting people there must be. Don't that say something about a nation? Why, there must be more good, decent and trusting people here in America than anywhere else on earth.'

He loosed off a volley of laughter that ended in a great and terrifying fit of coughing, the effluvial product of which he spat into the fire. After it had passed, he rose unsteadily and when I caught his eyes in the firelight, it crossed my mind that here might be a man perpetrating his greatest deception on himself.

'It's getting cold. I'm for sleeping in a bed tonight.'

He killed the fire and we mounted the tired horse which took us as far as the next town. 'What do you say, partner?'

I don't think I said anything but in getting up behind him on that bay, I felt I had thrown in my lot with Hope Scatter-good, the snake-oil Dickens man.

Chapter Eight

I SHOULD SAY right off that, regarding opportunities down South, Hope Scattergood was on the money. I later took his advice and profited by it and here I am, all these years later, with more than I can wisely spend and the kind of power that would have made a monster of someone like Melik Merriweather. I have a grand town house in Washington DC, convenient for the Capitol and a restored mansion which I share, when duty allows, with my wife and two of my four grown children, near Natchez. I have lackeys at my business and valets and servants share our home. I dress finely and am everywhere driven in my own carriage. I call myself William and sometimes wonder what survives in me still of the gawky stripling that was Billy Talbot. I guess that I have all I ever dared hope for and yet I know that I was happiest all those years ago, when I had nothing to sustain me but a handful of coins and the friendship of a man called Hope Scattergood.

It's true that I might have chosen a more reputable companion than this *chevalier d'industrie*; this self-confessed arch swindler, whose association would have confirmed Pop Bullock in all his opinions of me; but we had been thrown together by circumstances and from the beginning I was in thrall to this curious individual who had the effrontery to stand before a thousand people and call himself Charles Dickens.

Lest you should have in mind the nankeened impostor of the Louisville theatre, let me tell you now that in actual appearance Scattergood bore not the least resemblance to even the poorer prints of Charles Dickens and that any verisimilitude he did achieve – and there were those that saw Dickens and were taken in by Hope Scattergood – owed mostly to the sheer force of his personality.

We slept the first night in the best hotel a small town could offer and the next morning I met him in the lobby, looking so different I might have walked past him, had his pale and fluid eyes not flashed in my direction. We shared a pot of coffee and I noticed that the waiters that had served him with instinctive deference the night before, did similarly today and seemed no wiser than I had been that here was the same gentleman in different attire.

The eyes had caught my attention and these were blue and deep-set below a high forehead that was topped with a smart black hat. The wispy beard of the previous night was gone. He was clean-shaven, except for a pair of sideburns which he had sharpened with his razor. His face, with its aquiline nose and broad mouth that cut it in two when he smiled, was thin and of a part with the rest of his figure, which was angular and wiry. What his maroon vest of the night previous had concealed I didn't know, but dressed in his close-fitting grey frock coat and matching pants he appeared to have lost about thirty pounds.

His boots were highly polished and sharply-cut. He looked like a dandy, but his eyes told of wider experience than the ballroom and salon. What strength was in a man like that you couldn't say; not much, you might have thought, had you seen him bend double as his lungs sang their protests and he grasped the wheel of a coach for support. But then you wouldn't have seen him as he was born to be seen, before a crowd that savoured his every word, when he would draw himself up, breathe in power and return it as seamless oratory.

II

Over a breakfast of fried ham and hot coffee, Hope Scattergood was thumbing through a bunch of dog-eared newspaper clippings. A paper of a recent date lay denuded of some pieces of interest, upon the table. I said nothing while he clipped some new item from a paper and broke off to cough into another handkerchief, this one much too dainty to be a man's and suggesting itself as a keepsake from an old flame. I noticed how graceful were all his movements.

'Dickens,' he said, 'has been in New York. I have the account of it here.' He added the new cutting to the rest. 'Know your man, Billy,' he said. 'I have reports of his readings in England and every one he's given here. Details count for much.'

The manager presented his account with a small bow and said he would have Mr Appleton's bags sent to the front. He trusted he had enjoyed both nights of his stay and would honour them with his custom again. Scattergood seemed oblivious of the attention and we were bowed and scraped out of that hotel like we were gentlemen of the first water.

I was resolute that my companionship with Hope Scattergood would be a strictly temporary arrangement, something that answered to the exigencies of my present position. I scorned his values and his con-man ways, regarding myself as a man of morals to whom this present course would, under normal circumstances, be unthinkable. My own snobbery enabled me to persuade myself that this Dickens deception was a lesser evil than the litany of petty crime that was Hope Scattergood's history. If these people were too ill-educated to realise that they were not getting the real thing, well, so much more the fools they. Perhaps they would be getting what they deserved.

In any case, some help with his readings would be the full extent of my connection with this Scattergood. My new partner was a charismatic man. I could see how easy it would be to fall under his spell and have the world turned upside down and for a body to see black as white and evil as good.

However, within only a few minutes of leaving the hotel, I had cause to doubt my own resolution. Scattergood had said that to work the Dickens lay properly, we must look the parts and while he was satisfied with his own appearance, mine, he said, would decidedly not do. He took me to a store where he picked me out a coat, some new pants, a couple of shirts and a neck tie. The storekeeper, who treated me with a respect that I found entirely novel, suggested a hat, but Scattergood said, no, he kinda liked the one I had. I left the store well pleased with the new image I had seen in the glass. Who in Hayes would recognise this sharply-dressed gent as Billy Talbot? I felt that I had discarded my artless self with my old clothes. But at the back of my mind was the idea that Scattergood had put his stamp on me and that I now wore his livery. 'Livery' was our next port of call. Scattergood had been out and about betimes that morning and had already exchanged his horse for one more fitted for the work he had in mind. Behind the stables, we were shown a contraption looking like a huge bath on wheels, a home-made affair not quite coach and neither quite carriage and smelling like its last use had been for hauling hogs to market but Scattergood was enthusiastic, said that it just wanted a good sprucing and was a reg'lar knock-down bargain at the price.

And it did look much improved and nearer the part after I had cleaned it out and washed it down and repainted the more obvious signs of dereliction. Scattergood was pleased with the result and said this way we would arrive in town in some style like we would be expected to. When the horse was fed and harnessed, he stowed his bags and we both climbed on top. He flicked his whip and the wheels began to rumble over the earth. 'Gid'lang,' he said, cracked the whip again and we were leaving town, headed East, bound for I knew not what.

The coach was marvellously slow and I had time a-plenty to take stock of my new and curious position. I suspected that my integrity had been compromised, my character somehow blemished but my pragmatic self admitted that I was at least travelling, no matter how cautiously, in my intended direction and must at some future time, find myself on the Eastern shoreline, although I avoided considering whether Dickens would still be in America, or even alive.

My partner kept me distracted from thoughts of such a remote future with his speculations about the possibilities inherent in 'the Dickens lay' and what we might expect to rake in from inhabitations of different size. Ours, he said, had been a fateful encounter; my knowledge of Dickens would be worth, well, he wouldn't like to speculate on exactly how much right now but I should hang on to my hat if I was going to be teamed up with Hope Scattergood.

And hang on I did, as we rolled shakily through a number of small settlements that day: clusters of wooden houses with just enough people and chickens to give themselves a name on a shingle and some villages with enough pretensions to call themselves towns. As we passed through, I noticed that Scattergood was in the habit of stopping to chew the fat with the inhabitants. He told me that this was the way to see how the land lay and from these encounters he could judge whether anywhere nearby might be suited to our purpose.

However, I couldn't help but notice that nearly all of those with whom he talked were girls and generally pretty ones at that. He would slow down, until we were travelling no faster than a girl walking a little way in front of us, tip his hat back upon his head and call out his 'Excuse me, ma'am's' in a voice so laden with friendly promise, that the girl was usually half-smiling when she turned about.

He was a great talker, but, more unusually, he was a good listener, too, and had a way of making you feel that he was truly interested in you and your concerns and it surprised me that he had little trouble in drawing from me, as we rumbled across the dirt roads of Kentucky, the whole miserable story of my grand passion for Cissy Bullock.

This seemed to afford him not inconsiderable amusement. He digested the history of our too-brief courtship, my expulsion from their porch and our subsequent separation and he had the bad manners to suggest that Cissy herself might have been avoiding me after that. I had already allowed to myself that she had not been forward in finding ways of furthering our courtship but I figured that some girls were like that and that my love, being noble and true, must eventually win out, as it did in the books – even Pip and Estella had made it in the end.

We had been on the road some two or three hours and had turned up our collars against a chill wind. My thoughts were turning to blazing fires and some warm negus in a good hotel somewhere up ahead – we still had sufficient funds – but Scattergood had determined to give me the benefit of his own experience with women and I soon stopped noticing the cold and the rain that had begun to fall, as Scattergood recounted his adventures with the other sex.

I cannot but have been fascinated and somewhat appalled too: I, who had known but one love and had placed her upon a pedestal and worshipped her as something more than perhaps she was. Here was an out-and-out adventurer who had known more women than he could remember and who had taken them up and cast them off like worn-out shoes. He talked of rendezvous in barns and liaisons by moonlight. Then, warming to his theme and unwitting that he might be pouring it into ears untested by outrage, he told of cuckolded husbands, gaudy nights in bordellos and of one improbable coupling inside a moving coach. Girls of good family, girls who should have known better; women in respectable situations, matrons of virtue, all had succumbed to the fascination of this rogue. I had not thought such things possible. I observed him as he talked, his eyes fixed upon the road up ahead, but his mind elsewhere. There was no doubting his charm, but I was puzzled that the appearance of this roué should be found so universally attractive. He was handsome; that is, you could see he had been so once. But now, at whatever age he was, (fifty? sixty?) his countenance was deeply scored with age and his eyes were sapphires sunk deep in yellow-brown skin stretched taut by the daily action of the sun and the wasting effects of his disease.

We encountered a girl of fifteen or sixteen with another, who carried a baby and they responded to his call but when they saw him and their mistake, their mouths lost their coquettish pouts, their eyes their sparkle and both adopted the suspicious looks that some small-town folk reserved for strangers. His charm was by no means fool-proof. Scattergood didn't remark the incident but it suggested to me that the campaigns and victories of which he boasted had all been fought a long time ago, when Hope Scattergood was a healthy man in the prime of life.

He mentioned a few affairs of more recent vintage, only with these he was more sketchy with details and he often neglected to mention how pretty were the prizes. I was sufficiently innocent of experience to be amazed by his tally of conquests but despite my innocence, or maybe because of it, I asked him directly, had he never, in all his born days, found love? He didn't answer at once and I was forming an apology for being overpersonal, when he started to tell of a black-eyed girl from a place on the Bayou, whom he had indeed loved but who had in some way betrayed or failed him. But by then we were approaching a big town and Scattergood broke off to outline the plan of attack.

IV

The scheme, and those in the other places in which we read, worked in the following wise. We found an out of the way boarding-house and put up there in our workday clothes, under assumed names. We scouted the town and hired a suitable venue and if there was time, we tested its acoustics,

135

Scattergood reading from the stage, myself trying various places in the hall for audibility. We avoided being too public, but if we did find ourselves in a saloon, we made out we were travellers busting with exciting news for this burgh: Charles Dickens was heading this way. Shortly after that, handbills would appear all over town and anything we could do to boost the excitement and puff the event we did.

The next night we changed into our other clothes and 'Dickens' sat inside, while I got up top and drove him to the best hotel in town. This was always a gamble: it rather depended upon the success of the reading as to whether we might be able to settle the bill on the morrow. The actual booking of the venue, the settling of accounts and even, amusingly, the dealing with the correspondence and requests for autographs that were handed in at the hotel desk was done by me in my role of Dickens' manager and under the pseudonym of George Dolby. If one reading had gone well news of it would be all over town in an instant and I would have deputations at my door with petitions and even demands for the best seats.

We had worked out from newspapers that Charles Dickens read only on Mondays and Tuesdays and Thursdays and Fridays, reserving the intermediate days for rest or travel. Therefore we tried to restrict our own appearances to Wednesdays and Saturdays and hoped that no sharp-minded citizen spotted that Dickens had given a reading in Philadelphia only hours before he had made an appearance in a small town in Kentucky. This worked well in the hayseed towns in which Scattergood practised and perfected his performance. I wondered if our luck would hold when we reached somewhere a little more cosmopolitan such as Cincinnati.

I can't deny that I found my new role stimulating. I took the money at the door and ensured everyone was seated before checking that all about Scattergood's appearance was right, that his padding was in place and beard securely affixed to his chin. Then I had only to allow the crowd to achieve just the right degree of excited anticipation before taking my seat in the wings, signalling Dickens to walk on and myself become as one of the audience while Hope Scattergood delivered one of his increasingly authoritative and convincing readings from the works of Charles Dickens.

We read in towns of recent origin where civic pride had taken root with the earliest foundations and was expressed in a stone-built bank, an imposing city hall and a grand theatre. These were embryonic cities that became his proving grounds and these he treated with all the gravitas of players upstate polishing a drama destined for Broadway.

But there were places that were just too small and too insubstantial for Scattergood to take quite seriously, try as he nearly did, at which the performance might be mounted in a barn and where it was clear that the farmers who attended, attracted by the promise of novelty, had no more idea that the Dickens of advertisement was a great and famous writer than they did the precise nature of the entertainment itself and to Scattergood, these events were pure recreation.

I believe that he meant no harm by his erratic behaviour at such places and that at bottom he never had the intention to make fools of his audience, whom I truly believe he respected. His sympathy was reflected in the entirely nominal charges we made for admission, with half the audience being let in free or in barter for local produce or a flagon of home-made liquor. However, there was no gainsaying that these folk got something worlds different from their big-town cousins.

Hope was certain that even had some known the name of Dickens, none would be word-perfect in the stories he chose to tell. They might at best have had their essence imparted orally and this probably much changed by Chinese whispering. Nevertheless, he took quite unpardonable liberties, with both the text and, I thought, with me. Though he could conjure ghosts and summon Scrooge and Bob Cratchit with no more exertion than that expent on matters of expression and tone, he argued that a little exaggeration was just the thing for such unworldly folk. I allowed that there might be something in that but resulting cannonades of laughter also strongly suggested to me that I had been gulled and that Scattergood was having mighty fun at my expense. Once – but once only – he persuaded me to hobble about the stage behind him, aided by a borrowed crutch and feebly uttering, 'God bless us every one.'

The readings, whatever the venue, seemed at first to be markedly beneficial for his health. His cough had subsided or he had learnt to keep it in check. He was anxious and nervous before every reading but a change came over him the moment he opened his book and no one would have suspected that here was a man troubled by a severe illness. When he left the stage, now almost always to rousing applause, he was optimistic and hopeful: he glowed with success and talked of bigger and better venues, of tours in the South and sometimes Europe too.

I reminded him that Dickens would return to England and he must regard this as a thrilling but temporary measure. But he would not be put off and told me that it didn't have to stop with Dickens. 'I heard tell of a fellow down Pennsylvania way,' he told me, as he towelled his face in a dressing-room, 'swore blind he was Nate Hawthorne, as lately died. And there's accounts of a species of Herman Melville operatin' in Georgia and the Carolinas, too.'

He straightened his beard and admired his flushed reflection in the mirror. 'Dear boy,' he said, 'I'm very much of the opinion that here is a field of endeavour in which we may anticipate not a little success. I expect great things to come of it.'

V

I remember the long days we spent in that conveyance and the uncomfortable time we had of it. It seemed always to be my turn to sleep inside when we hit rough road or a stretch of corduroy and I was bounced about like a die in a cup, yet whenever it was Scattergood's turn, the carriage found tarmacadam and launched itself upon it like a ship onto calm water. But mostly, we both sat up top and chewed the fat as we rumbled past desolate hamlets, whose children and animals flew from one-roomed dwellings to mark our passing, or drove into thriving mining towns and lost ourselves in the hurly-burly.

These places, with their scarred hillsides, calvaries of winding wheels and thumping steam engines and armies of workers tramping to and from the mine gates fascinated Scattergood. He watched the wives shopping in the company stores, the craftsmen and mine workers threading their way through mud-stuck carts and teamsters' wagons towards busy saloons and billiard halls and was amazed that a single enterprise could support so much. He took in the multifarious scene, digested it all and pronounced 'Possibilities, Billy.'

We were obliged to make a halt at one such town while a blacksmith repaired our broken axle-tree. The locality offered a handful of diversions but there was no mistaking the Blacklight Hotel as the liveliest place in town. Wild, screeching music filled the street, drowning all noise of braying mules and even beating steam-hammers, whenever its doors burst open and some unseen agent propelled a customer into the street. I was for giving the Blacklight the widest of berths, but Scattergood said it was likely the only place in town to suit our purpose and strode through the doors, sucking me along in his wake. My apprehension was justified. When my eyes had adjusted to the gloomy interior, which was barely relieved by candle stubs and a few poorly-trimmed oil-lamps, I saw that the saloon was a smoke-yellowed box decorated mainly by rents in its wallpaper, some faded prints of George Washington and peeling posters advertising auctions of historical vintage. It was filled to capacity with carousing miners and aping the men were their boys who stood among them with their own glasses of beer and smouldering pipes. Away from the walls with and without infants and children, sat wives and mothers, smoking and spitting like their men-folk. Their eyes and even those of the wild-haired musicians, whose fiddle-scrapings had been suddenly suspended, were fixed upon us.

'Let's go, Hope,' I whispered, but Scattergood, conspicuous as much for his scrubbed skin which no coal-dust had tattooed as for his dandified clothes, seemed oblivious that he was attracting any special attention.

If you have ever kept company with someone whose very presence is always a liability and a threat to public order and whose conversation or demeanour may at any moment be the spark that ignites a conflagration, you might understand why I would have had sooner as companion the glaze-eyed and salivating madman in the rebel cap, than Hope Scattergood as his glaringly dainty walk took him towards the bar. In the down-South inflection that was native to him, he ordered not the beer and whisky of local favour, but a vermouth, cold.

His white and manicured fingers lifted a grubby glass to his lips and he savoured the taste of the aromatic wine before taking a case out of his pocket and from it, selecting a cigar. I never saw anyone take so long to light a cigar. He ran it under his nose, rolled it in his fingers and made an interesting spectacle of its decapitation with his pocket knife. Only when he was sure that no other avenue of invention remained, did he strike a match and with a great flourish, apply it to the leaf. He was immediately lost behind a great cloud of thick, blue smoke.

I waited for our moment's novelty to pass and listened for the music to strike up again but it was evident that we held some fascination for these people, above and beyond the patent fact of our strangeness in those parts. The silence was broken by a heavy footfall, as a great, black-bearded fellow, three-parts grizzly bear, separated himself from the crowd and advanced upon Scattergood.

'Waal,' he said, looking Scattergood up and down, as perhaps he might appraise some appetising morsel, 'who's the Lousiana lily?'

The door was probably ten paces directly behind me and I took one of those backwards steps as the miner loomed over us and sneered, 'You're company men, ain'tcha?'

There was a low hum of talking that ceased when a yellow-toothed individual with eyes so pale I could barely make them out in the gloom, said, ' 'Course they are. Come to move the engines. Or help flood the mine, maybe.'

I took another step back as Grizzly Bear's friends advanced for a closer look but Yellow Teeth saw what I was about and adroitly stepped behind me. There was silence; Scattergood was expected to reply but he only sucked upon his cigar and loudly ordered another vermouth. The barkeep hesitated until Scattergood added, in a voice that brooked no rebuff, 'if you're sure it's no trouble.'

I know I would have left him, denied his acquaintance, had that been at all possible.

'Well?' said the man, maddened by Scattergood's insouciance. 'Come to dance on the grave, have you?'

Scattergood put down his glass and met the man's gaze and said in a forthright and condolent tone that was without a hint of patronage, 'Grave? If someone has died, then I sincerely beg pardon for my intrusion. But it seemed to me there was some celebration in progress here.'

'This ain't no celebration,' said the man, 'it's a goddamn wake!'

'I'm a stranger, just passing through,' said Scattergood. 'A wake for whom?'

The man was clearly enraged but at that moment I had hope that the cause was not us alone. 'For all of us,' he spat. 'You really ain't heard? You ain't one of them?'

'I can hardly say. One of whom?'

'The owners and their pestilential blacklegs.'

'I know nothing of the doings here. What is it that these people have done, that angers you so greatly?'

Grizzly Bear looked about him as if referring our fate to the judgement of the crowd but it appeared to me that they were more urgent to have their story communicated to strangers than to vent their anger on the same.

'They're closing the mine. The owners reckon they'll make

141

more over at Johnson Ridge. They're closing down here and opening up there. When there's still coal to be had here.'

A boy hollered, 'And floodin' the mine so's no one else can git it.'

Everyone in the saloon began to talk at once. A hundred complaints choked the smoky air. I could hear some bad-mouthing the company but others were clearly looking to exercise their anger on us.

Yellow Teeth was by no means satisfied. 'They've sent spies among us afore now,' he said. 'Reckon these are the same breed.'

'Take 'em in back,' said a man who held a stout pick shaft. 'Show them what they get when they try and kill a town,' and I was held, by two strong women, who took an arm apiece. I tried to explain myself but the words were stillborn as the man approached, swinging his club as he came and I don't think I ever was so terrified in my life.

But I could detect no fear in Scattergood as he said, as calmly as he might order the replenishment of his glass, 'A moment, gentlemen, if you please, I would have my say.'

Only those who ever heard Hope Scattergood speak can have any idea of the powers contained in the range of noises that were his voice. A few words from Scattergood could bring reason where there was desperation before, belief where there had been doubt and more often, a sale, where there had been hope of none. And now, no one offered the least interruption as he said, boldly and clearly:

'Forgive me. I understand that you will be suspicious of strange folk at times such as these. But I hope you will grant this stranger the chance to prove that he is not as you suspect but one who believes in your fight and would be your friend.'

'Sweet words,' said Yellow Teeth. 'Just like them the company's fed us this last year. And all the time they was makin' the plans to shut the place down and starve our children. I say we teach these birds some Kentucky manners.'

'I believe I can prove I am not your enemy,' said Scatter-good. 'Let me endeavour to do so and if when I have done,

142

you are still of the opinion that I am a blackguard in the employ of those people, you may do with me as you wish. Is not that fair?'

Grizzly Bear came forward and whether out of justice to us or because of some long-standing feud with Yellow Teeth, ruled that the stranger would have his say.

'My name,' said Hope Scattergood, as he mounted a chair and threw out his coat tails, that his hands might rest upon his hips, 'is Willis Hope. I am a teller of stories. I work the carnivals, the country fairs, I work wherever there are people who will listen to the tales I have to tell.'

He already had his audience. They had stilled their commotion and wanted to hear more. It didn't need the querulous voice of Yellow Teeth to pipe up with, 'So, tell us one of your damn stories and let us decide what you are or what you're not.'

Scattergood appeared to hesitate. He appealed to the crowd. 'Is this the time?' he said. 'I would not have mere entertainment make mockery of your troubles.'

'We have all the time in the world,' said one of the women who held fast my arms.

'Then let it be so,' said Scattergood. He looked about him and waited only seconds while the shuffling and fidgeting, the coughing and expectorating, ceased completely. He drew a whistling breath and said, in a voice that, despite the rawness of his lungs, might have been heard clear out in the street, 'It was the best of times, it was the worst of times.' You may imagine what I thought was to follow, but instead of the tale of Lucie, Darnay and Sydney Carton, Scattergood told of a coal mine in West Virginia and of its terrible owners who asked all from its starving workers and gave next to naught in return.

Nowadays, they say I am a good speaker and that my words have the power to turn men's minds and it must be so; no one rises to a position of real wealth and influence by hard work alone, no matter what they say. This much I owe to Scattergood but I have never possessed the power to ensure the most mundane story unmade men and caused women to cry. This

Scattergood proved he could, as went to work hewing out the tale of a mine owner named Lewis and of his frivolous wife Mary, whose days were scarcely imaginable by those who paid for them with their sweat, their hunger and often, with their lives.

Scattergood's audience stood hushed and almost reverent until roused by anger or sympathy, when they expressed their approbation in shouts and wails; I had seen fire and brimstone preachers work to lesser effect.

Scattergood wiped his brow as he shovelled contempt upon the mine owner's head. Lewis barely ever soiled his boots near the mine and spent his days with his fine horses, which he raced there in Kentucky. Mary grew fat on costly delicacies and frittered her days on French novels or in the company of lovers while terrible hardship gripped the town. When the price of coal was depressed, wages were further reduced and men laboured all hours to feed their children and those without work became drifters on the road and begged their bread or else died.

The company stores grew rich on high prices and exhorbitant credit. Lewis's manager laid off the weak and replaced them with workers from neighbouring counties, who were in equally desperate straits.

'This ain't no story,' said a voice, 'it's the truth!'

'I can testify to that,' said another.

Sensing he was winning his audience, Scattergood made the most of building up his hero, a young man named Cragg who had endured 'a bellyful of Lewis and his kind'. He rallied the men; won over their wives, too; united the whole workforce and took a list of requests to the mansion on the hill. He asked for nothing that was beyond the means of the company and he promised that output would increase, were Lewis only to meet these reasonable demands. But Lewis would have none of it and Cragg returned with empty hands and a heart filled with hatred.

Scattergood began to intrude upon his own narrative and to suggest how Cragg might have duped Lewis and turned the crisis to his advantage. It seemed a cunning ploy to me and one through which none might have suffered and all enjoyed some benefit though it was but a compromise and only fulfilled the most basic of the miners' demands. There was a rumbling amongst the crowd and some catcalls too. He didn't need me to tell him that this was no time for the offering of sensible solutions. The man was swinging his club again and you might have read the change in mood on a barometer.

Scattergood was sensible of this. 'So they struck!' he exclaimed. 'They closed down that mine and posted pickets so neither the teamsters nor the managers got within a half mile of its gates. Cragg's men stood as one: they held that mine for six weeks and when news got about, people sent food and money too. No one knew how long they might hold out because now these men had been given back their pride and with that came courage and great resiliance.

'The only loser then was Lewis and his backers. They sent in the militia but the men were local boys with no stomach for turning their guns on their own. Then Lewis's son was found in an alley with his throat cut. He had been discovered with a local girl; he was killed, the girl tarred and feathered.'

Scattergood paused, hoping, I thought, to bring the listeners with him as he changed tack and with his awful retailing of the bloodshed that followed, make some point that anything might have been better than that. But Yellow Teeth, or one of his kind, called out and demanded to know the fate of Cragg, in tones of menace that the truth could not have placated. I later learned that Cragg had been wrongly accused of the murder and hanged, but to have told them that would have risked their wrath. Scattergood looked down upon me; I was still held fast and the man with the pick shaft stood at my side.

'Revenge,' he said, in a voice low and cold, 'was the only medicine. Cragg took his best men and they stole past Lewis's guards in the dead of a black night. I believe that Cragg's intention was only to reason with Lewis, man to man and face to face and never to harm him or his family. But revenge had fired his following and when they came upon Mary Lewis, they gave her over to their women, who dealt her such a fate as my words can hardly encompass.'

'And Lewis?' said Yellow Teeth. 'What'd they do to that son of a bitch?'

'They slit his throat,' said Scattergood. 'Cragg tried to stop them, said it would only be the worse for them. But their blood was up and Lewis's own poured forth in buckets. He died like a slaughtered pig, there upon his bedroom floor.'

Scattergood stopped and stood like a man concussed. I wondered that he had given too much of himself and might presently fall from his chair in a faint and I made to wrest my arms free from those who had held me close. But I was a prisoner no longer. I looked about me and saw that the eyes of all were upon him but still the mood of the crowd eluded me and I was ready to risk all in one deperate bid to pull Hope down and rush with him to the doors, when there was cheering, begun, I think, by Grizzly Bear and this grew louder and then hats were thrown and Scattergood pulled from his perch, clapped on his back and made invisible to me by a mob of well-wishing people.

As his friend, my hand was pumped, too, and I shared in the bounty his story had earned. There was much drinking, none at our own expense, tales of iniquity and heroism were the coin of the day and once again, with some misgivings, I wondered if there were ever such a man as Hope Scattergood.

It was late evening before I could extricate him and we were able to collect the coach, the cost of whose repairs had been mysteriously met. We got up top and rolled back down the street, Scattergood drunk as a lord and me hardly the better. Scattergood was in triumphant mood but I was unsettled, some doubt remaining in my mind regarding the moral tone of his story.

'I gave 'em what they wanted, Billy,' he said. 'Didn't you see their faces? They were alive!'

'I don't know, Hope,' I said. 'Maybe it wasn't wholly responsible.'

'Responsible?' he ejaculated. 'I brought those people happiness, Billy, happiness!'

And we trundled down the street, until we again passed the Blacklight Hotel from whose portals Scattergood's audience were now emerging and joining others who held flaming torches. We pulled up to watch them as they congregated and their numbers swelled. At a signal from some dark figure of the same proportions as the fellow I call Grizzly Bear, they began to march up the hill, with, I thought, fell purpose.

VI

We had left the mining town some miles behind us and Scattergood was waxing eloquent, as ever he did after drink.

'We'll read in Cincinnati,' he announced, 'and then in West Virginia and Pennsylvania too. It might be a little warm for us to try more so far East – Dickens is up and down that coast like a shuttle on a loom but I have other plans to occupy us, once we are there.'

'I wonder it's not too warm to read in Cincinnati,' I said. 'It's a big city full of educated folks. We could be found out.'

'Have confidence, Billy,' he said, 'that's all it takes. If I have the confidence to take the biggest place they got and walk on that stage as Charles Dickens, they'll believe me, all right. It just takes a good night in Cincinnati and some little time rounding up cash in New York and then I'll be on a boat for Switzerland and get my cure.'

'Is he good, this doctor?' I asked.

'He's a miracle worker. People a while lot sicker'n I am have come back completely cured. The secret's in the sweet mountain air. Just a few weeks of that and I'll be good as new, then me and you will head South, where the real money's to be made.'

That was Scattergood's dream. To drum up enough money to patch up his lungs and go on living, just the way he had. Maybe his doctor was something special, maybe he could cure this condition that crippled Hope on some days and let him alone to dream his dreams on others. I couldn't say. But that was his dream and he was so certain of success and a bright future that I would have lost an arm rather than gainsay it.

I too had a dream, but mine belonged to someone else. Mine was the dream of Elijah Putnam and the more I thought about it, the less inclined I became to pursue it. But here I was, still heading East, still telling Scattergood we must part there, as I had my own business to attend to.

It wasn't long before my easy-listening partner had got out of me just what was my business. He attended thoughtfully as I told him all about Elijah Putnam, my mother and what had happened, the first time Charles Dickens had visited America. 'If that don't beat everything,' he said, slapping me on my back. 'You are my bastard son? My boy, you have made me very happy. You may give your father a kiss.'

And so amused was he with this turn of affairs that he laughed so hard his cough returned in force and he all but laughed and coughed himself from the top of the coach. But when he had become possessed of himself, he inquired deeper into my history and said he was of the opinion that I might or might not be son to Charles Dickens and that the writer might or might not recognise me as such; but it was such a possibility that it could not be left untried: that would be like leaving money on the street because it might be counterfeit. We would go to New York and when it was possible and convenient, I should wait upon Charles Dickens.

Cincinnati was bigger that any place I had been before and as soon as I saw its magnificent streets and fine waterfront I was convinced that we were biting off more than we could chew. The theatre was immense and I doubted I could muster the temerity to walk into its manager's office and demand its hire. Scattergood took it all in his stride and after reconnoitring the city, he gave me a letter of introduction and instructed me to secure the theatre, have printed the tickets and to make myself known to the mayor of Cincinnati. If you had suggested to him a month before that Billy Talbot could do all that, he would not have believed you himself. But I did and was accepted, and even courted, as George Dolby, manager to Charles Dickens.

It was at Cincinnati that we first encountered the speculators, who bought up the first six rows of seats and began to sell them immediately, at double their face value. I was dealing out these tickets, six at a time, when a red-faced fellow in a Homburg hat looked sharply at me and said, 'You ain't Dolby.' I thought he must see the beating of my heart as it pounded through my waistcoat but I collected myself as best I could and said that of course I wasn't: I was merely Mr Dolby's agent and that Mr Dolby would most likely show up on the night of the reading. He appeared satisfied and took his tickets, but I was anxious that there might be repercussions. I was everywhere known as Dolby and wondered anew if, with Cincinnati, Hope Scattergood and I had not overreached ourselves.

If I have gall now – and my adversaries have indeed called me arrogant, brash and overweening, though I say it is only enthusiasm and confidence overspilling their bounds – then it has its beginning in these few days we spent in Cincinnati. I had no chance to waver: Cincinnati was do or die. As usual, I had scouted the city and put up bills and had arranged for the immediate printing of the tickets. Then I made time to wire Elijah Putnam, informing him that I would be delayed in arriving at the boarding-house in New York but that once there, I would try and execute his commission as faithfully as I could. I still figured the least I owed Elijah was to give his scheme a try.

Arrived at a magnificent theatre, I mustered sufficient courage to arrange a meeting with its manager, Mr Garwick, who, far from ejecting me as the impostor I thought it must be clear I was, invited me into his private drawing-room, sent out for my lunch and offered me a cigar.

'It's an honour, Mr Dolby,' he told me, 'a very great honour. And such a relief for the city. It had been rumoured that Dickens was not to come to Cincinnati, but I never believed

149

it, not for one minute. Of course he had to come. After what he wrote. I have it here.'

He took a volume from his well-stocked bookshelves and proudly recited Dickens' unqualified praise for the houses, gardens, streets, schools and people of Cincinnati, without glancing at the page more than once.

'Where will you stay?' he asked.

I named a couple of places I had seen which I had thought more majestic than anything I had seen before but Mr Garwick said that would never do, not for Dickens. It must be the Grand. He would make the arrangements himself. I told him that Dickens would arrive by rail the next day (we had purposely put up some few stops down the main line to Cincinnati) and when nightfall came, I boarded the train back to where Scattergood was awaiting in a high state of anticipation.

The next day we were met at the station by a deputation of the worthies of Cincinnati, deposited in a brougham with the mayor and his wife and followed into town by civic dignitaries, a marching band and a variegated following which cried up the news that here was Dickens; Old Charley had arrived just like he said he would.

There were flowers and a whole deck of visiting cards at our suite, to which we retreated as soon as decency allowed, Scattergood apologising that he was fatigued and in need of rest before the rigours of the evening. I closed the door against a knot of waiters and inquisitive meddlers but even then we had to draw the blinds before we felt safe from the gaze of spectators in windows across the street. We inspected the furnishings of our sitting-room and adjoining bedrooms and Scattergood read out some of the gilt-edged invitations.

'Spurn them all,' I advised, 'these are important folk. They'll see through us like glass.'

'Would they? Sometimes I think I could deceive my own mother. But I suppose you're right. Most of them will be at the ball, anyways.'

'What ball?'

150

'The Dickens Ball,' said Scattergood. 'The mayor's fixed it for tomorrow evening. The whole town will be there.'

'And we're going?' I said, appalled. 'We're not lighting out with the money, right after the reading?'

'I'm surprised at you, Billy,' said Scattergood. 'How on earth can they hold a Dickens Ball without Dickens?'

Chapter Nine

I

IF YOU ARE given to reading novels (and to this occupation I devote more time than my public duty strictly permits) it is unnecessary that I report the ball in Cincinnati in full. In its presentation and mechanics, it differed very little from the thousand and one similar events that smother whole chapters and rarely advance the action, unless it be significant that the heroine is *twice* asked to dance by the dashing Captain Popinjay.

I find that such scenes pall by their very familiarity and I approach a ball or a picnic or a grand dinner party with similar apprehension. They appear to me as artificial conceits in which characters whose paths may otherwise never cross are intimate with each other against a backdrop that would look better on canvas than paper. But although I had encountered such gatherings between the covers of Elijah's books, I had never the actual experience of any grander occasion than the night at the Particular, when a gentleman guest had given a great dinner for the commercial travellers, in honour of his two unmarried daughters.

Because of this, I was a little in awe of the enormous crowds that packed the ballroom, the sparkling crystal chandeliers, the deafening music and hubbub of chatter that was only to be avoided by stepping out into the cold night air of the terrace. Given the chance to remove myself to some distance – the gallery, perhaps, although that too was busy – and to become merely an onlooker, I might have recognised all the types familiar from my reading: chaperones with charges eager for their freedom, mothers offloading their daughters, whispering gossips and jealous old dames, young bucks tipsy on punch, obnoxious drunks, knots of men who knew their own importance and single floundering guests caught in the sights of fading wallflowers.

But we had been swept up carpeted stairs and confronted with a brilliant assembly that hushed at our entry and spoke to us only through the mediums of perfume and camphor and thick cigar smoke while we were announced as 'The Most Revered and Respected Writer and Honoured Friend of America, Our Beloved Boz: Mr Charles Dickens. With his manager upon this historic tour of the United States, Mr George Dolby.'

I doubt there was more than a second's silence between this and the applause that followed but that was time enough for me to experience profound terror: I scanned the expectant faces, half-expecting an arm to raise and a finger to point and a voice to roar 'That's not Dickens! And that's not Dolby, either!'

But such was the spell that the name of Dickens had cast over the city that no one discovered us. Some noticed a disparity in appearance between this Dickens and his resemblance in recent likenesses, but I heard it said more than once that 'Mr Dickens is better looking in the flesh.' He said little, allowing others to talk instead and give him their opinions of his works or tell him what he ought to think of the improvements that had been effected in Cincinnati since last he was there.

A dangerous moment occurred shortly after our arrival when among the dignitaries presented to us appeared an old man, whom it was said, Dickens must surely remember from

154

his earlier visit. The man had taken off his hat and was tending a tremulous hand. I noted the positions of all possible exits and braced myself for the acrimonious explosion that must follow our exposure as mountebanks who had insulted the entire city of Cincinnati. When I looked again, I saw that Scattergood was shaking the man's hand warmly, greeting him as an old and dear friend and the aged man was nodding and dividing his attention between Scattergood and some water ices on a tray, suggesting to me that he had achieved that superfluity of age when the mind is apt to wander.

Dickens entered the ballroom and was greeted with deference by the great and the good of Cincinnati. The famous writer was then handed about the crowd, fussed and fought over, his beaming smile and booming laughter assuring me that he at least was undaunted by the grandeur of the occasion. In fact, he was patently relishing the attention as he shook and kissed hands and accepted tributes as his due.

I too was launched amid the throng. I felt as a pressed sailor on a dangerous voyage and learned quickly how the safe conversational shallows of money and travel could suddenly shelve precipitately into the murkier depths of personal history and mutual acquaintance. I speedily began mastering the art of safe navigation.

These were dangerous waters. I feared there must be others who had seen Charles Dickens in Cincinnati and I was far from sure that the passing of a quarter century would sufficiently explain the differences between Dickens then and Dickens now. And might there not be some travellers who had already seen him read upon the Eastern Coast? Scattergood had assured me this was unlikely and that himself would be 'too many' for any problem that might arise. 'You only need confidence, Billy,' he told me and maybe he had been right. The more I forced my smile and approximated what Elijah had once told me was a passable English accent, the better people seemed to like me and the more amusement I had.

The ladies of Cincinatti begged to hear adventures I

exaggerated out of all recognition or borrowed of Hope Scattergood's plentiful repertoire. Some of those about me were plain and some pretty but all were attentive and patently thrilled to have the attention of Charles Dickens' manager and companion. Their adulation might have turned a lesser man's head but I was not such a fool as to believe them attracted only to Billy Talbot and reminded myself that my new-found success was accreditable to the magic of Dickens' name. And yet, as I passed a great and ornately-framed mirror, it crossed my mind that perhaps I was something more than the ugly duckling I was accustomed to think myself. I might have considered the night well-spent if I could only have continued spinning my yarns and webs to my admiring audience and I was mightily displeased when the good ship Talbot became snagged upon a shoal that introduced itself as Mr Hans Steiner.

This short, rubicund and whiskery individual had forced his way into our little circle, drawing in his wake a small and worried woman, wearing the curls of another age. He grasped my hand as if making an arrest and was immediately effusive and fulsome with his praise of my achievement as Dickens' manager. I cared little for his excessive civilities when I saw my adoring disciples melting back into the assembly.

'I believe I can do you a great service, sir,' he said, pumping my hand so hard I thought I should begin spouting water. 'I have no doubt Dickens' success in Boston and New York owes much to you, sir, but here in the hinterland you're a fish out of water, ain't that right?' He dealt me a card which proclaimed him an Official and Important Somebody. 'That's me,' he continued. 'I have at my disposal the City of Cinicinnati and I'm going to offer to you my considerable services. Well, what do you say, Dolby?'

I must have looked baffled because he immediately explained. 'Why, partnership, Dolby, partnership! I'll help you look after Dickens while he's in Cincinnati and make sure he doubles, nay, trebles his receipts.' I recognised immediately a type we had met with annoying regularity. At every place we stopped, we could expect to be approached by someone wishing to hitch his wagon to Dickens' star.

Before I had time to consider a reply, Scattergood hove into view with the timely suggestion that I sample the punch and I was relieved to be immediately cut loose by Steiner even though I was given charge of his wife, a pale and tremulous thing, from whom a goose might expect no rude fright. She mustered her courage and asked a question of Dickens, 'Where do get your inspiration?' but before Scattergood had properly begun to expand upon his debt to the muse, her husband had interrupted and from then on, he entirely monopolised the conversation.

The substance of his soliloquy was of no great interest or originality. Though he dressed it up in fancy words and boasted of his good works among the orphans and fallen women of Cincinnati, whom, he said, would be the prime beneficiaries of his own share in the suggested partnership, the message was the same that we had heard from a succession of sharp-eyed opportunists and only differed in tone and vocabulary from that of the masked men who held up coaches on the road. After each sententious burst, he looked to Scattergood, nodded as if Dickens had expressed his total agreement and went on as before. In all, he expelled so much hot air that had he been a balloon he must have ascended to a great height.

There were other impediments to our smooth progress. Two officers of the Union army insisted on restaging the War for the benefit of we who had missed it and our time was bought up by adventurous merchants who had visited London and, thankfully, preferred showing off their own geography to questioning ours. But, mostly, people were friendly and so pleased and honoured to make our acquaintance that I felt not a little uncomfortable about perpetrating upon them such a gross deception.

Encomiums and plaudits were Scattergood's and some little part of the glory I had too by association. Scattergood was further honoured when the mayor presented his daughter and asked if he would do them the honour of leading the dancing. He requested that the other ladies excuse him and with a look of rueful *noblesse oblige* took her arm in his. The crowds made way, the band struck up a waltz and I beheld the novel spectacle of Hope Scattergood dancing in an accomplished fashion, with the official belle of the ball.

While this was in progress a man I had noticed in conversation with Scattergood introduced to me a girl whose name was Katy Pearson and this young lady had the biggest eyes and the prettiest curls and the ripest red lips, that parted to say how delighted she would be to partner me in the next dance. I took her slender arm and led her upon the floor and we began to dance. I remember her flashing hazel eyes, her flushed cheeks, the feel of her soft skin beneath my hands and her slim fingers about my neck.

Just yesterday I caught a breath of a woman's scent as she passed me on the stairs and I recalled at once exactly how it had been when Katy and I had whirled about that dance floor, my face so close to hers that I was overpowered by the perfume on her skin and the fragrance of her hair. I had remembered us alone but now I can bring to mind the others who danced, both the gracefully proficient and the cheerfully inexpert. I can even remember the waltz they played and how certain I was that those who looked on saw only me with the girl who must surely be Cincinnati's finest flower. I blazed with pride as it struck me that there was not a man-jack present would not have paid hard cash for an hour in her company. And I thought that I had known love? Oh, that Cissy Bullock might have seen me then!

The waltz had ended and people were clapping. I felt Scattergood's hand upon my shoulder and his breath in my ear. 'Well?' he whispered. 'Are you *happy*, Billy?' And I was too filled with that emotion to form a reply. In all my memories of my time with Hope Scattergood, this is the moment that keeps its warmth still. We were at the height of our powers: we were rich, the takings were already secured in the hotel safe, we were celebrated, possibilities abounded and I was in love.

Katy Pearson said it was hot inside and could we not take a turn in the gardens? I thought the night air chill, but seized the chance to be alone with my new-found love. Below the terrace were some neat and well-tended gardens and I gave her my arm as we strolled across them, in and out of patches of light cast by the windows of the ballroom.

We walked this way and that, exchanging small talk and I never thought that our perambulations had any objective but once out of sight of anyone upon the terrace, she led me down a flight of steep and slippery steps into regions uncharted by any gardener, a wasteland that had perhaps been the garden to an earlier edifice and had yet to be incorporated into the new grand design. Katy guided me about the rubble of broken and abandoned monuments to a dark corner, where tangles of vine appeared to limit further progress. She located a narrow opening and I pushed into the dense bush, emerging in a corner of the garden where was an old summer house.

She opened a door and we entered a musty and mildewed space in which were faintly discernable the shapes of tables and chairs, furniture for the garden, in store for the winter. We crossed the threshold and when she turned I could barely see her face, which was turned up towards my own.

'Well?' she whispered and I felt the warmth of her trim body pressed against mine and smelt the hair that tickled my nose as she buried her face in my chest. I took her and held her close and swelled up with bursting love and pride and should have certainly kissed her there and then had not Katy freed herself from my embrace. For a second I thought I had been too forward with her, but she was opening her jacket and loosening her blouse, removing a ring from a finger that fell to the floor and rolled on the boards and then she was taking my hands and placing them above her stays and I could feel the softness and warmth of a woman's breasts.

She lifted up her head and her hot breath was upon my lips. I kissed her own full and beautiful mouth, all thoughts of

Cissy Bullock, Hope Scattergood, Elijah Putnam or any other atom of my previous miserable existence extirpated in this one moment of unparalleled being. Her hands were beneath my coat, the tips of her fingers pressing lightly in the small of my back and I thought that moment was everything and unsurpassable but then she broke away and busied herself with dustsheets and some old clothes which she threw on the floor.

Then she was upon the floor herself, pulling me down with her, upon her. I could not resist, nor would have. I had not a thought for the rights and wrongs of the business so eaten up was I with desire and the hunger for consummation. She removed her dress and asked me to help her with her stays. She coaxed off my own jacket and shirt and released me from what was left. I was frantic, ungainly, desperate but she was cooler and guided me towards a better knowledge and more perfect satisfaction and I shuddered with supreme joy as the longed-for relief and the celebration came. Tears welled and made shimmer the white moon. I was laughing and crying all at once. Indeed, I felt like crying out but I could not but be aware of and considerate for she who had forsaken her honour to give me such joy.

I bent to caress her forehead and stroke her hair, to reassure her that what we had done was not wrong. Despite what the preachers and praters said, how could *that* be wrong? But she was already rearranging her clothes and hair and folding up the sheets and rugs.

'Quickly,' she said to me, 'before we are missed.'

III

This happy state of affairs, this unbounded happiness, lasted for perhaps an hour during which I danced with Katy Pearson and, flushed with success and brimming with new confidence, I talked to all and sundry and entertained them with a ready wit I was hitherto unaware was in my possession until, at the height of my felicity, the attention of my audience was diverted to the mayor who was to make a speech of welcome to Charles Dickens. He stood beneath the enormous banner that already said as much as he intended and began his task, Scattergood standing at his side, looked suitably abashed, though whether by the mayor's flattering remarks or by his own audacity, I couldn't decide.

Hope Scattergood thanked the mayor for his cordial welcome and Cincinnati for the generous reception it had given his readings. Scattergood had read to a full house, the largest audience I had ever seen him face and yet he had not faltered and seemed more convincingly Charles Dickens than at any other time we tried the Dickens lay. I guessed he was the sort to rise to a challenge. There was not a hint of uncertainty now as his eyes twinkled and he began his reply by applauding the open and trusting nature of the American people and then went on to praise American womenfolk, whose charm far exceeded that of the ladies of London. As an aside, he hoped it would go no further than 'these four walls' if he were to say he had some experience in that department.

He took advantage of a ripple of hearty laughter to drink from his glass of punch. 'My friends,' he said, 'you are the best of people and I am unworthy of the honour you do me.' He raised his hands to still murmurings of dissent. 'After all, what have I done? Have I felled trees and carved out farms from wood and prairie? Have I built a magnificent and thriving city as you have done in Cincinnati? No, it is you, my friends, who are worthy of honour. All I have done is written a few poor books for the amusement of those with the time to read them. What is it to take white paper and make upon it such marks that a publisher finds pretty? Why, anybody might do the same. I don't deserve your praise. No,' he held up his hands to quiet further protest, 'I really don't.'

His self-deprecation puzzled his listeners. Then someone at the back piped up with, 'Hell, yes, we done good here but you done good too, Mr Dickens!' and that provoked a rousing cheer. When there was calm, another voice, that of a tall man

161

who had already introduced himself to me as a schoolteacher said, 'Sir, your modesty does you credit but you cannot underestimate your achievements. Your genius shines from every page. Your characters alone . . .'

'Ah, my characters,' said Scattergood, 'they are my friends.'

'It's as if you know them, I suppose?' said the schoolteacher.

'I *have* known them,' said Dickens. 'In fact, I'm related to some. Martin Chuzzlewit, old Martin, that is, was my grandfather. And my cousin Nick Nickleby accompanied me to the boat. We made quite a gay party. Dick Swiveller and Bob Allen came along to see me on board and we raised many a glass to my expedition and to the United States of America.'

Eddies of consternation spread through the audience. It was like a millstone dropped in a pond. Scattergood must have seen this but appeared unruffled.

'The boy Smike,' he began again, 'and I'm sure the transformation that Nick effected in his unhappy circumstances will justify me in unmasking him here, was inspired by the unhappy early days of my friend Dolby, there. You see before you the original.'

All eyes turned towards me and I cursed my friend through gritted teeth. I already knew Scattergood for someone who would always go a step too far but at least my corporeal presence added some substance to what he was saying even if now his listeners were clearly perplexed.

A woman at the elbow of the schoolteacher asked, 'But David Copperfield? Ain't that really you?'

Scattergood said, 'Bless you, no, ma'am and I shall have royal fun with Copperfield when I tell him that. I will own that he's a particular friend, though, and I always knew that the true story of his eventful life would make an appealing publication. No, ma'am, David Copperfield, eats, breathes, drinks Madeira wine and might be seen any evening, promenading with choice spirits in Covent Garden. However,' he added, 'I did accede to his request that his name be altered for the purposes of publication.'

The woman, in conspiratorial tone, whispered, 'What was it really?'

'It was,' said Scattergood after pausing for effect or perhaps, for inspiration, '*Daniel* Copperfield.'

I began to laugh, I think, at Scattergood's monstrous presumption but some others joined in, then some more saw the joke. I heard someone close by say, 'Irony, don't you see? Dickens is really a most amusing fellow.' And from that moment, anything Dickens said was greeted with the most exuberant hilarity and I think he might have read a page of obituaries to the same effect.

Once persuaded that Scattergood was not about to scuttle us, no one enjoyed his performance more than I but my pleasure was to be curtailed by an unpleasant distraction. I had become aware of a figure standing by the French windows whose attention had fixed itself not upon Charles Dickens and the mayor of Cincinnati but upon me. I tried to follow the mayor's speech but the uncomfortable sense of his presence grew stronger. He was always there, a black mote in the corner of my eye. I hoped my fears were groundless and here was not a man who knew in person the real George Dolby.

He moved and by some gesture beckoned me. I turned reluctantly and recognised Silas Amory, the editor of the Hayes *Bugle* and confederate of Melik Merriweather I disliked him and was disposed to ignore him but Silas Amory was, as he liked to say, a man to be reckoned with and I doubted not that his presence here had some special purpose. He observed me coolly, as I excused myself to Katy. I was loathe to quit a scene of such conviviality and would gladly have heard the remainder of Scattergood's address with Katy at my side. But I obeyed his summons just as I always did at the Particular when Merriweather was as happy for me to satisfy his friend's whims and fancies as his own.

'Mister . . .' – he cut the end from a cigar – 'Dolby,' he said, ponderously. 'I wonder if you might spare me a minute of your precious time?' I followed him through French windows

and we stood upon the terrace, which we had then to ourselves. Amory leaned against the parapet, his face dark against
the gas-lit streets of Cincinnati, except for where a red ember
glowed fiercely when he sucked on his cigar. I waited for him
to speak, but he seemed in no hurry and continued to smoke.
Finally, he said, 'Well, well, Billy Talbot. I find you considerably
changed.'

'Has Merriweather sent you?' I asked.

He snorted. 'I should send that witless fool to hell before I
let him order my movements.'

'Why are you here?' I asked.

'You've become impatient, too, I see.'

'Whatever you're here for, can it not wait until tomorrow?'

Behind the glass, Scattergood's speech was being received
with tumultuous laughter.

'I can see how this might be inconvenient for you,' he said.
'But I'm here as a gentleman of the Press. Surely it would be
a dereliction of my duty to miss the appearance of Charles
Dickens at Cincinnati?'

'What do you want, Mr Amory?'

'All in good time. You recall an evening walk you took with
your blind friend, Mr Putnam?'

'We often walked in the evenings.'

'Let us say I was clearing my head of smoke with a
nocturnal promenade and it so fell out that our paths crossed
and I was unable to avoid hearing some titbits of startling
information.'

'What did you hear?'

'Oh, only that you may be kin to Dickens and were to
intercept him during his stay in this country.'

'And that is how you have found me?'

'I was in Cincinnati for quite another reason, although it
suits my purpose to catch up with you. When I discovered the
town had caught Dickens fever, I felt it likely I should find
you here. You may imagine my surprise at witnessing your
triumphal arrival. To begin with, I thought that you were
already installed as Dickens' long-lost son. Then I heard you

164

called Dolby and surmised that if you were he, then that' – he indicated the form of Scattergood, who was barely visible amid a colourful cloud of satin and silk – 'was not Dickens.'

The doors opened and curtains parted. Light shone upon his face and I saw that he was smiling and I knew we were undone. The euphoria and confidence, the sherry-fuelled bonhomie and the victoriousness of only minutes before, were gone and in their place was creeping fear. I turned to peer through the windows, an outsider looking in. It seemed incredible that in the brightness and warmth of the ballroom were people still laughing and making merry and a girl who was perhaps a little bit in love and yet only steps away, in the night air which was beginning to freeze, was a soul empty of anything but the most hopeless dread.

A boy and his girl had come out onto the terrace in search of privacy but they were followed by a couple of businessmen who talked in conspiratorial tones and by a woman I took to be the girl's chaperone. A drunk stumbled out too and thought to strike up a conversation with Amory but he saw the set of the other's face and thought the better of it. A man with whom I had talked earlier looked out of the doors and called, 'Halloa, Dolby! We need you inside, you know!'

'This is impossible,' said Amory. 'Be so good as to meet with me at this address once this festival for fools is over. There is some business to be done. You know me, Billy. I would not hesitate to see you exposed before all Cincinnati if you try and cross me. I shall know it if you attempt to leave town.'

He flicked his cigar over the parapet and slipped down the steps to the lawn where he was soon consumed by the shadows. I re-entered the ballroom, where Katy was being amused by another gentleman. I had not a thought for her at that moment. I stood at the back of the crowd, my face no doubt as black as midnight and awaited the moment when I could privately tell Scattergood, who was then receiving a loud ovation, that we were in trouble, very probably in danger too.

Chapter Ten

I

THEY SAY A man can sell his soul to the Devil. I don't know if this is true or not but I have now a handful of colleagues who are routinely reported by this city's newspapers as having done just that. Whether these are first-hand reports, taken down by accurate stenographers in the presence of both parties or are merely hearsay, I'm sure I don't know.

But selling his soul, or pawning his very essence, is what a man does when he decides to break the fetters and ties of conventional morality and treat lightly the laws of man and God. There are such people but so great is the boldness and daring required that they are few. Think, for a minute, of what must be required of the man who says that the way he lives now is not enough and that he will discover what might be possible if he allows nothing to stand in his way. Consider the man who pursues his designs at any cost – any cost at all, so long as *he* does not pay. He only needs courage and the fruit of the earth might be his.

One can only speculate on the liberation that might be entailed in fully exploring one's potential and finding out what one might be. The creation of a new set of rules, the chance to start afresh, would be exhilarating, I'm sure. I can understand those blasphemous freethinkers who consider it the greatest thing a man might do. But what it must do to those men, in the end, is beyond my comprehension. These are not solely bad men. They are neither mere animals, made slaves to their lusts and hungers and barely cognisant of their folly as they blunder from one brutish act to another. Nor are they such as I was, which is neither good nor bad but in some middling state. These men, for all their audacity and courage, are evil and such a man, I think, was Silas Amory.

I never caught him arm-in-arm with Lucifer and nor were cloven tracks ever found outside the grimy offices that were the home of the Hayes *Bugle* but had anyone told the child Billy Talbot that Silas and Satan were on first-name terms, I can say for certain that he would have taken it as Gospel.

I was on Main Street when Silas Amory first showed up in town. He wasn't a newspaper editor then. It had been raining all week so hard that the whole town looked in danger of slipping its moorings and sliding down the hill to coalesce with the mud of the Mississippi. Water had gotten everywhere, had seeped through roofs, spoilt crops, made new ponds of hollows and collected in deep wheel ruts from whence it turned low-lying Main Street into a little creek.

Teamsters hollered for help when their wagons not only got stuck there but began to sink and folk were laying out boards on the road and hoisting wheels and horses from this morass of rainwater and black, glutinous mud when I showed up, basket in hand. This was my third visit to Hayes that day. No one at the Particular wanted to quit the comparative dryness of Rodericksburg, which was perched on the summit of a bluff, for the stinking mire of the main town. Being at the pecked end of the pecking order, I was despatched by Merriweather or Irving, Cook or even Mary Ann whenever any little thing was wanted from town and I was getting mighty tired of trudging through heavy rain in boots caked in clay.

I was stood by the dry-goods store, waiting for old man Baker to come and open up after his lunch and the rain was streaming off my hat and coursing down my neck while I watched the drivers whipping their horses into vain attempts to jerk their loads out of the mud and up upon the boards when my attention was taken by a cart newly-arrived from out of town. It too began to stick. Someone shouted, 'Lose some weight or you'll sink.' The carrier threw down a couple of sacks but the spectator, whom I had seen direct several similar operations already that morning, said, 'More,' and then I saw the driver rolling a much bigger sack off the tailboard, which landed heavily in the deepest and darkest patch of mud in the street and which distinguished itself from the other sacks by beginning to move.

'I could have done without him anyways,' called the teamster. 'Was drunk when he got on board, been drinking ever since.'

I watched as the thing rolled over in the black mud and slowly rose up upon one and then both hands. I couldn't make out any feature, mud had clogged everything and, as he ran a hand across his brow to clear his eyes, it was like seeing some ancient creature crawling from the swamp. Slowly, it rose to its knees and unsteadily found its feet. Onlookers had gathered and were staring as they will but the man stood his ground and waited for one of their number to break his gaze and depart before he slowly crossed the street upon the boards and asked of them if anyone knew where was the hotel of Melik Merriweather. From where he had come I never knew. To me he was always a thing spawned of the mud.

For a time, he was a guest at the hotel, though I doubt he was the paying variety. He seemed pretty thick with Merriweather, who bought him a suit and may have lent or given him money, because the thing of the mud evolved suddenly into a lean and sleek gentleman, who sported well-groomed hair and moustache and who dressed about as well as you could, in those parts. Whatever history Melik Merriweather and Silas Amory had shared I never found out but I doubt not that the connection was unsavoury. Amory stayed at the Particular and very quickly made himself known to those who counted in the hamlet of Rodericksburg and in the town of Hayes. But although he was very soon known by all, I never heard of anyone professing to like him. How he raised the money to buy into the ailing Hayes *Bugle*, and shortly after buy out his partner, was another mystery but however he got it, you can be sure of one thing – someone else lost out by it.

At first people were encouraged by his entry into journalism, prepared to give him the benefit of the doubt. He had found a proper job and through the newspaper, might perhaps provide a service for the community. But then the calumnies appeared. The mayor was discovered involved in some petty corruption and publicly disgraced in the town newspaper. Others were also pilloried. Someone tried to set fire to the *Bugle* and the lead story of the first paper to appear after the damage had been put right lamented the mysterious murder of a citizen who had brought a suit against Amory and the *Bugle*, although whether the two events were connected was anyone's guess.

It became clear that Silas Amory had bought the Hayes *Bugle* as a means of establishing himself in a position of power. He used the power shrewdly and the *Bugle* held sway over town elections. Silas Amory was courted by all factions and often endorsed the most unlikely candidates. Amory quickly got richer than you might imagine possible for a small-town newsman. He seemed everywhere at once and so many of my childhood memories are marred by his presence, a black shadow flitting hither and thither, sleuthing, we were given to suppose, some great story but to my mind always involved in some other dark and secret work.

Recently, it had been said that Amory himself would enter politics. Everyone knew of his ambitions to become mayor of Hayes but opinion had it that Amory saw this as only a stepping stone to a Governor's mansion and beyond. Amory had won influence among those who mattered but not among the general electorate and it seemed likely that the embryo of his political career would be stillborn. Others said that the only way in which he might succeed quickly in politics would

170

be as one of the breed they were calling 'carpetbaggers' who were then drifting into the defeated Confederacy and paying the newly enfranchised electorate for political power with a bagful of empty promises. Amory, they said, was just the kind to succeed in that line. I didn't care what he did just so long as his chosen future led him away from Hayes and Merriweather's parlour in which he was so often comfortably ensconced and where he delighted to taunt and often frighten the callow boy in the stovepipe hat.

I might have been callow with much still to learn about man and his ways but by the time I met him in Cincinnati, I knew enough about Silas Amory to be certain that his appearance there boded no one any good, least of all Billy Talbot and his new friend Hope Scattergood.

II

Scattergood remained composed as I broke the news. I was surprised because following his official welcome he had shaken hands with and received the approbation of probably every pillar that supported the society of Cincinnati. He must have felt himself upon a pinnacle. He merely remarked that it was a regrettable setback but one that must be expected in a precarious line such as this where the risks were great but the rewards commensurate. However, he added into a glass of French champagne, he rather thought it would take more than some blackmailer from the boondocks to bring him low. We would simply have to be somewhat more circumspect in the manner of our departure.

I told him all I knew of Silas Amory, of his shady dealings and of how he was so often suspected of sinister crimes but never taken up for them, let alone convicted and so convinced him that this was a man most unlikely to take chances. I was never more sure that if we failed to keep the appointment the whistle would be blown and the morning would find us behind lock and key if nothing worse.

He saw that there was no question but that we must comply,

171

though I wondered if he might also be genuinely curious to discover what sort of a man would dare to pit himself against the wits of a Hope Scattergood at the peak of his powers. We followed Amory's directions towards the river, past rows of new warehouses and along the quay, where a great steamer was berthing and a gibbous moon made silhouettes of crumbling edifices on the older part of the waterfront. I became apprehensive as I found our path taking us among these abandoned warehouses where rotting derricks creaked like gibbets and the faint stench of an obsolete tannery yet lingered.

We arrived at a two-storey wooden building in an advanced state of dilapidation. No doubt the Schwarz whose painted name was faintly discernible had once pioneered some river trade here but small trace of his business survived. I lit a candle that perhaps was provided for our use and illuminated a counting house, its antique desks lying broken on a glass-strewn floor, where faded pages from a calendar showed early days in the city's history. There was no sign of Amory there and we were obliged to mount the stairs which groaned and complained as they announced our coming. Above the counting house was a great dry-storage room whose floor, where it was not encumbered by broken chests, timber and rat-chewed sacks, was striped narrowly with the moonlight that shone in through small broken windows.

'Over here, gentlemen, if you please.'

A match flickered and the wick of a lamp burned brightly as Silas Amory divested himself of shadows and stepped into a small office. Scattergood hestitated for a moment and then followed.

'So it is Mr Amory, is it?' he said, taking one of the chairs at a desk on which burned the lamp and behind which sat Silas Amory. Before him was a five-shot, pepper-pot pistol that was alarming and yet at the same time somehow familiar. 'Well, we are here. What game would you play with us?'

'Every game has its winner and its losers,' said Amory. 'I'm glad you take it in that part.'

'And what is to be my forfeit?'

'You must guess that. The receipts of your readings in this city.'

'And if I don't choose to hand them over? You will expose me before all of Cincinnati, I suppose?'

'I had thought to.'

This was insupportable. Only hours before, we had been feted by the best, centrepieces of a brilliant tableau. We were unstoppable, invincible, ready to conquer the world. 'This is my fault,' I said to Scattergood. Then to Amory, 'I suppose I was followed from the Particular?'

'Followed? I wasn't looking for you.' I heard again the throaty gargle that passed as a chuckle. 'Odd you should think that,' he said, 'because Merriweather and the folk in Hayes believe I've been doing exactly that.'

'Why?'

'I convinced them that you were in on the robbery. It wasn't difficult, following your mysterious departure, after which, by the by, I gave you a head start and alerted Merriweather. He said he had shot at you but I see you are none the worse for it. I volunteered to track you down; thus would no suspicion attach itself to me when I left town on certain business of my own. Who could have foreseen it? Billy Talbot, a fugitive!'

'But I had nothing to do with that robbery!' I exclaimed.

'I know that with certainty. No, it wasn't me,' he smiled, forestalling my question. 'I was seen at the offices of the *Bugle* at the time it occurred.'

'But it must have been someone who knew the hotel . . .'

'I shall lose nothing by confiding in a fellow criminal,' said Amory. 'I discovered that the bartender, Irving, is wanted in Wyoming and I made a confederate of him. He would empty the safe and we would meet at a pre-ordered date and divide the spoils. This was my business in Cincinnati.'

'Then Irving is here too?'

'He is here but my business with him is concluded. I should have left town had I not seen you posing as Dickens' manager.

173

I perceived what you were at and knew then that there were further pickings to be had.'

He examined one of our handbills. 'At $4 a head, less the hire of the theatre, I guess you might have cleared somewhere above $2000 these past days. That's not at all bad. I congratulate you upon such a neat scheme. You have a considerable talent, sir.'

Scattergood sat immobile and expressionless, his hands neatly clasped in his lap.

'Where is the money?' said Amory.

Scattergood's dilatory answer was delivered as though each word were $50 that he was reluctant to part with. 'In a hotel safe. It can only be released to myself or to Billy, in person.'

'That's of no consequence. I should hardly like to be seen collecting it anyway. One of you must fetch it.'

'I'll go,' I said.

'No, you will stay,' said Amory. 'He will get the money.'

'I have no intention of giving you anything,' said Scattergood. 'A game, we said. Does it occur to you that the playing of this game might be the all with me and that I would rather take whatever consequence than lose to such as you? Call the authorities if you will. I've faced down such things before. But I shall denounce you and you shall have nothing from me.'

'You will go and you will go now,' said Amory in a voice brittle with rage. He snatched up the pistol and levelled his arm so that its cold muzzle brushed my lips and the reek of grease and cordite filled my nostrils. 'Make no mistake, if you are not back within the hour, alone and with the money, I shall kill him.'

Scattergood stood slowly. I tried to turn, to read his intentions in his eyes, but Amory kept the gun in my face and I could see only Amory as he glared fiercely at the man at my side. 'Lest you doubt me,' he said, lowering the gun, to my great relief and turning the handle of a door behind him, 'look in here.'

He opened the door and the glare from his lamp lit up a

small adjoining room. 'Take the lamp, Billy,' he said. As the light mushroomed and the dishevelled cot, the fireplace full of white ashes and the bits of poor furniture defined themselves, it was immediately clear that what had appeared in the gloom as a big black sack was something more significant.

'Look more closely, boy,' he said. I entered the room, in which was a faint and sweet smell like that of bruised peaches and light fell upon the broad back of a man who lay across a rocking-chair. Its near-side arm was broken off and over the other the man was full-stretched as if reaching for something placed on the floor beside him. His long black hair mixed with the dust on the boards.

'At his face, boy, look at his face.'

He took the lamp while I dragged the thing from the floor and with some exertion righted it in the chair, into which it fell back heavily. Motion gave the lifeless form a ghastly animation as it rocked in and out of the glare of the lamp and I could see that something was terribly wrong, above and beyond the fact of its death.

Nausea swept through me; I felt faint and was only kept from swooning by Scattergood, who gripped my arm tightly and murmured some supporting words. The light was moved and what I had taken to be a shadow on the face, I saw was a hole on the left side about where the nostrils must have been. The wound, bad as it appeared, was disguised and further disfigured by the track of a dark channel of blood, now dried, that had run around the mouth and had pooled in the hollow of the chin. What remained of his face was yellow in the lamplight and the eyes were whitely rolled back, as if fixed upon heaven. Some seconds passed as I stood petrified by this ghastly object before other faculties resumed their operating and I recognised Matthew Irving, who had kept bar at the Particular Hotel. I retched and pulled out my handkerchief but too late to stem the eruption that came forth and mingled with the blood and matter on the floor.

When I have recounted this episode since on the verandas of
wealthy neighbours or to men in clubs who always enjoy the
story and never believe it, I have asserted that I never wavered:
not for one moment doubted that my friend Hope Scattergood would return with the money and that Silas Amory
would not have recourse to the lump of grey metal that sat
upon the desk between us and which he occasionally span
with his finger. But of course, it wasn't like that and I did
doubt him. Why, after all, should this consummate adventurer
and cheat return with the proceeds of his most successful
scheme ever and hand it over to a dangerous man whose next
move would even then be uncertain? Surely, he would collect
the carpet-bag full of cash and slip out of town as quietly as
he could. But if I thought that then surely Amory had weighed
it too. I was greatly puzzled that he had let him go. Perhaps
some accomplice watched out for Scattergood. I doubted it.
Even when conspiring with Merriweather, I always thought
that Amory had his own, private agenda. He was the sort to
work alone.

The knowledge that I might have only an hour to live was
strong upon me. Less than that – for how much time had
already passed as I sat there, weak with terror and dazed by
this savage and sudden reversal of fortune? Only Amory knew
and he wasn't telling. I began to calculate my chances of being
shot by Amory. What I had seen in the next room left me in
no doubt that he was quite capable of the act. Getting rid of
me would mean that I could never dispute his account of the
robbery at the Particular. And, of course, and this was the
gloomy clincher, there was only me and Scattergood to link
Amory with the death of Matthew Irving. Whether or not
Scattergood returned, and I could hardly think that he would,
I was already dead.

I realised that in the dead of night the sound of a gunshot
would carry a very long way and must put Scattergood to
flight if it didn't actually alert anyone else. He would wait the

full hour and if Scattergood didn't show he would then kill me, cut his losses and decamp from Cincinnati with what he had and an easy mind.

'How long have I got?'

Amory had been absorbed in meditations of his own and was slow to respond and when he did acknowledge me, I thought he did so for the sake of some amusement.

'Got? I don't follow you.'

'Before . . . Mr Scattergood is due back.'

'Scattergood? Is that his name? Is it an alias?'

'How long have I got?'

'Do you know, I think I know him. Under another name, perhaps.'

'Until you kill me,' I said. 'How long?'

This got me his attention. He looked surprised. 'Kill you, Billy? I don't mean to kill you. For goodness' sake, boy, I'm a newspaper editor, not a murderer.'

'But,' and I looked into the blackness that seemed to seep from the half-open door at Amory's back. 'Irving?'

'Irving was an accident, Billy. He wanted more than was his share and pulled a gun on me. This gun. His gun, you see.'

Now I knew why the pistol was familiar. It was the weapon Irving had kept behind his bar, in case of trouble.

'He would have shot me and taken the money. I was fighting for my very life.'

'You ain't going to kill me? Really?'

'I should not like to,' said Amory. 'Once I have the money we shall go our separate ways and I don't expect our paths to cross. You will keep in mind that you are a wanted man in Missouri, I hope.'

'But what if . . .'

'If your friend doesn't show? He will, I have every confidence.'

'Why?' I forced myself to say. 'Why are you so sure? Why didn't you go with him?'

'I doubt I would have been able to take you both at

177

gunpoint through a busy town and into a busy hotel. This way is better.'

Amory spun the pistol again and then picked it up and peered out of the battened window. 'He'll be back,' he said, 'because he is weak.'

'How is he weak?' I said, shortly. Amory couldn't know of how valiantly he had fought to keep his illness at bay.

'I know his type. Never spends long enough with one woman that she gets close to him; never gets to care for her and risk some hurt. No close friendships with men, neither. No one's got a lever on him. Sound like your friend?'

'Maybe,' I allowed.

'But he thinks a lot of you. I've watched you together. I saw how he was with you, how he delighted in your success and your conquest. Oh yes, I saw that too. It was a father's love for a son. Some fathers, anyway. I think you are a son to him and that is why the fool will return and not with some of the money or with a few bills at the top of a bag of rubbish but with all the money.'

He laughed as a thought occurred to him. 'Maybe that old fool Putnam was right in a way. You are Dickens' son . . .'

He became silent again and we were both left with our thoughts. I knew nothing of his but for myself, I was thinking that I was no more certain that I would not shortly be the resting place for one of Amory's bullets. I strained my ears for Scattergood's booted steps upon the stairs but the only sounds were the lapping of the river against the wharf, the whistle of wind through the shattered windows and the distant noise of a steamer on the Ohio.

IV

I had recited the Lord's Prayer and done my deals with God and had even been pleased with myself that I included Scattergood in my transactions and trusted that He would be as merciful with this great sinner as with Billy Talbot, who hadn't had the opportunity for much sinning up to now. But

178

then I recalled the events of earlier that night, remembered the heat of Katy's body in the summer house and though it brought a glow of pleasure, I knew that in regard to being prepared to meet the after-life, I was maybe no better circumstanced than was Hope Scattergood.

Dawn was breaking and I had started into the Psalms when I heard the sound of a door opening below. Amory heard it too and his gun was levelled against the entrance as Scattergood walked in carrying, I saw, his carpet-bag. I need not say I was never so pleased to see anyone in my life. I thought he looked changed. He had rid himself of the beard and padding with which he built his Dickens and now, without a full change of clothing, seemed somewhere between his two selves and there was uncertainty in his manner and even in his gait. He placed the bag upon the desk. Amory rifled his pockets for some newly-concealed weapon before motioning us back against the wall. He opened the bag, moved the lamp and glanced at its contents.

'You see that I was right, Billy,' he said. He took out a bundle of bills and began to count them.

The moment was electric. My throat was dry, my heart thundering and every nerve alive as I awaited my fate. Just two slim chances might save me. One was that Amory would not kill us but this seemed unlikely. I had already foreseen how our deaths might look conveniently like thieves falling out and how Amory would then be suspected neither of the robbery at the Particular nor the the shooting of Matthew Irving.

The other was that Scattergood had some some card unplayed, some trick up his sleeve. Surely such a sharp operator would not walk naked into the lion's den? He would not be brought low by such as Amory: I had heard him say that. I waited for one of these men to make a fatal move. Amory continued to count the money. Scattergood only put a hand upon my shoulder and whether it was done to comfort me or to support himself, I could not tell.

Some minutes passed in this way. I have no idea how many.

Time expanded, contracted, stood still and hurtled onwards. Amory thumbed slowly through wads of dollar bills, each piece of paper resounding flatly as it was flicked through his fingers. In the next moment, fifty dollars disappeared in an instant while he fanned through another wad of bills. But two thousand and eighty dollars must be accounted for some time and when it was, Amory snapped shut the bag and smiled at Scattergood.

'You have kept your part of the bargain. By my reckoning you can hardly have held anything back. But perhaps that is not so very singular. Anyway, I shall keep mine. I am leaving now. I only require you to stay here until I am safely away. The door will be locked from without but it should not be beyond your combined wits to discover or construct some egress in the space of one or two hours.'

He took up the bag and we heard a key turn in the lock and, a short time afterwards, his quick step upon the stairs. We sat upon the floor in silence. I felt marvellously relieved to be alive and grateful to Scattergood beyond measure but I was also uncomfortable. I knew what he had denied himself for me. Only hours ago he had ruled supreme as Emperor of Cincinnati – now we had lost all because some part of my past had caught me up. I wanted to ask him, 'Why did you return?' but I knew then that I wouldn't chance the discovery that Amory had been wrong.

My friend looked pale and ill and his breathing rattled in his throat. Perhaps he had overexerted himself making haste to the hotel or otherwise the shock and shame of this defeat was too much for his frail constitution. He appeared sick and despondent and I thought to offer some consolation. At least we were undiscovered, I said, and might try the game again. What could Amory gain by unmasking us to the authorities or, more likely, to a newspaper? As a journalist he might think he had a strong story but I doubted he would risk connecting his name with ours in such a case.

If he had killed us it might be different. I could see how he might have wished our characters to be blackened before our corpses were found and we were reviled as murdering swindlers who had fallen out. But he had not. Amory, I suggested, was only another sharper looking out for easy money. And now he had it, he would light out for some other place and leave us be. But still Scattergood said nothing. I was about to offer a second helping of homespun homilies when Scattergood jumped up.

'Smoke!' he said.

I was suddenly aware of the smell of burning and saw wisps of grey smoke rising from where they were snaking beneath the door.

'We're on fire!' I said redundantly, and immediately a terrific rustling and crackling filled the air and we both knew that beyond the door, whose panels and handle I discovered were already hot, a big fire was building. Now there was a new sound, like a drowning man gulping breath as the fire sucked in oxygen and some new store of combustible materials became part of the conflagration.

The office was filling with smoke. Scattergood tried to stem its entry but wherever one ingress was stopped up, it found another, seeping in through cracks in the wainscot and now, alarmingly, filtering up through through gaps in the floorboards. We had immediately tried to dislodge the thick battens that were nailed firmly about the single window but whoever had secured them had not spared the nails. Where we could see past them, we saw orange light flickering on the river and knew that some part of the building below must also be ablaze. I took a chair and beat it against the battens but not one moved an inch and I only succeeded in breaking the chair.

Scattergood applied his handkerchief to his mouth again and I followed him into the adjoining room where Irving watched our frantic movements with supreme disinterest. There was neither door nor window here but the inside walls were markedly hot as flames scorched their sides. It could only be a few minutes before they broached that wall and everything there and in the office too, was consumed.

I think I was for some mad idea of taking up the heavy

desk and heaving it at the window, a feat which, even had Scattergood been in prime health, we might never have managed, when I noticed that beneath the desk and mostly hidden by an old and rotting rug, was a rusty hinge. Spluttering and choking, we shoved away the desk and discovered a trapdoor, so large that the lamplight and grey dawning had failed to reveal its shape. A ring fixed in a timber above me indicated it had been used for hauling up goods for dry storage.

'Good boy, Billy!' exclaimed Scattergood but I saw that a great padlock secured it and, our lungs burning, we tried to break its rusty mechanism. It wouldn't shift. I thought that we might have played our final card but Scattergood had his clasp-knife from his boot and was succeeding in loosening and prising the screws that fastened the hinges. When the job was done, we dug our nails into the rotten wood, secured some handhold and slowly the great door shifted, rose just a fraction but sufficient to force bleeding fingers under it and then, slowly, to raise the trap.

I thanked God that we were met with no great bellow of flame. Some part of the walls below were catching fire but the loading area was open to the river and much heat and smoke had escaped into the open air. We pulled back the trap and Scattergood pushed me forwards. I swung my legs into the void, slipped down and tried to limit my drop by catching hold of the rim but my fingers had been damaged and refused to grip. I dropped heavily and crashed upon boxes, which were so old and rotten that rather than breaking my back, they gave way and broke my fall. I looked about me. The side doors were chained and the third wall already hotly blazing. The only escape was by way of the river. I called up to Scattergood who had caught the lip of the trap and for a moment dangled there like a hanged man before his grip gave and he too fell.

The boxes having already given, he fell much harder than I had and lay crumpled upon them. For a moment I thought he had broken his neck. I tried to help him upright but before

I could assay his injuries, a great and terrible noise jarred: a grating, splintering, renting and roaring cacophony, of timbers screaming and joists cracking. Above us, in the seat of the fire, the ceiling began to give way. The wormed and fire-eaten wood ripped and succumbed to the weight of the burning boxes and heavy lumber which creaked and groaned above. I grabbed Scattergood and with every pound of strength I had left in my body, I dragged him roughly towards the river. Suddenly the boards gave way entirely and the monstrous mass of blazing lumber and flaming floor timbers crashed through and exploded upon the ground. In the same instant we were out, spat into the freezing water by a gale of dust, debris and hot flame.

Chapter Eleven

I

SCHWARZ'S WHARF WAS twelve, maybe more, feet above the level of the river and we fell headlong into icy water and I broke the surface gasping with shock and cold.

Scattergood had come up nearby but was just about to sink again, knocked senseless by some river debris. When I swam behind him and took him under the chin we would have struck out for shore but no safe landing offered itself on the sheer quay walls, above which terrific flames leapt out and coloured the water with a hellish hue.

We were beginning to drift and I knew I couldn't support him much longer without jeopardising my own chance of survival. I looked for some supportive flotsam among the leaves and sticks and garbage that floated past and occasionally struck our straggling forms. Then something large approached, a broken corner of one of the great rafts that carried timber down the Ohio and into the Mississippi.

There was a moment when I thought it would run us both down but I managed to take hold of a spar and pulled Scattergood in close, hooking his coat upon a big nail while I used my last energy to haul myself and then Scattergood's unconscious form aboard the raft. The river was running quickly and there was no way of steering this precarious vessel. I was obliged to let it decide its own course while Scattergood slowly regained consciousness and stared uncomprehendingly at the fast-passing parade of clouds above him. It wasn't to be a long voyage: within only a few hundred yards, the raft entangled itself in undergrowth in a bend in the river and I was able to drop into waist-deep water and drag Scattergood off and on to dry land.

Scattergood was in a bad way. He couldn't walk and needed warmth and shelter. Hidden by trees was a small, ramshackle boathouse and into this damp, fetid-smelling place I dragged him. His water-logged clothes had about doubled his weight and it was all I could do to get him upon some drier boards, remove his coat and pants and wrap him in the only dry thing I could find, an old and dusty tarpaulin I ripped from a broken boat. I said I would go for help and Scattergood mouthed something about a place he knew but he was so faint and I was too impatient with panic to make much of it. I told him I'd be back in no time at all and hurried away. I stumbled through woods that fringed the river and found a road that I judged must skirt the wharves where I knew there would be much activity as soon as the alarm was raised. It was early morning and there was as yet little traffic upon the road but in my wet and clinging clothing I cut a conspicuous figure and avoided anyone in my path, making use of back alleys and circuitous routes. My sense of direction was good or perhaps I was only lucky because I soon found myself within a block of where Scattergood had been received by the mayor of Cincinnati an age ago, it seemed.

It was a Sunday morning and while most people had the newness of dress and sobriety of manner to suggest that they were church-bound, some others were hurrying towards the river. Fire bells were ringing and a pall of smoke could be seen rising from the wharves. There was no chance of concealment now as the concerned and the curious rushed past me but none commented upon my strange appearance. Hoping to find out how safe the city was for us then, I apprehended one of these who was pulling on his shirt as he ran and asked of him, 'Is it a fire?' I thought he might shake off my hand in his haste but he turned and spat, glad to have found someone who hadn't heard the news. 'Aintcha seen the *Enterprise*? Big-shot in town yester-eve was no more Dickens than you nor I – they say he's killed some feller 'n' hid the body on the wharf. There's people going down there to look right now! Say, what happened to you?'

But before I could arrange an answer, he had hurried on, leaving me to curse my luck. So Amory had planned our deaths all along and had used his contacts in the newspapers to spread the story of our duplicity after all. Our charred bodies alongside Irving's would tie up a lot of loose ends. Now we found ourselves wanted men – as villains sufficiently audacious to pull off the grand Dickens scheme there would be small reason to doubt the rumour spread by Amory that we were responsible for a burnt cadaver with gunshot wounds. They would only think that we had got the drop on them and high-tailed it out of town. They would pursue us but with no more zeal than would Amory who would be desirous of finishing what he had started before we found some way of turning the tables and exposing him.

I abandoned any hope of soliciting help from a citizen of Cincinnati. Nor would there be time to make the long and possibly dangerous journey to the house out of town, where we had put up before making our first incursions into the city. However, I was reminded by my proximity of the summer house in which had been clothes and dustsheets which would serve for bandages and hurried thither. It wouldn't be much but it would be dry. I would find a little food somewhere and hasten back to Scattergood before he was discovered.

Rushing through the tangle of vines, I stopped dead when I saw the glass door close with a small click and some sign of movement behind the dusty glass. I edged closer, intending to await the departure of whoever was within. After a moment, the door opened and a woman stepped out, pushing a ring onto her finger. I heard her say, 'Reckoned that was gone for good,' and recognised Katy, her hair and dress unlike anything they had been last night but my girl just the same.

'Katy!' I hissed and broke cover. She seemed not to know me at first but then asked me what was I doing there when the whole town would be up and after me soon. I told her enough of our business to satisfy her that we were not as black as some folks were busy painting us and then informed her that my partner was presently laid up by the river, in a bad way.

I was gratified to find that she had a heart of gold. No sooner had she heard of this sinner in need than she seemed possessed and took me from the garden by a back way and we disappeared down many a street until we arrived at an unremarkable house in a district that was some way from being salubrious. She bid me wait while she talked with an older woman, who harried a Chinaman until a horse was harnessed to a wagon, a bag of necessaries was thrown in and the Chinaman was driving the three of us in the direction of the old boathouse.

The older woman turned to where I was hanging on behind her. 'How bad is he?' she asked. 'And how'd he do it?'

'He got hurt falling through a floor.'

'Huh, I always said he would one day,' she remarked and sucked upon an extinguished pipe as she urged Chinaman and horse to greater endeavours. We passed an intersection of streets and down at the end of one we could see the crowds and fire-tenders and the wall of Schwarz's from which plumes of black smoke were still rising. It looked as if two of the paddle boats queueing up to dock had slowed up early to give those on board a look-see at what was going on. I directed the Chinaman back down the track and at its end I helped Katy off the wagon and ushered everyone into the dark and quiet boathouse.

Scattergood remained conscious but looked empty of any volition as if all the fight had been washed out of him in the river. He sat swaddled in the tarpaulin and registered no surprise when he saw we four looking down upon him.

'Like a washed-up river-rat, aintcha?' the older woman said to him as they helped me lift him aboard the wagon. 'You get a little money and take off like a Marky Polo but you ain't no better than Marky Velly and back you comes with your tail between your legs, every time.'

'Don't be hard on him. I think he's hurt real bad,' said Katy.

'Oh, you always were a fool for him and his ways. One day the scales will fall from yo' eyes, girl,' the woman replied. But she chuckled and leant over and patted Scattergood who flinched with the pain. As we approached the intersection to which the sightseers were now returning, she pulled the tarpaulin over our prostrate passenger and we made our way through milling crowds of talkative people, some of whom seemed careful of giving us more than a scant glance.

II

We returned to the house and the woman, whose name was Mrs Currabell, and Katy Pearson tended to Scattergood. A doctor was called who appeared to be at least an intimate of the house and he bandaged Scattergood's chest and pronounced that his ankle was only sprained and not broken. The calamity had knocked the wind out of him and it was clear from what the doctor said that we would not be able to get out of Cincinnati for several days. Much of this time Scattergood spent upon an enormous maple bed, his slender form all but lost among the blankets and patchworks that were heaped upon him by Mrs Currabell.

As well as Mrs Currabell and Katy Pearson, there were two other girls living at the house, a jet-haired German named Frieda and a Georgian girl called Anna Lightfoot. Katy addressed Mrs Currabell as 'aunt' and before I heard the girls speak, I thought that Mrs Currabell was a widow with the care of three delightful nieces. The fifth member of the household was the Chinaman, Mr Foo, who cooked every meal and did the laundry. His sacred domain lay at the rear of the house, where saucepans clattered and knives ground and this place he considered inviolable as I found out when I went looking for something to eat, the first morning.

I encountered Mr Foo, dragon-like with pegs for teeth, at his backyard lines where bed-sheets and clothing billowed and blossomed like sails and colourful kites. When he had extracted his pegs and hung the last of his washing, he looked sharply at me and said 'You stay long?' in a voice that recommended any other course of action. My warm reception in the house had not prepared me for this. 'I don't want to be no trouble,' I said as he marched me back through the kitchen. Pots and pans and kitchen tools hung from hooks overhead and these jangled in the breeze that followed our entrance. Foo reached down a knife that flashed on its hook and I couldn't prevent myself jumping back in alarm but he only smiled and began to whet the blade against a stone. 'Your friend,' he said, as sparks flew from the grindstone, 'has brought bad spirits to this house before. I think you take him away real soon.'

It was soon borne upon me that Foo was more than some jack-of-all-trades or paid lackey. After long connection with the household, he had taken it upon himself to be its fierce protector as he proved that first night, when he routed a small party of loud and drunken young men. Foo's duties appeared to include everything possible except those which I discovered that the girls themselves performed, every evening and Sundays included.

I don't know how long it took me to realise the obvious but perhaps it was something longer than it might have taken other young men of my age. When first I saw that three gentlemen had come calling it pained me that Katy might be walking out with a young man but this was as nothing to my grief later that night, when I had to stop my ears to the abominable noises from overhead. I need hardly detail these here but they were not the sort that might be expected from three dutiful girls under the chaperoning eye of their aunt.

The worst of it was the cruel realisation that Katy Pearson had been paid by Hope Scattergood to give herself to me in the summer house. A few weeks ago I would have bitterly resented such monstrous presumption but experience was changing me and after a few hours of moody reflection I was forced to conclude that he had meant the best by his action. There were moments of awkwardness when I encountered Katy but I soon realised that all the awkwardness was on my part and she continued to be breezy with me and to treat me if not as her intended, then at least as a huckster might a favourite customer. I admit, though, to some pangs of jealousy when I saw how tender and selfless were her ministrations to my sick partner.

Time and tending, rest and chicken broth did more for Scattergood than any doctor could have. Though recovered from his recent misadventure, he was still patently a sick man and was worse than ever I had seen him. He could do nothing now to disguise the severity of the fits of coughing and on the first of many such spasms the whole house stilled, even the cook his pans, as Scattergood's awful hacking filled every corner. I saw the girls exchange glances. Once, Katy, her cheeks wet with tears, buried her face in my coat and made me promise I would look out for him. And then he would seem to recover and become again something like the Scattergood I had known before, talkative, restless, ravenous for amusement as I was to discover on the last night of our stay at Mrs Currabell's.

As it was deemed dangerous to be abroad in Cincinnati we stayed inside and were entertained by the girls, as they readied themselves and the parlour for the evening's business. I was advised not to leave the house, as successive newspapers and trusted customers of Mrs Currabell's made it clear that our names were on everyone's lips for the worst of reasons. We were enjoined to remain silent and keep to ourselves while the girls were entertaining their clients. Mrs Currabell said that to have suspended business would not only have compromised their income but would probably have aroused suspicions too.

Every evening, Katy and the girls would put their house in order. I had at first been dazzled by the splendour and primped opulence of the parlour. It looked like a palace and if Mrs Currabell were its unlikely queen then Katy was its enchanted princess. I had never seen such an abundance of strange furniture and interesting novelty and I had no doubt at all that the White House was just like this. There was a great abundance of knick-knacks and curios: pottery figures, miniature busts, glass animals and more ticking, whirring and chiming clocks than might be required by a whole race of particularly punctual people and these were littered upon delicate tables and rosewood cabinets of unusual design, any remaining spaces being taken up by jungles of luxurient plants. Brightly-papered walls were all but completely obscured by framed pictures, depending on chains of varying length and the tone of these pictures was often of a piece with the mantle's slate clock, whose pediment was supported by a pair of nude caryatids. After dusk, the coloured glass covers worn by the lamps cast the strangest hues upon eyes and skin, wallpaper and brocade but in daylight I saw that I had been duped by novelty. The carpet was old and recorded a history of dropped cigars and spilt drinks. Table-tops were deeply scored, marquetry chipped, curtains were frayed and the sofas old and lumpy. But the girls worked hard at making the most of it all.

'It has to look nice,' said Anna Lightfoot as she polished a mirror. 'We cater for the better end of the market.'

'We have standards, you know,' said Katy.

'Don't you ever want to do something else? How can nice girls like you –' I began.

'Do something like this?' said Katy. ' 'Sakes, we're just selling another commodity. I have enough money to buy pretty dresses and I even got savings. One day I'll get out of here and set myself up with a business in another town. But not just yet. We got teachers and professors, lawyers and judges coming here. If it's all right for them then I guess it's all right for us. Where's the difference, Billy?'

192

I shrugged. 'How come you get folk like that?'

'We're the best,' said Anna Lightfoot.

'Constance,' Katy indicated the door to Mrs Currabell's room, 'hooked most of 'em years ago. Our trade is pretty regular.'

'She's an uncommon woman,' I said.

'She's that all right,' said Katy and beckoned me after her as she opened the door of Mrs Currabell's private office. This was less well-furnished than the room without but more homely. A small writing-desk stood against a wall under a portrait in oils of Mrs Currabell herself, painted perhaps twenty years previously. Her large figure, great bones and sharp blue eyes had changed little since. She was just the same, only there was now a little more of her. Above a comfortable sofa, on which sat a row of china dolls, were Oriental prints depicting sages and fishermen and a bay window overlooked a small yard whose only feature was a withered apple tree and an unhinged back gate.

Katy closed up the writing-desk and picked up a couple of books from off its top.

'Behind you,' she said and I turned to behold a library arranged along polished shelves. The books themselves looked expensive and there was no doubt that I was intrigued to find so many in the private room of a whorehouse madam. Yet there was something wrong. I looked along the shelves and for some moments the names of Benvenuto Cellini and Machiavelli, Rabelais and Chaucer, blinded me to the obvious but then I perceived that the volumes were arranged only by order of colour and size. The morocco covers were all in a block; black and calf leather in another, cloth-bound on a shelf of their own. Others were assigned a homogeneity because their bright gilt lettering was of the same typeface; I could see no relation in their authors and subjects. Katy watched my puzzlement.

'She don't read 'em, least not that I've ever seen.'

'Then why does she have them?'

'They're gifts from customers. I don't how it all started.

Maybe she asked someone for a book but as soon as they knew that books were what she wanted, her best customers got in the habit of making her presents of them. That was all right, 'cept a few of 'em thought it was a great joke and I heard them laughin' about how they would outdo each other to bring her the most scholarly book. Anyways, she's got this library now and it keeps on growing.'

'But what does she do with it?' I asked.

'About once a week, if we're not busy, she gets down all the books, polishes up the shelves, blows out the dust from each and every one, wipes the covers and puts them back like they was all pieces o' Meissen chiny. I sometimes seen her looking closely at them that has engravings but most don't. I seen her sitting on that sofa holding a book in her lap and just feeling the leather. She says she can tell a good book by the quality of the binding and the toolin' of the letters. I was good at my schooling, afore I took it into my head to go and see what was around the next corner and I reckon I know that Chelleeny and Chaucer ain't kin just because they got the same fancy covers. All the same to her, though.'

Mrs Currabell, I decided as I turned the pages of an illustrated Malory, was as queer as anything else in this house 'Katy,' I said, suddenly seized by a romantic notion. 'I want to take you away from all this.'

She smiled, as if I had said just what she expected. 'You're a very nice man and I'm sure glad 'bout what happened in the garden and all. But Billy, I ain't the one for you nor you for me. I ain't saying this here is perfect but it's my home and I ain't going anywhere just now.'

'But you do care for me?'

'Why of course I do, Billy. You ain't like a customer. I couldn't do business with you, not now. You're special.'

'Then why not come with me? We could go to New York.'

'Billy, I care for you for yourself, of course, but also because you take such good care of Hope,' she said. 'He needs your help. Without you, I reckon he'd be lost. Lord, I ain't known him long as Connie but long enough to know him for one of

God's own. I couldn't bear anything to happen to him. Me and you'll be friends though and any time you come by Cincinnati, I'll be here for you.'

I left Katy arranging her hair in Mrs Currabell's glass and looked forward to the day we could get out of there and on to New York.

III

One afternoon, as the rain beat on the tin roof and Scatter-good lay in his bed by the window, I asked him about Mrs Currabell. I was fascinated by this big, pipe-smoking madam, not just for what she did but because of her odd habit of peppering her conversation with what were obviously in-tended as learned allusions. 'The whore and the gambler,' she had winked to Scattergood, 'build the fate of nations.'

Constance Currabell, Scattergood told me, had been orphaned as an infant and taken in as a ward by a friend of her father's, called Mr Eden. It was a mixed blessing: Mr Eden was kind to her and she remembers him still with great affection but his wife was waspish and spiteful and resented the intrusion. While her own daughters were educated by a private tutor, Constance was sent to help the kitchen maids.

In the evenings the girls worked their samplers, gossiped with their mother, did whatever it is that women do. The father took to his library after dinner, where he was fond of dipping into his books, of which he had many hundreds. One such evening, while fetching himself refreshment from the kitchen – he rarely employed a servant to do that of which he was capable himself – he came upon Connie sat upon the stairs, wearing the grubby apron in which she had spent the long day working and evidently looking quite disconsolate. He took pity on her and invited her into his library.

He knew what was the matter: he could hardly have failed to mark the way in which his ward was treated, kept separate from the girls and used as an unpaid servant. But the man was weak and would always avoid confrontation with his wife.

That said, he could still be sympathetic and had taken a liking to Connie and after that evening she visited his library regularly and he talked to her about his books and though she could not read, she was fascinated by the colourful illustrations he pointed out to her and by the potted histories, summarised classics and the novels whose essence he imparted.

It wasn't long, of course, before his wife noticed the special attention being lavished upon the girl and she forbade the nightly visits and instead, Constance spent her evenings in her attic, with books she had borrowed from the library but without the skills to read them. Nobody had inspired her like Mr Eden. She did not resent him for being too meek to take her side against his wife but rather was grateful to him for the tantalising glimpses he had revealed to her of the vast wealth of experience and possibility that this life had to offer.

Shortly after her banishment from Mr Eden's library, Connie was summoned before Mrs Eden and told that she was being sent to a school upstate where she would receive the education to which she obviously considered herself entitled. Connie was glad of the news and eagerly awaited the day on which she should make a start for a new life.

But disappointment was in store. The school was little more than a discreet and secure depository for unwanted children and bastards. Jonathan Malahide, who oversaw this terrible place, was a brutal and ignorant man, no more capable of imparting an education than Melik Merriweather. There were no vacations and there was no remission of suffering for those children forced to endure Malahide's harsh regime of beatings, insubstantial diet and an absence of any medical attention. Connie suffered all this for several years, until she was grown into her teens.

By her own admission to Scattergood, there had been lovelier flowerings of youth; her frame was large and her nose Roman. Yet by comparison with her ill-nourished fellows, she might not have been considered ill-looking. At least not by Malahide, who had noticed this and on several occasions had tried to force his attentions upon her. She was by then big enough in stature to make some defence of herself against the tyrant and all Malahide's attempts came to naught until the day Connie awoke from a deep and troubled sleep to find Malahide's bare and repulsive form upon her own and her honour plundered. She screamed and would have beat Malahide from the room with the candlestick but found herself incapable, recalling the drink that Malahide had offered her the night before – a rare demonstration of unwonted generosity – and deducing that she had been drugged.

The following night, fearful of a repetition of the heinous act, she absconded from the school and walked into the nearest town, without any thought of what she might do there. Frightened that she might be returned to the school she decided against reporting Malahide to the police.

What does a young girl do who has no means of support? She begged for work, but being too young, found none. She begged for food and shelter without success. This world being what it is, it wasn't long before some gentleman offered his protection to the girl on the sort of terms you will easily imagine. Since that day, in one city or another, Connie had plied the oldest trade but always ensuring that she bartered with only the best class of customer. She had just enough learning to reassure her clients that they had not strayed too far from their social station and each one was encouraged to impart some little of their own particular fruits of knowledge. In this way Connie Currabell had become the strange thing she then was – 'the wisest whore in Christendom', as Scattergood had called her.

The girls told me that Hope and Connie had known each other since the dawn of time, when Scattergood had turned up on her bordello doorstep selling bibles. Sometimes, they said, there had been more to it than friendship and there had never been any hint of a business transaction. Though men of standing became hypocrites as soon as they overstepped the threshold of that house, Hope and Connie never pretended to be other than they were, in their own company, at least.

The whore and the gambler were as true to each other as they were able to be.

An incident occurring in the middle of the night spurred us on to New York sooner than we had intended. Our company had dined well and although Scattergood's appetite was too faint to admit of his taking much dinner, he had his compensation in generous glasses of Mrs Currabell's brandy. We retired not so very long after the girls had gone about their work, but for an hour, or perhaps two, I was unable to sleep for the loud locomotion of bed-springs and the climactic groans and heavy sighs that were the storms before each lull. Equally inimical to repose were the cod squealings of the girls and unusually, this night, the smart stroke and lachrymose response of a scourging. This was all most exceptional for a young man who had been innocent, until recently, of all but intention. Still, I was curious and allow that I might have experienced a little vicarious gratification had it been unalloyed by the realisation that one of those honeyed tones that enticed and suggested, pandered and cozened, must be that of the girl I persisted in calling 'my Katy'.

Tormenting myself thus, I was alarmed by a great thunderclap; rather, it was the report of a pistol, discharged directly above my head. A girl screamed and I heard boots on the back stairs and both front and kitchen doors slamming. I pulled on my breeches and raced into the hall, where I nearly collided with Mrs Currabell and Mr Foo.

'Upstairs!' she pointed. 'Katy's room!' I took those steps five at a time, no matter that I was unarmed, unlike Mr Foo, who followed, just as unsteadily, with a cocked Colt. The door was closed and I turned the handle with racing heart, dreading not an assassin's bullet but that I might find Katy Pearson injured or even dead upon the floor.

There are now, on stages in New York and in New Orleans, so I have heard, tableaux vivants that bring to life well-known works of great art. The French painters, especially those who have produced famous nudes, are well represented. I'm told that these can present quite singular spectacles yet I doubt any was ever so strange as that created by Mrs Currabell when she turned up the low, flickering gas of the wall-lights.

Hope Scattergood stood by the bed in his underwear holding a pistol by its muzzle which suggested that he had snatched it from the grasp of a bald and fat, ruddy-faced and naked gentleman who guarded his modesty with the corner of a bed-sheet. Katy Pearson sat up in the bed, wide-eyed with shock and seemingly unaware that she held in her grasp the stock of a horsewhip. Above her the plaster was shattered about a small hole.

The tableau collapsed as the florid gentleman picked a pile of hair from off the bed-post and positioned it upon his head. He began to complain to Mrs Currabell and to accuse Hope Scattergood and suddenly I recognised Mr Steiner, the wearisome humbug of the Dickens ball, who now threw the bed-sheet over his shoulder and looking less like the Roman senator than perhaps he imagined, he turned again on Scattergood.

'Confound it,' he said. 'You're the scoundrel everyone's looking for! I knew there was something wrong about you the moment I clapped eyes on you. What kind of a low-down villain are you? You make sport of the dignity of Cincinnati and now you attack its citizens in their beds!'

'I had only lost my way in the hall. You appear to have lost yours,' mused Scattergood, as he examined the weapon, 'metaphysically.'

'Ten-dollar words won't get you out of this,' he said. 'Do you know who I am?'

'I seem to remember you for a man of good works. You must make your wife proud.' He appeared to notice Katy for the first time and bowed. 'Someone, as you say, must take an interest in fallen women.'

Scattergood picked up his clothes which he had folded neatly on the chair, oblivious, it seemed, that Steiner was already in the bed. Whether my friend had been equally unconscious that he was in Katy's room presented a problem I had trouble resolving. Before he left, Mrs Currabell ushered

Steiner into her private office and helped him see how matters then stood. She explained to him how exposing us would make matters very difficult for himself. He had seen sense and would, she assured us, be 'silent as a man sent to Covingtree'. But of course, we could remain at the house no longer, both for our sakes and that of Mrs Currabell. It was decided that we would push on for New York.

The Dickens lay was too hot for us now but Scattergood maintained that New York was a place where men of initiative could always make money and he thought that once there, we should very easily be able to raise sufficient for our daily existence and with luck, enough to pay his own expenses for treatment abroad. He was insistent I should at least try and meet Charles Dickens while he was still in the States and to appease him, I said that I would go with him for that reason but by then my object was only to look after Scattergood and if possible, see him sent off for the long-shot treatment across the seas. However, he seemed satisfied that in making the journey to New York himself, he was helping me achieve my own dream. Twenty dollars that Scattergood produced from the lining of his coat was augmented by a loan from Mrs Currabell which was made on the condition that we travelled by rail all the way to New York. I had an address of a boarding-house given me by Elijah Putnam, which he had used himself on a visit to the city and which he assured me was still in existence and run by a very respectable woman of the name Hodges and there, after long hours in which Scattergood sat huddled over the stove or sleeping on my shoulder as we rattled through Pennsylvania and New Jersey, we arrived.

IV

After reading Dickens and Boswell, Daniel Defoe and Henry Fielding, I had often fancied I would one day find myself in London, strolling down Cheapside or Cornhill or patronising a theatre in Haymarket or Drury Lane. My books had familiarised me with much of London and I thought I would not be at a loss were I ever to visit. Strangely, though I had many times projected myself beyond the great Atlantic Ocean, I had never imagined myself walking the streets of the great American cities of the East Coast. Though Broadgate and London might be half-known to me, New York and mighty Broadway were decidedly beyond my ken.

It appeared that all the world had chosen that day to visit the city with us. As we pushed through the crowds outside the New York and Harlem Railroad station, I thought I had never seen such a vast assemblage of people and carriages nor imagined that they could, every one, be in such a terrible hurry to get wherever they were going. My first instinct was to turn around and flee from this pandemonium. Scattergood, however, seemed revivified by it all and we walked briskly down broad sidewalks where packed bars were noisy with excited chatter and hammer-blows on ice and shops over-spilled with a plenitude of colourful produce. Brightly-lit windows exhibited expensive and presumably fashionable clothes and interesting bookshops, new publications and gay prints. Everything we passed spoke loudly of business and bustle and a lot of money. We walked on, into the shadows of the distance.

It was apparent that although we had continued upon the same street, the district we were now entering was less salubrious, perhaps more dangerous. Houses here were older and poorly maintained. Some were empty or overrun by gangs of young boys who leered or spat at us from glassless windows and packs of mangy dogs scavenged in dark alleys. Still we walked, though my legs ached and I longed to find some small eating place where we might rest a while with a coffee or something stronger. There had been a place by the station called, auspiciously, 'The Putnam House', from whose portals the most appetising aromas had wafted. But Scatter-good had said we must go on; it wasn't far.

I had hoped in vain that the tall and dilapidated tenement into which Scattergood led me was not our destination and that he had only entered to ask directions. I gave Elijah

Putnam the benefit of the doubt and almost believed him. Perhaps Hodges' Boarding-House had indeed been a clean and respectable establishment when he had put up there. He had assured me that at this establishment I would have a safe base for my operations in New York. Arrived there now, it was clear that the intervening years had not treated Hodges' kindly. On the ground floor we progressed through several litters of children who clamoured for pennies and candy. We had already been robbed of ten cents by two larger children, who sat muffled against the cold on either side of steps, like animated gargoyles. An urgent young man accosted us as we climbed rickety stairs and insisted we buy his coat or if not that, his pocket watch.

I mistook a woman sat in a well by a second-storey window for Mrs Hodges and said we wanted a room for a period. She asked for two dollars, right away, which I thought to be a deposit or the payment in advance but she pocketed the money and said 'Bless you, Mrs Hodges has been in her grave these past five years. O'Leary's the man you want. Ask O'Leary.' I didn't have to part with more money to discover the whereabouts of this O'Leary. There came the sounds of a violent struggle from the floor above and the voice of a woman calling out, evidently in great distress. I bounded up a flight of stairs, turned upon the hallway and saw a flame-haired man assaulting a woman whose features were obscured by his broad, shirtless back.

'If you can't pay I'll take what you've been selling. It's only right and fair.'

He had hold of both her wrists and I cannot bear to imagine what might have been her fate had I not intruded and made myself known to Mr O'Leary. The man reluctantly released the woman and looked like he might have turned on me, had he not seen the glint of money in my outstretched palm.

The woman appeared from behind him and threw herself in my arms.

'Oh Billy,' cried my mother, 'I thought you'd never get here!'

Chapter Twelve

I

THE SNOW HAD descended like an avalanche from a barn roof and by midday the choking mass of wheeled traffic that had clattered continuously about the streets had been magically transformed into so many smooth-gliding sleighs and a foot of sudden snow had achieved the impossible and hushed New York.

The fresh fall that moustached the lintels of great hotels and iced the porticoes of monumental banks fell also upon the empty sockets of crumbling tenements and made hard walking for rich and poor alike. But then the steam ploughs had begun clearing the tramlines and the city started to breathe again, the energy of inexorable movement slowly melting and despoiling all, until puddles and rivulets of black water besmirched dresses and bespattered the sharp-creased pants of the regiments of men of business who scuttled over crossings and stopped briefly on corners to exchange paraphrased anecdotes and shorthand news, always urgent in their pursuit of the dollar.

I too walked briskly, as far as my leaking boots and great fatigue would allow, flapping my arms or burying my hands deep in my pockets, where was the reassuring touch of new-gotten money. It had been a dreadful night but I was fired by recent success: I had sold all of the tickets at prices that might have shamed me had circumstances been entirely different.

However, the night itself had hardly gone as planned. The mark I had hired to stand in line overnight had failed to show and I couldn't replace him in time. So, rather than relieving some paid dupe in the early morning and having only a couple of hours to stand with the other speculators, I had queued the whole night and would now only briefly keep an appointment with my partner before I retired to my bed.

I lost my footing on the last couple of steps that led down into the old-fashioned oyster bar and my noisy entrance occasioned a head to shoot out from between the grey curtains of a secluded booth. It was Scattergood, whose pale eyes and wan complexion argued poorly for his state of health.

'Well?' he said, urgently. 'Went it well, Billy?'

'It went well, Hope,' I said as I sat in the booth and showed him a fistful of money.

'Good, good,' he said. 'Have something to eat. I'll just take a restorative.'

He ordered a glass of whisky and I, two dozen oysters.

She had been sitting quietly in a corner, but then said, 'I'll take a shot too, Hope.'

That we were sat in so dismal a place when I had money in my pocket was of a part with the precarious existence that had been our lot since we had arrived, almost penniless, in New York. Our fortunes fluctuated wildly: they were up and down in a day and the money we always promised would be put aside for Scattergood's passage to Switzerland or for my own future usage always found some other purpose. But even when we were up and could afford something better, it was to this low tavern, with its walls of crudely daubed eagles and presidents and forts and ships and with its oft-drunken, sometimes dancing mulatto woman, that Scattergood was like to go, because, I understood, it was something like a place he had known in his heyday.

204

Behind the curtains, I counted the money. 'I had to stand in line the night through,' I said.

'Oh, Billy, not in the snow?' she said.

'I'll go next time,' said Scattergood. 'Look at this! See if I don't make the same or more.'

She touched his arm. 'You can't go again,' she said.

'Leave it to me just this one more time,' I said. 'You're in no condition.'

'Condition?' he exploded in a fit of coughing that he stifled with his handkerchief, before roaring, 'You think I was in no condition when I read at Cincinnati? Or at Boston?'

'We never were at Boston,' I said, while cold nausea welled in my stomach. 'Maybe you're confusing it with one of those places in Kentucky. Or Ohio?'

He whipped out the tatty bundle of clippings and waved them triumphantly: 'Do you think a man in *no condition* did all this?'

My mother's face reflected my own unease. 'Hope,' she began; he stood and for a moment I thought he was going to damage himself with a further outburst. But he took up his glass and began, quite softly, to sing, 'There's a good time coming, boys, a good time coming . . .'

She shook her head and blew her nose. I avoided her eye and we both pretended that nothing of any significance had occurred and that Hope Scattergood had not mistaken himself for Charles Dickens. The moment, strange as it was, had passed and while my mother and I ate our oysters, Hope took more restorative. He talked of our plans to make a killing at the next sale of Dickens tickets – though George Dolby was making every effort to outwit the average speculator. He was no match for our combined talents, we agreed. (Dickens' manager, just like his *doppelgänger* Billy Talbot, was responsible for ticket sales. He was capable of making life difficult for we honest traders who wanted only to buy up as many tickets as we possibly could and resell them at up to five times their face value.) We also talked of the high times we would have when Hope Scattergood came sailing home from Switzerland.

Whisky and his own good spirits made him look better than I knew he was and I was always aware of what battles he fought to keep his disease at bay or at least to conceal the outward signs of his suffering. His pinched and pallid skin and deep-sunken eyes told a story no amount of joviality could suppress. I guess he knew that we comprehended what was his true condition but there was a tacit understanding between us that none should mention it, unless it were allied to what even my mother now must have known was a fiction, that Hope Scattergood was going to Switzerland.

We did what we could to care for him, which wasn't much. I volunteered for more than my share of night duties and tried always to take my turn when the temperature had dropped way below zero as it had on several memorable occasions. We bought him medicines and once spent all our money on the services of a reputable doctor, but Scattergood wouldn't let 'the quack' near him.

All we could give him was our support and my mother, her love. I had been aware for some time now that the affection that had sprung up between them since the day they met at O'Leary's Boarding-House had become something much deeper. The little services my mother did for him and he performed for her were expressions of their budding and then blossoming love. She was ever at his side, always taking his arm, supporting him spiritually, on some occasions physically too. And now I saw her look with loving and careworn eyes into his own and saw her hand taking his and squeezing it gently.

The mulatto came and took our money and as we left the table Scattergood was singing again: 'Way down in Ca-i-ro . . .' escorting my mother up the steps and into the light.

II

Charles Dickens continued his gruelling itinerary of readings, dividing his time chiefly between Boston and New York. As we had foreseen, it would have been madness for Scattergood to attempt a reading anywhere in New York or Massachusetts: newspapers reported the great writer's whereabouts daily. However, Scattergood had told me, as the passenger car from Cincinnati finally approached New York, there was still money to be made out of Dickens. Hope, who had witnessed the fevered trading of tickets before Dickens' first appearance, announced our intention of entering into that line, using the scant resources we had left as capital.

Only days after we had arrived in New York and settled at O'Leary's, we saw that tickets for the next reading by Dickens were already being advertised in the newspapers. Some of the advertisements were official and placed by the promoters. Others, inserted by private individuals, guaranteed that any number of tickets could be acquired for those who could pay for them. The tickets were to go on sale at nine a.m. of the morning after the puff appeared but just after sunset on the previous afternoon Hope Scattergood and I had walked over to the theatre to see how the land lay and to decide on how we might best place ourselves in order to succesfully complete our business on the morrow. Perhaps some sheltered doorway might be secured as protection from the biting night air.

We rounded a corner and saw the playhouse and also the lines of customers already forming along the wall by the doors. We had no choice but to join the throng and stick it out there until the sale began. The street might have been ill-lit but I could see that our neighbours were, for the most part, as unlikely votaries of a man of letters as I could imagine. We were keenly regarded as we stepped up to the end of the line by men who looked like they might defend the ground on which they seemed rooted to their last drops of blood. Of course, these were speculators, a sample of which species I had already encountered at Cincinnati. They were an unwholesome crew but something like them we must become if we were to succeed in our present design.

We staked our places behind fellows that I might have taken for swells had I met them anywhere else but here. These men stood with elegant easy poise, immaculately turned-out in expensive and well-tailored clothes. I learned from their confident conversation that they were professional speculators from Brooklyn, Jersey City and Philadelphia who had considered it worthwhile to take offices in New York for the duration of Charles Dickens' stay in the United States. Scattergood's instincts hadn't failed him; here was money for the taking.

Others began claiming their places behind us, many of whom had manifestly yet to get hold of that money. A shabbily-attired attorney's clerk was joined by two more of his calling. All three, I discovered, were to be paid by their employers for standing in the lines. Behind them, like some cigar-smoking colossus, towered a tall, rough type, who planted his boots firmly apart upon the sidewalk, daring the encroachment of any other. A second line had formed alongside our own and standing in that were some sad and, I thought, desperate individuals, for whom matters of personal appearance were no longer important and whose clothes were wretched rags. There were opportunists, looking for an easy dollar but others had more pressing need of fresh funds, such as the fellow who shifted and twitched as if afflicted with a nervous disease and popped his head from the line to search for some unseen nemesis among the crowd. 'I'm being dunned,' he complained. 'And these fellers don't bother with the law courts.'

We were obliged by proximity to listen to a babel of chatter in which laments for lost chances and disappointed hopes were qualified with the most optimistic expectations of what might be made through the resale of Dickens tickets. During the night we saw many more hopefuls heading down the street to swell the numbers at the ends of the lines. We were often importuned for our own places but we were hardly there for the sake of five or ten dollars.

The New York speculators were well organised and had come prepared for the rigours of a January night on the streets with mattresses and blankets, bottles of bourbon and bags full of meat and bread. We had nothing yet Scattergood insisted upon staying the night with me. It had been his idea and he would not be dissuaded, though the cold and long hours upon his feet could not but be injurious to his fragile state of health. Snow still lay upon the ground and even had we our neighbours' straw mattresses, proper sleep would have been next to impossible: the whisky drinkers behind us had begun singing loudly and when they left off, others took up the song and two or three entertained their fellows with wild breakdowns and jigs.

Instead, we stood propped against the wall. I hovered between waking and sleeping and then, tearing myself from a stupor in which nightmare scenes were flickering before my eyes, I found that the nightmares were all on the waking side and two men were fighting with broken bottles, before a roaring bonfire.

Something overheard during this night put me on my guard for the rest of that night and on every subsequent day I spent in the city. I was alerted by the words Cincinnati and Dickens and was idly wondering what sort of sensation the arrival of the real Charles Dickens might have created in the city. But then, as clear as if my neighbour had spoken, I heard a voice from a little way down the line say 'Passing themselves off as Dickens and Dolby, as I have it.'

I looked behind me but the men I saw in conversation had the bonfire at their backs and were only to be seen as two silhouettes, one tall and lean and wearing some kind of muffler that obscured his face and the other a short gentleman who must once have hit upon the idea of compensating for his stature by the purchase of a very tall hat.

'Lotta gall, lotta damn gall,' said his tall colleague and laughed loudly.

'Sure they have,' said the short man. 'And I hear your man doesn't look at all like Dickens but who's to know, out in Ohio?'

'Lotta gall, Rory, I take my hat off to 'em.'

'Well, to be sure, yes, but did you not hear what these fellers done? They went and kilt a man and set fire to him, so they did. Because someone was on to them. That's the kinda fellers these are.'

'You don't say? They been arrested, Rory?'

'No, them boys ain't been took yet, though the newspapers are making a great hullabaloo 'bout it all. Well, it's an insult to America. Here's Dickens being treated like he's the Holy Father himself and there's those fellers making fools out of him and everyone. And going and shooting folks into the bargain.'

'I never heard about them before,' said the tall man, removing his muffler to scratch at his neck.

'No reason you should, it's out of town they've been operatin',' said the short man. 'Only now the papers have taken it up because somebody's seen 'em here.'

The tall man swivelled his head and I might have sworn he looked at me. But the short man in the big hat said, 'Not here, you eedyut. In New York City. And everyone's looking out for them because of the big reward.'

'A re-ward, is it?' said his friend, looking, perhaps, directly into my eyes and making me feel more vulnerable than I had been since we had arrived in this big and menacing place. There was no doubting that Scattergood had heard this exchange too, but at that moment he was gripped by a fit of the most brutal kind and I held him close as he brought his paroxysmal frame back under a kind of control.

After dawn, there was activity in the queues as some part of the watch was changed and the fresh faces of employers now took the places of those they had sent to stand in the lines. There was more distracting novelty across the street, as a restaurant opened and waiters began ferrying hot food and drink to those with sufficient ready cash to meet the day's inflated tariffs.

At last, a conveyance rumbled along the lines and its occupant, a large and ruddy man, was recognised by many who stood there. A little man in a jaunty red cap shouted out: 'So Charley's let you have the carriage, has he?' and others followed with raucous calls and jibes. 'How is he, Dolby?'

210

'Don't drop the tickets, Dolby!' 'Look alive, Dolby! We'll freeze to death out here!'

I craned my neck to get a better look at the original of the name Scattergood had conferred upon me for the purpose of working the Dickens lay. He looked a jovial man, his face reddened perhaps by exertion as he hurried through the theatre doors with his small portmanteau, or, more likely, by the hail of chaff that was showered upon him by the speculators. He took an age to arrange himself and his tickets behind the office window and then there was a further delay as one of his agents came out in the street and made the extraordinary announcement that today, tickets would only be sold to those customers wearing hats. The consternation of our neighbours sang in our ears.

'Is he mad?' I said.

Looking up and down the line, I saw that nearly all the speculators were wearing caps. Dolby was trying to avoid all the tickets falling into their hands. Before even the sharpest of the speculators had decided his answering action, Scattergood had already solved the problem. He had gone off down the queues, commanding me to guard our place and I lost sight of him for a few minutes but shortly afterwards, he was back. Clutching a great pile of hats of all colours and condition, he whispered, 'We just went into the men's millinery line.'

He changed his own hat for a slouch that had taken his fancy and the rest he sold at extraordinary rates to clamouring speculators. Not long after that we had our tickets and on the night of the next reading, we were able to resell every one outside the door of the theatre like they were small stakes in a gold mine of good prospect.

III

But nights such as these were hard on Scattergood's constitution. After what we had been through, it was hardly any surprise that his rate of deterioration had begun to accelerate and his failing state of health made us always anxious and sometimes despondent. His system had taken a beating these past few weeks and it was a wonder that this sick man continued to function as he did. Ever since we had fallen in the river, or no, a little before that, I think: perhaps at the point when he had made the decision to return to Amory with the money, he had begun changing, becoming less like the ebullient confidence man of old and more like the near-invalid he was now.

There were days together when he stayed abed and I was forced upon my own resources, but I became adept at pressing some craft I had learnt from him into our own service and could usually raise a few dollars here or there to stave off the pangs of cold and hunger. Most times I preserved some semblance of self-respect and got my money through some small but ingenious trick. However, I confess that on one or two occasions, I was brought low enough to pick a pocket. I was never easy about this. In my mind, there was a sharp distinction between the skilled confidence trickster and the common thief.

Then, when there was a sale of tickets for a reading by Charles Dickens, I could count on earning enough to keep us like kings for a week or more. My own artfulness surprised me. I was growing up and quickly, too. There was no room here for the feckless boy from Hayes and he only reappeared when he suited the purpose of a con. Self-reliance would be everything now. I aimed to make myself as smart as the New York City sharpers or freeze in the attempt. Our adventures had nearly killed my friend but they had made a new man of me.

On a morning like any other in that dismal place, Scatter-good was slumped in a chair, snoring loudly, the bowl of thin soup my mother had prepared balanced precariously in his lap; I had slept the morning through and might have slept longer but O'Leary had hammered upon the door, de-manding his rent and I had given him the money that we had made from selling battered hats to those in sudden need of such items.

We were occupying my mother's room, an L-shaped affair, of which Scattergood and I shared the main part and the bed. My mother made do with a blanket and the floor. We had pleaded that she keep her bed but she had taken me aside and told me that my friend was very ill; he should not be kept out all night and nor should he be left to sleep on the floor. Something of Scattergood's old charm had survived the ravages of his disease, I figured; and though it might now be too faint to catch the notice of the girls we passed in the street, my mother had seen it and become enamoured of it. Or perhaps there was that spark of humanity in her that I had yet to grow to recognise. She was caring and tender towards him from the moment that they met. But it was of another man that she was speaking now, as she sat upon my bed, her hair hanging loose over her face as ever it was in the old days, obscuring eyes that might have been filled with tears, for ought I could see of them.

'I was always a born fool,' she was saying. 'But surely I should have seen through Dwight Howells. Billy, he didn't want to marry me at all. He just wanted what little money I had or could get hold of and he hoped that by promising me the world, a new life away from the scenes of my suffering, I would . . . well, maybe you can imagine. He didn't know what Merriweather had made of me at the Particular or he wouldn't have gone to so much trouble to get what he wanted. I guess that was why I was taken in. He treated me like I was a lady.'

She began to sob, softly. 'He used me, Billy,' she said. She turned from me and buried her face in her apron. 'I had been asking him about his business, because I'd heard him boasting about it to his buddies and the way he told it then wasn't at all like he told it to me. I wanted to be quite certain it was all on the level. He said he had only been fooling with his friends and he had details that would prove it, in a drawer in his hotel room. He began to make up to me but I said I wanted to know all, to find out what I was letting myself in for. He was so drunk he told me everything: he was just taking folks' money and running off. He thought it was very funny and he

213

was the cleverest man on this earth. I should have seen it much sooner. I asked what was to become of your money and what of the house that we had the plans for?

'He said that was all right, that was safe but I didn't believe him and I told him so. I called him a liar and he turned on me like a dog. He beat me and then he raped me. I tried to stop him, Billy, God help me I tried but there wasn't nothing I could do about it. In the morning, he was still so drunk he didn't hear me when I took all his money, which wasn't much by then and got the hell away from there.'

'Where did you go?'

'I had nowhere to go. I went to Springfield, Illinois, because I had the address of a man who once said that if I ever wanted anything, I could get him there. Well, he wasn't there then. And I didn't know where you would be, so I went back to the only place I knew, Hayes and the Particular. Elijah had been moved into run-down rooms above the stables in town, which some operator had told him were real swell apartments. The smell must surely have told him otherwise. He wasn't pleased to see me, 'til I said I had seen you.

'He was frightened. He said the newspaperman, Mr Amory, had been to see him about you. He wanted to know if you had returned to Hayes and if not, where you were headed. Mr Putnam had never liked Mr Amory and wouldn't tell him but Mr Amory cut up rough. I reckon it was him gave Mr Putnam the black bruise he had on his face. Mr Putnam said he had gotten the wire you sent, soon as you got to Cincinnati. Amory said he knew that and that you were wanted for murder in Cincinnati and that if Putnam didn't come clean he'd not only have him to deal with but the law as well. Amory said he knew all about your quest to meet this Dickens and so Mr Putnam knew he was beat and told him you had been heading to New York, though he says he didn't give him this address.'

'That's a small mercy. I only hope it's true.'

'I knew you could never have done no murder and when I had heard that Silas Amory and maybe the law as well was on your trail, I was frightened for you. Elijah was in two minds.

He said he had no wish to aid a felon but I said he was a fool and knew you better than that and it was like he had just turned loose the dogs on you. I said I would find you and warn you. I had used the money I took from Howells in Illinois and I had to ask Mr Putnam for an advance.'

'But Elijah already gave me his savings,' I said.

She looked uncomfortable.

'Well, he had a little left over,' she said, 'And 'sides, I can always raise a little money if it's really needed.'

She changed the subject abruptly: 'It ain't true, Billy, 'bout the murder?'

'No, it ain't,' I said, shortly. 'Silas Amory done it.'

'That about figures,' she said. 'So I came to New York and this awful place. I didn't know what to do when I found you weren't here. I had no money nor nothing; I had counted on you being here.'

'How did you live?'

'I got by. Where were you, all this time, Billy?'

'I was laying low. In a house in Cincinnati.'

'With friends?'

'With ladies of the night,' said Scattergood. I don't know how long he had been awake, but he seemed much refreshed now and was laughing loudly at his own joke.

'Oh, Billy!' said my mother. 'That's not true, is it?'

I began to try to explain how I came to be living in a cathouse but the more I said, the more mixed up it all must have sounded and there was certainly no way in which I could account for it satisfactorily, without damaging the character of Hope Scattergood, a man whom my mother currently held in some regard.

She looked at me in a new light and the awkwardness of a minute ago was gone. 'Ah, Billy,' she said. 'And I thought you were different!'

IV

Sometimes there was money but most days we lived from

hand to mouth and were obliged to fall back upon less glorious devices than trading in tickets for the readings of Charles Dickens. We eked out a tenuous living while we awaited the return of the great man, from Philadelphia. Up to then, Charles Dickens had read in New York and Boston and we had hoped he might confine himself to these places.

But now he was in Philadelphia and the intelligence we bought off one of Dolby's less scrupulous agents revealed that he would soon be in Washington and then he might be reading in further flung and less convenient venues. The good news was that arrangements had been made for the hiring of a chapel in Brooklyn and four readings would shortly take place there.

These were heady days but hardly free from care. Scattergood's parlous condition worried my mother and it must have been a black incubus in his own mind. On top of that was the ever-present fear of discovery, either by Silas Amory, who, for all we knew, could be in New York now, searching for us with a pepper-pot pistol in his pocket or by some money-grabbing informer who had seen us read at Cincinnati. What the speculators had said was true. That same day we were news in two New York newspapers and there was a small piece the next day, recounting two supposed sightings of men thought to be those wanted in Ohio. Someone in Cincinnati, whom I guessed wanted his name in the newspapers almost as much as he wanted revenge, had put up $1,000 as reward for information directly leading to our capture. I didn't need to see H. Steiner's name at the bottom of the article.

Whenever possible, we went abroad with my mother, that we might appear as a regular family enjoying a promenade – which, in truth, I often felt us to be – rather than two fugitives from justice. There was no knowing to what lengths Amory might go to ensure our silence nor whether we were wanted beyond the Ohio state line. All we could do was to keep a watchful eye, be careful and trust to luck while we raised enough cash for Scattergood to go to Europe and for my mother and I to go somewhere else, Canada perhaps, while I worked out how we might safely clear my name.

It was not an easy time and the anxiety of it told upon us all. I would be irritable, especially if what we made fell short of our target, which it almost always did; my mother fretted over Scattergood, who was sometimes too ill to remain long out of his bed where he would lie mumbling and the substance of his haltering speech was that he believed himself to be Charles Dickens.

We planned to make the most of the Brooklyn sales. We heard that Dolby was now allowing only six tickets per purchase: to circumvent this restriction, some of the better-heeled speculators had fielded up to fifty dummies in the last sale and now Scattergood too had persuaded a small army of hungry destitutes to swell our ranks, on the promise of some small remuneration. By then, we shared the view of fellow speculators that George Dolby was our arch foe, to be outwitted and bettered at every opportunity.

Meantime we had a couple of days to spare, which we filled so pleasantly together with walks in the park, or discovering what wealth would buy on Fifth Avenue. A whole day was spent at Barnum's Museum, which Scattergood revered as a Mussulman might his temple. He suspended the amiable cynicism with which he controlled his every action and allowed himself to become as one with the slack-jawed tourists and excited children who gaped and gawped at every amazing novelty.

And then we were crossing the East River to Brooklyn and as the ferryboat cut the water, we and others of our kind rubbed our hands at the thought of the money to be realised on that far shore. I thought that there must be a future for Scattergood. He stood at the rail like Columbus at his prow, his long hair streaming in the wind and his sunken eyes flashing in the dying sunlight. He looked so proud and so certain that I was persuaded that here wasn't the man to be overcome by the limitations of the human condition. He seemed strong enough as he turned to me and enthused about the chances of buying up whole blocks of pews at Ward Beecher's Brooklyn Chapel.

'This is where we make our killing,' he was saying. 'With what we make here, we can bank half and use the rest to dog Dickens on his travels. I mean to squeeze this lay 'til it's dry.'

'Follow him?'

'Certainly. I have one of his agents in my pocket.' He took a pull from a whisky bottle which was newly bought but already half-emptied. 'You can't leave business like this unfinished. We're only beginning to make it work for us. If the other places are even half so lucrative as these have been, we'll have enough to skedaddle down South and make some real money.'

'But what about Switzerland?'

'Of course, I must go for my cure. But, I thought perhaps before we did that we might just see what's afoot in the old Confederacy. A whole lot of building going on down there and then there's all those new votes . . .'

'Votes?'

'Well, yes. It's something I've been thinking much about, lately. Politics. That's the new lay for men like you and me. See, Billy, there's a whole fresh electorate now and who d'you think they'd like to vote into office – the old masters with their old ways or maybe Yankees, who brought them their freedom? And if I can pass for Charles Dickens I'm damn sure I can pass for a Yankee!'

'Politics, Hope? You?'

'Well and why not? I've worked every kind of scheme but I never got a shot at the big time. Look at this.' He pulled out his bunch of clippings and showed me a new one, but the light was too poor to read by. 'It says here that the Southrons ain't co-operating with the major generals the Government put in place down there. Ain't even putting up candidates for office, reckoning they'd be Yankee puppets.'

'Where does that get you?'

'As I see it,' said Scattergood, 'the way's clear for anyone with ten cents' worth of ambition. Why, I reckon I could be governor of one of them states in no time at all. There's carpetbaggers down there now with no more'n the clothes on their backs and a lot of empty promises, doin' real well for themselves. If a blockhead like Johnson can be president, I don't see why I shouldn't get along in that line.'

'I'm sure you could,' I said, 'but as soon as we have the money I'm going down the shipping line office and booking your berth to Europe.'

'I wouldn't want to miss out on the opportunities they got for fellas like me,' said Scattergood, thoughtfully.

'Damn it, Hope,' I said, 'you won't have no opportunities if you don't go to Switzerland!'

I said I was sorry and that wasn't what I meant at all but he said I was probably right. What troubled me was that I was sustaining an illusion. Unless Swiss doctors had some science that the rest of world hadn't heard about, they couldn't cure Scattergood and in supporting the lie was I denying him the chance of pursuing his dream. But to give up on Switzerland would mean that both he and I would have to admit the inevitable, that he was going to die.

'We'll do all that, just as soon as you get back, I promise,' I said, cravenly. 'We'll hire detectives, Pinkerton's maybe, and clear our names. Soon as Amory's behind bars and we can hold up our heads again, we'll go down South together.'

'That's just what we'll do, Billy,' he said. 'Soon as I get back.'

I turned my back, made it look as if I was watching the fiery finish to the day, as the sun set over the great city of New York and made silhouettes of seamen aloft in the sails of berthed merchantmen. Perhaps it is only a sentimental memory of an old man, but I think that I had turned not to witness the glory of the sunset, nor the spectacle of the great ships disgorging produce from the world over but so that no one might have marked my tears.

I can never be sure, because the moment was shared by one of sudden danger; a whistle screamed and I beheld an old passenger steamer crossing our bows, so close that I could see alarm on the face of the helmsman. Our ferryboat missed being holed by inches and nervous laughter rippled along the rail. I watched the steam packet as it wheezed black smoke and slowly progressed down the river and reflected that Dickens must have arrived, all those years ago, on such a craft: Elijah too. As seagulls swooped about our prow, catching morsels of bread hurled by children and a suggestion of the salt water spray of the great ocean filled my nostrils, I felt I knew how Dickens and Elijah must have felt as young men setting out to conquer the New World. Maybe I would meet Dickens and maybe all would be well. Was it like Scattergood always said – all things were possible? But I cut my contemplations short as the new buildings of New York's dormitory loomed and the ferryboat was soon tied to the quay.

My mother had sent us to work with bags of meat and bread and Scattergood had a full bottle of good whisky under his coat, now much reduced. Our mattresses were rolled in bundles beside us and we and our fellows must have looked for all the world like some new kind of water-born gypsies. We closed with the Brooklyn shore and all about us, men picked up their bundles and prepared to disembark. We tramped down the gangplank like an invading army but once ashore, the speculators with their mattresses and bundles and me helping Hope Scattergood, all ran pell-mell through the streets, towards Ward Beecher's Chapel, that the best places in line might be secured.

I had never been to Brooklyn; its speculative new developments and older timber buildings were strange to me and yet I thought I knew its name. There was no time now to call the connection to mind; like everyone else, I had thoughts for nothing but the cold. It was bitter and where we stood in line we could expect but little benefit from the enormous fire that would be kept up all night. Scattergood had installed his dupes and we had all arrived in good enough time to obtain prime positions in the lines. Not too near the front – for Dolby often refused to sell the best seats to those at the head of the queue, expecting them all to be speculators – and, of course, not too far down it.

The cold and wind that funnelled through the streets made

this night harder to bear than any previous. There was more drunkenness and more fighting and no one was in a very good mood as we awaited the frosty dawn. For no more than an hour we tried to rest upon our bedrolls but there could be no sleep amongst such a loud and argumentative mob and when two squabblers pitched forward and fell upon us, we resigned ourselves to another night upon our feet. The night was long and there was little to divert us from the searing cold but the antics of drunken revellers around the bonfire, whose flames were too distant for us to derive any benefit. Scattergood finished his whisky and stood in silence with his coat pulled tightly about himself and his face set hard in an expression of grim determination.

Rumours passed up and down the lines. Dolby would not be selling the tickets that day but would be sending instead an agent, who would be easier to manipulate. Or it was said that no one would want tickets for a reading over in Brooklyn and that anyone buying up the tickets now would be sure to lose money and I would have wagered our ticket money on that last suggestion being the work of one of the more astute speculators. I saw no one leave the lines. A sale of Dickens tickets had failed no one yet. Once again, I caught a fleeting mention of 'that feller who made out he was Dickens, in Cincinnati'.

Someone lost in the darkness had a banjo and struck up some popular songs. His high and tremulous voice caught the ear of all who were near and brought a measure of order to this unruly crowd until an upstairs window in a nearby house was flung open and a loud argument ensued between the awoken householder and the men in the line. Though he slammed shut his window, the bored and angry speculators did not concur that the matter was ended and when their profanities failed them, someone struck up 'The Battle Hymn of the Republic'. Those standing further down the line knew nothing of this small altercation and took up the refrain for their own pleasure and soon it seemed that every person in both the long lines was singing out the hymn at the top of his voice.

This little diversion ended, there was nothing for us to do but await the dawn. When finally it came, so did the police, who began to break down the bonfire. A fire hazard, they said, with so many timber buildings nearby. Why they had only noticed them now, I couldn't say. The people in the lines hurled abuse and then a bottle was thrown. Policemen waded into the crowds and pulled from it the culprit. His friends were too tormented by the cold and angered by the police action to allow this and vicious brawling broke out, firstly between them and the police and then between rival speculators, as vacated places in the line were detected and appropriated by interlopers from further down the lines. It became something like a riot as the fighting spread and I clung to the palings at my back as bottles and stones and then a burning spar soared overhead. Thuggish elements took advantage of the chaos and were now openly threatening and often attacking those with prime places in the lines and the faint-hearted took off there and then, while others made a fight of it.

I couldn't believe that these roughnecks would have the nerve to approach Scattergood. Whatever his health, I still regarded him as a powerful man capable of achieving anything, a mentor and protector, in whose keeping I still felt myself to be. The Brooklyn street-hounds, of course, saw only a frail old man. A hideously-scarred brute I had seen earlier, kicking his heels with impatience and emptying a bottle snatched from another speculator, had already made himself conspicuous by threatening those further up the line and his imprecations and obscenities had frightened away an old man and a boy. This animal, backed by three associates of similarly fearsome bearing, now looked for a weak link in our line and fixed upon the enfeebled figure of Hope Scattergood.

'Better shove down the line, old man,' the ruffian said and pushed Scattergood aside. I was for letting the matter go, it was only what you might expect in such dubious company. But Scattergood was furious and eloquent in his dismissal of this usurper and I couldn't prevent him laying hold of his

antagonist. Hope called him names the other would understand and the man spun about, vehemently cursing and
swinging a fist. A heavy blow sent Scattergood reeling to the
sidewalk. The scarred man became as a hyena about wounded
but dangerous prey. He pointed and taunted, said that no one
made a fool of Mick Mulligan, that didn't want his lungs
pricked with a sharp blade. Mick Mulligan, he proclaimed,
had fought the niggers and the Polacks, was king of the streets
and no foul-mouthed, queue-jumping old man would stand
in his way. As Mulligan and his men began to kick the fallen
Scattergood, I made my move.

I have always abhorred physical altercation but I am glad
to recall that I didn't think about this but flew straightaway at
the chief among Scattergood's attackers and would like have
done him real injury had I not been pulled off and sent reeling
by a hard blow from some heavy instrument made upon the
back of my head. When I had collected my senses, I saw
Scattergood lying balled upon the ground as he was kicked
repeatedly in his ribs. I tried to rise, but it was over and they
left him where he lay and assumed our positions in the line,
laughing as after pleasant diversion.

I picked myself up, my head pierced by sudden pain but
my concern was for Scattergood, who cried out in anguish as
I picked him up and helped him to stand. I tried to ascertain
how badly he was hurt but got no reply, only a rambling
senselessness that degenerated further into the sort of
whimper that might be heard from a beaten dog. I spent the
few coins I had on the ferry and a cab to take him home,
recalling at some point in our retreat that there once been a
great battle in Brooklyn.

Chapter Thirteen

I

MY MOTHER UNDRESSED Scattergood and tended his wounded body, sponging and dressing his cuts and bruises and covering him in a sheet, as lightly as she could. He was barely conscious but he cried out whenever he was moved or the vinegar-soaked sponge touched a painful place. His body was livid and raw, great purple blotches disfiguring his pale skin. She examined him as delicately as love would allow and found that ribs he had broken before, were broken again. She took her coat and said she was going out to fetch a doctor. I reminded her that we had no money but she went anyway and an hour later returned with a squint-eyed sawbones in tow. 'He don't look good,' he pronounced and administered laudanum before he began to bandage the patient's sides but when he still flinched in pain, my mother sharply admonished him to be more careful, if he wanted his fee. Then it was done and he left and my mother went with him.

For above a month, Scattergood lay upon his bed or sat by the window, gazing at decayed tenements that walled out the light and from which unintelligible and frightening cries arose in the dead of night, serving as unnecessary reminders of what a dangerous and unpredictable world lay just beyond our door. The beating, his injuries, the nights in the cold had all taken a heavy toll and he was weaker than ever. I would not have left him but I had to be about some business or other, making sure we had enough to eat and that all was in place for the next sale of Dickens tickets, when we all hoped that some real money might be made.

My mother stayed at his side, talking to him of this and that while he dozed, or mopping his brow in times of fever and listening to his rantings and delusions. There were times when the fantasies of his sickness remained with him, though the crisis had passed and he took his collections of clippings and again thumbed through them as if each contained a personal memory of which he was proud. I was somewhat in awe of the patience and attention with which my mother looked after my unfortunate friend. She bathed him and changed his bandages and cleaned him up when he had soiled the bed and I once returned to find my mother sitting by him, a book open at her knee, her fingers tracing the words as she made a stumbling effort to read to him.

Sometimes, Hope called me his son and while I was always happy that he should regard me as some surrogate for a child he had never had, it was all too often the result of some muddle in his mind and when he talked of discovering me after all these years, I knew that he was thinking himself Dickens again. Periods of lucidity, when he might opine acutely about the sensation of the day, which was the possibility that President Johnson might actually be *impeached*, alternated with those when his mind was clouded and his only conversation the most dismal and senseless rambling. He slept for hours at a time and then my mother and I talked of him, although we never addressed the great truths of the matter. We looked instead to that halcyon time when he should be free of his pain.

Some days he appeared much improved and lately we had come to believe that he was on the mend. We all were more hopeful and with some reason: I had been fortunate in my dealings and had saved some little money. We agreed that this should be invested in rail travel and that I must go wherever the tickets were on sale. Already, I had been in Boston. In Washington I had bought and sold my tickets amid scenes of monumental splendour, where builders and masons worked to consolidate and set in stone the victory of the North. I had made a very neat profit and now I looked forward to repeating my success and accumulating some money.

Slowly, Scattergood improved and at last he was well enough to be irritated and bored with his confinement and he took to going out. His pleasure was to inhabit the nearby basement oyster bar in which he drank too much whisky and regaled the customers with broken songs or his antics in bygone days. He could entertain the denizens of the bar but his conversations with my mother and I were increasingly intense and almost obsessive. He repeatedly warned me against wasting my golden opportunity and insisted that I seek an audience with Dickens and reveal to him that I was his flesh and blood. I assured him I would do so just as soon as I saw my chance but I might then have agreed to anything, so long as he became more tranquil and gave himself time to rest. The only action I accomplished to this end was to mail a note to George Putnam, whose address had been supplied by Elijah, announcing my intentions and requesting a written introduction. I regretted it as hasty and foolish the minute it was posted and was relieved when no reply was forthcoming.

II

I do not distinguish the individual days of this bleak period. Rather I recall what I felt: pangs of hunger and of pity; brittle insecurity, vicarious suffering; fleeting hours of hope and joy that rarely balanced the days of disappointment and despair. But, somewhere amidst all this, was the seed of something good. Then it was that the last reserve I felt for my mother was banished and in its place came love.

Hope Scattergood lay asleep, the remains of the breakfast, of which he had eaten almost all, saucing a plate by his side.

He had slept well the night before, too, which was a spring of great hope to us all, after so many in which his hacking had kept us all awake and he had been so weak as to need help to sit up and lean over the bowl into which he expectorated blood. Perhaps the laudanum and the whisky had helped, but he had woken early this morning and had chatted gaily about how much cash I ought to be able to raise when I went out selling my tickets, that evening. Then he had eaten and had fallen soundly asleep once more. My mother covered him with a blanket and kissed his forehead. 'He's mending,' she said. 'Look at him. So peaceful. I can't hear his chest, neither.'

I listened and agreed that his breathing sounded stronger than it had for a week or more. Previously, it had been shallow and whistling; now I thought he might begin to snore deeply, at any moment.

She smiled. 'I pray he'll get better. I never met anyone like him before, nor anyone who ever cared for me like he does.' She looked worn out by the care of him.

'I care, Mother,' I said and she turned, quickly.

'What did you say?'

I squeezed her hand, hoping to so express what I could not quite repeat.

'You never called me mother before,' she said and turned away, sparing me my discomfort.

'It's a nice day,' I said. 'We should go out. Get a breath of air.'

Still she sat by Scattergood, stroking the grey hairs at his temples. 'I can't leave him,' she said, but rays of strong sunlight were streaking through the dust-mottled glass and I could see she might be persuaded.

'A walk will do you good,' I said. 'You've barely set foot outside this door in a week. Get your coat; we'll take a turn in the park.'

She cast a last look at Hope who seemed quite at peace and we left him asleep on the bed and I took her out into the fresh morning air. She slipped her slender arm over mine and we walked block after block until eventually we left the crowded streets and entered the green sanctuary of the park, where the bright skies and a few tiny flowers betokened the coming of spring.

The pleasant change of environment worked its magic and as we strolled beneath budding boughs and among early blossoms, my mother became livelier than I had seen her of late, remarking how pleasant was this place. So it must have seemed, after weeks in which she had barely left the cramped squalor of our room, while she attended to her precious charge. Now, the wind on her face was a joy, the verdant space a beggar's elysium after her long confinement. She delighted in the thin and crisp carpet of unsullied snow, the dissonant chatter of passers-by and the startled squirrels that flew up trees at our approach.

The unexpected sunshine had brought others out to enjoy the park. Young men promenaded with their girls, matrons aired their babies and families shepherded children who chased hoops or clutched rag dolls. I was reminded of how circumscribed had been my world as ambassadors from the earth's four corners crossed our path and these of every station in life: ragamuffins and swells, the well-heeled and the down-at-heel were encountered in equal proportion, alongside drunken sailors, roving shoeblacks and hawkers of every kind of comestible. Men of business for whom the park was only a convenient route between two points went by at a clip. I was thinking that we should continue walking and watching folk all afternoon when my mother arrested our progress where a father was at play with his children.

'Kites, Billy!' she exclaimed. Two young boys sent aloft a big red kite to join that of their father, which soared and dipped high above the treetops. We watched transfixed as both performed gracefully against a background of high and feathery cirrocumulus clouds until the lines becoming entangled each with the other, the kites plunged from on high and smashed upon the ground. The protests I expected from the disappointed boys were immediately stemmed by their father. He picked up both and said they would directly go and buy two bigger and better kites. My mother was silent as we passed the boys. She marched onwards, now oblivious to all around her as she followed the planting of her own feet. It was some moments before she stopped again and then she said, quietly, 'You never had a kite nor none of those things children ought to have.'

She continued to find a fascination in her shoes but though her face was averted, I could see that her ears and her cheeks had reddened considerably. I hesitated to reply. She had spoken the painful truth and the occasions when I had wished to broach the subject of my childhood with her were number-less. But I said, 'That doesn't matter. What does it signify if I didn't have a hobby-horse or a kite?'

'It mattered at the time and you know it did,' she said. 'And all the other stuff mattered more. I wasn't there to help you when you needed me. All those years at that terrible place, slaving for that man. What you must have suffered. I did the world's worst job in raising you Billy, you know I did.'

I remember how I sucked in my breath and held it. Not so very long before, what she said just then would have dyna-mited a dam of accusation and reproach and a sump of bile I had accumulated in my dark young years would have found its release. But now I let out only a long breath. and said, 'I know I thought so at the time. I was mortal ashamed when I found out how you were used by Merriweather.'

She was weeping, standing there in the middle of the park, stifling her sobs as people passed by and looked enquiringly at this woman and the young man who hesitated to offer succour. I blew away the cobwebs of my past and took her hand.

'But now I understand how you were fixed,' I said, squeez-ing her fingers. 'And I guess I know you now for yourself and not for what Merriweather made of you. That life is behind us and I can't let you take the blame no more. Don't you remember what you said: "When big folk sweep little folk into a corner, sometimes there just ain't no escapin'?" Well, I can see that now. Maybe I've grown some.'

'You understand?'

'Understand? I'm saying it wasn't your fault. I know how you were hoodwinked and scared up by Merriweather. I know how young you were when you were brought there too. You couldn't have known no better.'

But it was clear she neither expected nor would accept any mercy until her confession had been made in full. 'I knew soon enough that what Merriweather had me doin' was wrong, Billy. I knew too that I should be doin' something for you, only I didn't know how I could change things at the hotel, so I could do that. I didn't have nothing I could fight that man with. I turned agin' him, Billy, a couple of times. I fought and I still got the marks. But I should have tried more, for your sake. Some time, d'you think you might forgive me?'

'I don't see there's anything to forgive.'

She looked up like a deer scenting something in the wind, uncertain for just a second whether it detected water or danger. 'You really sure about that? I cain't hardly believe you.'

'I'm sure, Mother,' I said. 'If anyone's got any apologising to do it's me. I behaved like a fool, a regular jackass.'

I heard her laugh. 'Well, yes, maybe you did, now you mention it,' she said and her smile returned and warmed me like no weak sunlight could ever do. It only required Hope Scattergood to have been there in good health and we might both have been content.

Our perambulations had taken us by the frozen lake, where skaters twisted over its glossy surface like black bugs on a mirror. 'Didn't have no skates, neither,' mused my mother. The skaters shimmied across the ice, a hundred men, some adventurous women and more boys than perhaps the ice might safely stand. The accomplished displayed their skills, describing graceful figures about others who had stopped to chat, or to do business.

'No skates,' I agreed, though there was neither shame nor accusation in this exchange. 'Nor regular candy. Or fancy clothes,' I added.

231

'Billy Talbot,' she said, 'it was me told Merriweather to give you that hat. I hope you ain't complainin'.'

We skirted the lake and passed among the brilliant colours and glinting equipages of fashionable New York as it assembled for a parade of affluence. Carriages lined the lake, horses snorting icy breath while women with hour-glass figures and fine hats talked with men in fur-lined coats, who smoked cigars and talked loudly about their business.

Though necessarily dressed for the cold, each of these women was exquisite in her turnout, every item beautifully tailored, every pleat keenly creased. Their expensive perfumes hung in the air like a fabulous ether of wealth. It was plain my mother had never seen the like. Their perfection far surpassed the elegance of those at the ball in Cincinnati. There, the prettiest girl was not as she seemed and I was forced to wonder if what I saw before me was counterfeit too. Money, I was learning, might make anyone magnificent and perhaps even beautiful. After all, the splendid people I saw here were not the blooded-gentry of my reading, who turned out on London's Rotten Row but ordinary people who had succeeded by themselves and congregated here to advertise that fact.

As we rounded the lake and began to retrace our steps, I thought upon the lots that had been drawn by me and my mother and came to believe the words I had recently spoken. She had not been at fault. She had been the victim of circumstance and the machinations of others and I, in my callowness and ignorance, had blamed her. I fervently wished that I might make amends. I decided then that I would raise myself from the mud and if not by the sweat of my brow then by the sleight of my palm, I should bend myself to improvement, so that my mother might one day wear such dresses and ride in a sleek black brougham and people should remark as we passed, 'There goes Billy Talbot the swell and his mammy. Mighty fine lady.' That would be something and if, by the grace of God, Hope Scattergood survived to sit by her side, what a family we should be. A confidence trickster, a prostitute and a bastard – a singular combination, that was true and yet our family would surely be held by stronger bonds than many we had seen this day.

How I should achieve my grand ends was a matter for cogitation I was happy to postpone by stopping at a refreshment shack by the park entrance and buying a couple of sodas. She drank quickly, her face and actions betraying agitation. 'We should be getting back to Hope,' she said. 'I didn't mean to be so long away.' To save time and my mother from further concern, we boarded an omnibus and alighted a few blocks from O'Leary's apartments. All the ride back, I had been thinking about how maybe we deserved as good as the fine folk in the park and I couldn't help revealing to my mother something of my intentions.

'Hope says you should go see Mr Dickens. Maybe he can do something for you. Get you a start in a good job, maybe. It wouldn't hurt for you just to see him, Billy.'

But by now I had seen Charles Dickens and upon several occasions. I had watched him hurrying through stage doors with George Dolby and a man who had charge of his gas-lighting or tightly maintaining a public face in the streets. I had heard him greet astonished well-wishers and seen him courted by the nabobs of New York. But these chance encounters were not what I had in mind, when I amazed my mother, saying, 'I *have* seen Charles Dickens.'

'Well, for goodness' sakes! What did he say? Does he want to see you again? But you never said – did something go wrong?'

'I've been dealing in his tickets. I was bound see him sooner or later.'

'You know what I mean, Billy,' she said, as we crossed an intersection, my preoccupation and her enthusiasm very nearly putting us under the wheels of a photographer's van.

'You mean have I been sufficiently forward to march up to him and introduce myself as his bastard son?'

'Billy! You know what I mean,' she repeated.

'Well, when I last saw the old man, as I recall, Charles

233

Dickens was standing as close to me as you are now.'

'No! When? What happened?'

'It was in Boston.' She nodded, though I doubt she had been sure where I was half of the time, as her attention had been entirely focused on Hope Scattergood's wavering state of health.

'I had spent the night in the lines again but I'd gotten enough tickets to have made it worth the trip. Once my business was done, I cut behind the theatre, this being the quickest route to the railroad depot. Round by the stage door, there was a small crowd gathered. None of the speculators was there and I could see at a glance that no extra business was being done. These people were being made merry by some diversion, perhaps being entertained by some unusual street entertainer. My curiosity drew me amongst them and towards the front, where I was shocked to find myself face to face with Charles Dickens.'

'No, Billy!'

'It's true, Mother. Expecting a pierrot or maybe a man with marionettes, I emerged between a big bald man, whom I later recognised as Dolby, and someone I thought I had encountered before, though exactly where, or when, I couldn't have said. Both these men were laughing heartily, the latter displaying a smile that was as barren of teeth as is Dolby's pate of hair. I had no time for further observations as the object of theirs, who had been addressing a young lady behind him, suddenly turned towards us and then Charles Dickens was looking directly at me. Petrified by my own guilt, I thought he had discovered one of those involved in what they're calling now the "Bogus Boz" scandal. I didn't want to worry you, but there's whispers we've been seen in New York. Rumours, nothing more, but when Dickens fixed me with those eyes of his I thought we were undone for sure and that he'd have us taken up for that murder in a twinkling or that between them, Dickens and Dolby might tear me apart. Dolby had the strength and Dickens the fervour.'

'Oh, Billy,' said my mother, as a hail shower forced us under

234

an awning advertising 'Segars and whisky'. 'So you told him who you was? And he couldn't prosecute his own son?'

'It was only my conscience, Ma. I doubt he even noticed me, then. He was telling a story and it seemed to me he saw only those folk we was talking about.'

'But you did speak to him, Billy?'

'All in good time, Mother,' I said. 'Let me tell you his story, as best I can, as it's something I thought I might work up and amuse Hope with.'

'I suppose you might tell it until the weather lets up,' she said, chafing that I would not immediately reveal what she wanted to know.

'You must imagine Dickens,' I said. 'Don't think of Hope as the two are not in the least similar. Dickens has a big and polished forehead, wispy hair thinning on top, beard like poor cotton, a vein upon his temple, here, that throbs like a bullfrog's gullet and eyes that would light damp tinder. You have him?'

She nodded and I discarded my customary, round-shouldered posture for Dickens' more manly bearing. 'Hearing I was in low spirits,' I began but the tone was too high, the voice too American. I tried again for Dickens' own alien brogue and this time succeeded as well as ever I might.

'Hearing that I had been brought low by the American catarrh,' I said and this time I thought I sounded not unlike Dickens, 'my valuable friends George Dolby and James Osgood resolved to mount an entertainment for my benefit. I must say I was gratified when it reached my notice. But what do you think was the notion that these two great minds hit upon? Amateur theatricals, you might think: my love of suchlike is well-known. Or a musical concert, Osgood performing on the piano whilst Dolby puffed into a tuba? Just the thing for a recumbent invalid, think you. But no! Not they! It was their idea – I had nothing *whatever* to do with this. I was not *even consulted*, I think – it was their idea and theirs only, to hold a Great International Walking Match!

'Don't tell *me* that Boston was snowbound or that the

235

streets were a grill of sheet-ice navigable only with skates. Don't tell *me* that an invalid such as myself should have been tucked up in his bed, rather than exposed to the freezing air, overseeing a battle of brawn. Tell them! There's Dolby now! Tell him! And may it do you more good than it did me, for they *would not listen to me!*

'I was assured that no less weighty a matter was at stake than the honour of the two greatest powers on earth. Dolby would be walking for her Imperial Majesty, Queen Victoria, her loyal subjects and the British Empire. Mr Osgood would be representing republicanism and the newly united states of America. He mentioned something about justice, freedom and equality for all, but I disallowed these and said he was walking for quite enough as it stood.

'I think by then my own part in all this had become less than insignificant. However, if a thing is to be done, it must be done well, I told them. They agreed and I sent them out upon a five-mile breather about Baltimore, from which they returned, wheezing and puffing smoke like a pair of locomotives in need of lubrication.

'When we arrived at Boston, I drew up articles of agreement, that, as I say, the thing might be done properly and that there might be no recourse to law or lethal weapons in the event of a disputed result. The competitors were allowed to use their sporting names. Dolby would race as the "Man of Ross", Osgood was advertised as the "Boston Bantam". The umpires would be "Massachusetts Jemmy" Fields and myself. My expertise upon that truly national instrument, the American catarrh, allowing me to claim the sobriquet "the Gad's Hill Gasper".

'Dolby and Osgood began training immediately. Perhaps you have seen athletes practising their art? In my circumscribed experience, they run, they lift dumb-bells, they shadow-box. I don't claim to be an expert in such matters and it might very well be that the best training a walker can do is to see *how high he can kick the wall.* I don't know. But it seemed that Dolby and Osgood thought so because I caught them engaged in this same competition and if you might imagine the Herculean figure of Dolby here kicking the bricks with the diminutive Osgood you will understand the reason for my astonishment, though Dolby says that for life of him he couldn't see it.

'You see that it hadn't escaped my notice that there was some disparity in the physical attributes of the two contenders and I did question, as umpire, whether some system of handicap should be adopted. Osgood said no, he knew that Dolby had an unfair advantage, on account of his bald head offering no resistance to the wind when dropped like a bull charging, but he, Osgood, was nearer to the ground and objects closer to the earth, he argued, have shorter orbits. However, he did object when Dolby sent home for a pair of seamless socks. I checked the rules and finding nothing to prohibit the use of seamless socks, Osgood could only grind his teeth.

'The agreed route was to be six and a half miles along the Mill Dam Road to Newton Centre and back. On February 29th, the competitors took to the field despite the most atrocious conditions ever recorded at a Great International Walking Match . . .'

The hail had ceased and my mother and I left our shelter and began to walk up the street. I suited my gait to the action of my story.

'They both started well. Here were the Bantam's legs going like a pair of tailor's scissors and there were Dolby's elbows pumping like steam pistons. For the first three miles they were neck-and-chest but after the turning the Bantam forged ahead and pegged away with his drumsticks as if he saw his wives and a peck of barley before him. There can be no doubting that Dolby had been complacent. The hare and the tortoise had taught him nothing. But as distance diminished the Bantam still further, the Man of Ross woke up. Down went his head and Dolby charged. I was certain that British baldness would win the day. The Bantam squinted over his shoulder and saw what Dolby was about. He clucked like he

237

had just seen the fox and off he went again, scratching ahead with no fox, but two hundred pounds of British beef on his tail. Dolby approached like a one-bull stampede and quickly closed with the Bantam, who had begun to flag. I, for one, thought it was all up with him.

'But this is where matters take on a murkier shade. Though a suitable appellation for a sporting fowl such as the bantam, I should not have thought to employ the words "foul play" in connection with the Great International Walking Match. But what do you call it when a lady *not entirely unconnected* with the Bantam side, drops into his mouth *bread soaked in brandy*! That, I regret, is what occurred and thus fortified, the refuelled Bantam streaked off towards the finish line, where his crowing began and hasn't stopped since.'

I paused here and checked my pace. Only now did I see that in my zeal to recreate the story with all verisimilitude, my mother had been obliged to maintain a brisk trot in order to keep abreast of me.

'And that was as Dickens told it, more or less. Now, do you think Hope will laugh? Can I read as Dickens as well as he?'

My dilatory speech had driven my mother close to distraction. 'Billy, you tell me about you and Charles Dickens this moment or I'll beat you for the first and last time, I swear it!'

'I was coming to that part,' I said. 'When he had done, I found Charles Dickens was peering at me again. This time there was no mistaking, he was looking only at me. "Well?" he said, his expression comically enquiring, his face only inches from mine, his breath sherry-sweet. "I thank you for your patience, sir, but you may give me your message now."

'I told him I had no message. "What?" he said, in a loud and theatrical tone, "No urgent telegram? No cable summoning me this instant to Buckingham Palace?" I shook my head. To speak would have then been quite beyond my powers. "Then I am perplexed and you have me at a disadvantage," he said. "Here I am talking with my friends, Mr Longfellow, Mr Dolby and some others whose friendship and acquaintance I value, enjoying private tête-à-têtes when blow me if, from the midst of this happy circle, your interesting poll don't pop out like a reg'lar jack-in-the-box."

'He and all present laughed until they shook, but there was nothing malicious about it. I was encouraged to see the funny side too and I thought that rather than laughing at me they were only amused by the turn of circumstance. But that could not prevent me from suffering the most acute embarrassment.

'Perhaps seeing this, Dickens administered the *coup-de-grâce*. "Was there something particular you wanted to say to me?" He looked at me earnestly, as if he knew everything, I thought. "You may speak to me privately, if you wish."

'This was it, the encounter I had imagined so often during my last days in my garret at the Particular, or on the road with Hope Scattergood. I had my chance. I had only to ask him to step back inside the theatre for a few minutes and all would be out in the open, come what may. I might have revealed all there and then but as you must have guessed, I didn't. I shook my head and said, "That was a real gaudy story, Mr Dickens."

'You said you liked his story?' said my mother, aghast. 'That was all?'

'Yes. He ruffled my hair like I was still a child and told me to get along. There would be an employer somewhere wondering where I had got to, he said. So I bid him goodbye and went on my way.'

'Oh, Billy,' said my mother, brimming with disappointment. 'Why ever didn't you speak to him?'

'Mother, I've given this a lot of thought. I don't know if Charles Dickens is my father. Maybe I never will know. Nor do I know what would come of telling him my story. Nothing good, maybe. But since being with Hope and you, it's come to me that I don't want to be what everyone else wants me to be. I don't care if I let down Elijah Putnam. I'm truly sorry if you and Hope feel I've betrayed you, but it's because of you that I didn't speak to Dickens.'

'Because of us? Billy, surely not!'

'I had been looking for a father. I had thought that father

239

was Dickens and in a way, so it was. But not the Dickens of English letters. The other Dickens, the one at home on his sickbed, Hope Scattergood. In these few short months he's been more of a father than I've ever had. And after all these years, I've got back my mother. I think that with you and Hope I have all I could want. It's enough.'

'I don't know about that, Billy, though it's sweet of you to say so,' she said, hurrying as we approached O'Leary's, where the usual urchins were littering the steps and lounging on the sills. A thin man in dark clothes and a hat pulled down over his eyes slipped down the steps and walked quickly down the street.

'I still think you may have been foolish,' my mother said. Her mind was upon my lost chance. Mine was with the stranger turning the corner of our block. Despite my enquiries, I had been unable to ascertain whether Hope and I were known to be in New York and whether we were wanted beyond the Ohio State line. The newspapers had mentioned the Ohio murder because of its connections with Dickens, whose name was as common as punctuation in the New York press. The speculators were still full of it for the same reasons. There was no saying whether the police or inquiry agents were not now combing New York for the cons from Cincinnati and a strange man leaving our building did nothing to ease my anxious mind.

The man had escaped my mother's notice. Having enjoyed a happy day in the fresh air and, I believe, being secretly pleased that I had chosen her over Charles Dickens, she was humming a popular tune as she turned the key in our door. We stepped into the dank and fetid room we called our home and saw that Hope Scattergood was gone.

Chapter Fourteen

I

SCATTERGOOD'S CONDITION had been cruelly inconsistent. After a week in which he had barely strength to turn himself in his bed, he might be granted a remission of one or two days and sometimes longer. At these times we seized upon new hope and talked of his future. Maybe we even believed in such a thing. We dreamed of Switzerland and the miraculous cure but Hope's mind was more often in the South, the place where he planned to be reborn as a successful politician. But perhaps that was no surprise. Politics was in the mind of everyone now as the President fought with Radical Republicans who were openly threatening his impeachment.

Hope Scattergood had become fascinated with the forces at work on the seventeenth president of the United States in those early months of 1868 and in his more cognisant moments had closely followed the drama as it was reported in the newspapers we brought to him. Johnson had been a disappointing successor to the visionary Lincoln, at least from the points of view of the victorious North. It wasn't so much that the President vetoed the bills to help the new Freedmen, although his neglect of the Negroes lent his opponents an attractive moral legitimacy, but rather that this awkward cuss from Tennessee was giving back to the South much of what the North had fought to win. Positions of power and influence which ought by rights to have been among the spoils of the victor were being awarded to old Confederates. This stubborn man had fought vigorously for the rights of homesteaders and had such courage of his convictions that his Southern brothers had called him traitor. Why then did he later overturn so much of what the North had won and do so little to free the Negroes from Black Codes that made the victory of the Union seem so hollow? This question had much exercised the mind of Scattergood as he had lain awake upon his bed. Once, he confided to us that he should do things very differently, when he was in office. But I cannot say that either Scattergood's fevered hubris or the President's crucial dilemma was of immediate concern to me as my mother and I regained the room and found that Hope was gone.

II

While he had been sick the room had been suffused with his presence. Some previous occupant of that room, fearful of cold or perhaps gripped by the terrible waking dreams of the terminally drunk, had nailed shut the windows and every breath Scattergood took was breathed over again by him and us all until the place was stale and stank. This overfamiliar stench met us as we entered, together with the sweet smell of his sweat, that had soaked sheets flecked with black-brown specks. Sometimes his breath had been misted with blood. So strong were the signs of his presence to our senses that it was doubly puzzling to find him absent in the flesh.

His bedcovers were strewn across the floorboards as if they had only reluctantly relinquished their grasp as he rose. Some food we had left for him stained the floor by the pieces of a broken plate. I saw at once that his clothes and his boots were gone. He had acquired an old carpet-bag of a fellow speculator and this too was missing, along with his other clothes. My mother ran out into the hallway, calling his name and accosting those loiterers there for information about the sick man in room twelve. She sent a boy out to the backyard privy and another to the roof, but to no avail. The window overlooking the street gave to her desperate strength and nails tore from wood as she cast it up and scanned the road below.

'Our fault, Billy,' she said, 'this is all our fault. We shouldn't have left him, I knew it all along.' She threw herself down upon the chair and beat her forehead with whitely-clenched fists. I restrained her violence and reminded her of how much better he had looked when we had departed and that he was surely only getting a breath of air. I didn't believe it. He was in no fit state to go promenading. Only some fantastic notion born of his sick mind could have impelled him from his bed and out on to the New York streets.

'This is all wrong, Billy, awfully wrong,' my mother said. 'He's never gone out without one of us, not since Brooklyn. We've gotta go find him.'

I could see no gain in going out upon the streets ourselves. There was always the chance, no matter how small, that he might return, but what could I say to this woman who was pulling upon my arm, her eyes bright with tears and her lips pursed with determination? I followed her down the stairs and out the door, where she frightened the urchins that played about the steps, demanding to know in which direction had gone the grey-haired man with the walking-stick. I tried not to show it but I was as anxious as she. Although he had slept well the night before and had appeared more rested today, his manner and state of health up to that time left me doubting he had made any sudden and wonderful recovery. I was sorely worried and would have liked nothing better than to see him heave into view around a corner and tell me he had been out and done the most wonderful business. However, I had not the faith to believe in such a miracle and doubted we could possibly find him in this immense and complicated city.

Purpose had allowed her a measure of hope. 'We'll find him,' she said, 'if we just use our heads, we'll find him.' She stopped on a corner and bit her fingers. Then she stepped off the kerb, forcing a cabman to pull sharply upon his reigns and swear loudly at the crazy woman and the troubled young man who were hurrying across the busy roads and creating further confusion among the current of pedestrians on the opposite sidewalk.

We searched in every place we had ever been, in shops and in saloons and even in the church where Scattergood had once successfully solicited a small donation for his mission to the pygmies of Africa from a credulous young clergyman. Then we inquired in the oyster bar and the mulatto said that he had been there only an hour before, 'Talkin' like a crazy man and lookin' like he was goin' to a masquerade.' She asked if we were 'goin' to pay for the whisky he drunk?'

My mother recalled that Scattergood and I had talked of my plans for this evening. I had bought up tickets for Dickens' next Boston readings and tonight I had intended going to the new Steinway Hall, where speculators often gathered to tout tickets for shows, lectures and anything that was currently 'hot'. I wanted to test the market for out-of-town tickets and just possibly avoid the necessity of travelling to Boston the next day. I agreed that we would at least try the Steinway before we returned home.

There were indeed some handful of men milling by the doors of the Steinway, among them some faces I knew. Long lines of people were filing into the hall, businessmen, from the look of them and a sprinkling of officers in the uniform of the Union army. Some speculators were making desultory forays among the lines with their tickets but even I knew a poor chance when I saw one. The faces of these men were not those of pleasure seekers looking for the best entertainment New York had to offer. I guessed this was a rally of some sort, very probably political. Though posters advertised musical concerts and some still the readings that Dickens had given there weeks before, I couldn't see one that explained this great gathering of generals and men of business.

Among a knot of disgruntled speculators who appeared to

have ceased any efforts at trading to this crowd and who now stood stamping their feet and talking amongst themselves was a gentleman who was always conspicuous at any sale on account of being dressed up in the blue tunic and powder wig of George Washington. People, he had once confided to me, were likelier to trust a man dressed so. However, he was a harmless soul who never appeared to do much business and was always ready to take time for a pipe and a chat. I hailed him and asked if he had seen 'the Duke' as Scattergood was known among the speculators.

'He's here, but he ain't selling,' said George Washington. 'Wouldn't stop for a talk, neither. Strode past like he didn't know us. I tell you, English, it's long weeks since I last saw him and he's changed. Looked a different man. Nothing wrong, I hope?'

'Where is he?' said my mother.

'He's gone in the hall,' said Washington. 'Takin' up politics, I suppose?'

Though we were both urgent to get within the walls of the Steinway and find out what Scattergood was about and how he was, we were unable to persuade any among the business barons and military men to allow us a place at the head of the queue and were forced to wait patiently as the line slowly moved towards the doors. From their talk, I discovered that the purpose of this rally was to demonstrate support for those parts of the Senate opposed to the administration of President Johnson, whose name was bandied about the line like that of some harum-scarum desperado. I knew by then that the opposition to Johnson was a subject that had greatly interested Scattergood, when his mind was sufficiently unclouded to admit such reasoning. I was surprised, though, that he had sufficient conviction to make what must have been a great and painful effort and walk several miles to the Steinway Hall. As my mother had said, this was all awfully wrong. If I could have pushed those gentleman on and through the open doors, I would have done just that.

III

When at last we had shuffled through the portals of the great new Steinway Hall, we took our seats and waited while the last latecomers found theirs. The hall was clouded with blue cigar smoke and loud with the greetings of men united with a common purpose. For above an hour, they attended and applauded a succession of speakers, who examined the problem of President Johnson from different angles but all were in complete agreement that their cause would only be served by the impeachment and removal of the President. His dismissal of Secretary of War Staunton, some said, gave them just the opportunity they needed. This is as I comprehend the state of affairs now; back then I could hardly make out what was going on and was only interested in trying to locate Hope Scattergood among the crowd.

I was beginning to think it was a hopeless task. The hall was darkened and besides, I couldn't see every seat in the place. I figured we should wait outside and meet him as he came out and was for escorting my mother from the building, that we might take up advantageous positions before the meeting came to a close. But then there was an interruption. The speaker stopped in mid-sentence and even from where I sat, I could see his expression change from quizzical to profoundly astonished. Then he smiled broadly at someone who was mounting the steps to the stage. He held out his hand and warmly shook that of the newcomer. 'Gentlemen,' he said, when he had recovered himself, 'here's a good omen for our cause. We have a surprise guest. And another speaker, too, I hope. Please welcome the great book-writer from England, Mr Charles Dickens!'

He paused until he might be heard above the applause.

'We are indeed privileged by your presence, Mr Dickens,' said the man at the podium. 'But it does not surprise me that you should be here, not a bit. I know that we are all glad that you have chosen to lend us your support but your reputation for fair play precedes you, sir and I'm sure you are as horrified as we at what iniquities this President is perpetrating in the name of the American people.'

As Dickens declined to make a reply and only remained smiling complacently at the filled seats before him, the speaker continued.

'Mississippi is reverting to its old ways, the Confederacy is being welcomed into the Union with no guarantees of equal rights and what of due reparation? President Johnson could overturn everything for which Lincoln strove and the Union army died for in its thousands.' There was noisy approval from the military elements, who loudly voiced their support and clumped their boots. 'I have no doubt, sir,' the man yelled above the hubbub, 'that this must go straight to the heart of a noble spirit such as yours.'

Dickens shook his head, his look one of great benevolence as if he were humbled that so many should turn out to see him. 'And now, sir, perhaps you would say a few words?'

I doubted that many of this audience would actually have read a word of Charles Dickens' novels but I could see that they were immensely gratified to have so august a figure associating himself publicly with their cause. Whether or not they had read Dickens, they were about to hear him now as the newcomer said in a voice that was clear and free from any sign of his recent suffering:

'With your permission, sir, I shall read a little from *Great Expectations*,' and produced a book from his coat pocket.

'Very appropriate, sir, very apt,' said the man and retired from the stage leaving Dickens alone, immersed in the limelight.

He began to read in strong and resonant tones that must have convinced anyone who had never heard an English voice and, for all I knew, those who had, that here was an English-man and a substantial one at that. He read two significant scenes from the book. He described the return of the convict Magwitch, with his 'long iron-grey hair' and said that his 'age was about sixty', and I thought he might be describing himself as he went on, blowing up Pip's expectations in his face. Then

247

he smiled and read another part of the book and I could sense that all around me, business magnates, cavalry officers and generals all, were spellbound as he told of Pip's last visit with Miss Havisham.

' "I looked into the room where I had left her,' " he read, ' "and I saw her seated in the ragged chair upon the hearth close to the fire, with her back towards me. In the moment when I was withdrawing my head to go quietly away, I saw a great flaming light spring up. In the same moment, I saw her running at me, shrieking, with a whirl of fire blazing all about her, and soaring at least as many feet above her head as she was high.

' "I had a double-caped great-coat on, and over my arm another thick coat. That I got them off, closed with her, threw her down, and got them over her; that I dragged the great cloth from the table for the same purpose, and with it dragged down the heap of rottenness in the midst, and all the ugly things that sheltered there; that we were on the ground struggling like desperate enemies, and that the closer I covered her, the more wildly she shrieked and tried to free herself; that this occurred I knew through the result, but not through anything I felt, or thought, or knew I did. I knew nothing until I knew that we were on the floor by the great table, and that patches of tinder yet alight were floating in the smoky air, which, a moment ago, had been her faded bridal dress." '

He closed the book and there was a silence in which you might have heard a whisper from across the hall. I had never heard him read to such effect. Then there came the applause which roared like an enormous rock-slide and was long in its dying. I thought that if you never read again, you know success now, Hope Scattergood. My mother pressed my hand. Dickens stood upon the stage with his head bowed. At last, the speaker who had welcomed him stepped forward, expressed the thanks of all present and asked if he might comment upon a very moving reading.

'I don't think I'm wrong,' he said, 'in presuming that in this Magwitch is a telling image of our villainous President, although he, unlike Magwitch, still awaits his conviction!'

Some part of his audience thought that this was a very good joke and he waited until the last titter had finished. 'Our expectations have been grievously disappointed, as were the boy's.' He paused, seeking, I imagined, to draw further parallels from the readings. It was clear this was proving no easy task. He covered the awkward hiatus by walking up and down the stage, smiling to one and all and nearly succeeding in giving the impression that he were enjoying some intellectual game. At last, he stopped by Dickens and held up a finger.

'And do I see in this terrible fiery end of the old woman, the calamity in store for our own great Union, if we here do not take matters in hand right away? I'm right, I believe, sir?' he asked Dickens, his hands upon his hips, smiling broadly at his own cleverness. But Dickens remained silent and stood immobile in the glare of the lights, as an object petrified, unsmiling now and peering as if at an object far away.

'Sir?' inquired the man.

'Billy,' whispered my mother. 'We must get him out. Quickly.'

I left my seat and began to make my way towards an aisle, from where I might approach the stage and, with luck, pull Hope Scattergood from it and get him out of the building. He began to speak again but he sounded ominously different. All traces of the oaken timbre and English correctness had gone and in its place was a distinctly Southern drawl. Also gone was his elegant poise. His pose now had become distinctly louche.

'Great expectations,' he said. 'Y' all have 'em. Well, don'tcha?' He looked out among the faces and some nodded. 'We all 'spect something, don't we? Some of us 'spect to get rich and others 'spect to get hanged one day. I know I do.'

He waited, as if for a laugh, but none came.

His shoulders convulsed. He coughed loudly and spat into his handkerchief. ''Scuse me, folks. I'm allus taking this snuff and I guess the kind don't agree with me.' He looked at the name. 'Peck-Snuff brand. Well it ought to, I guess!' Again he paused and smiled, as if hearing some laughter that had never been. 'You, sir,' he addressed a man in the front row. 'You use the Peck-Snuff brand, endorsed by me?'

'I likes a good chawing tobacco, myself,' the man said. 'I don't like nothing I have to stick up my nose.'

'Well, maybe you're right, sir,' said Dickens.

'Are you going to git on with this here story or not?' said a neighbour.

'Where was I?'

'I'm not sure I rightly know,' said the speaker at his side.

'It don't matter,' said Scattergood. Again, his chest heaved and he cleared his throat by spitting upon the floor. Then he lifted his head and spoke out.

'I knew a whore down in Louisiana,' he said, 'from the Bayou. She was a black-eyed French Cajun. Gentlemen, I fell in love with that whore. I took her from the very gutter and found her a place of safety. I bought her pretty dresses and furnished her home with every bauble and gewgaw a young girl could desire. We were fixed to be married in a little church in New Orleans. It wasn't going to be no big affair, just her brothers and some friends of mine, because my parents didn't want to know.'

I had reached the stage now and was calling softly to Scattergood but he seemed oblivious both of me and of the whole assembly, many of whose members were now making audible their consternation and dissatisfaction with the turn proceedings were taking. Somewhere far behind me, a door opened, there was a low murmur of conversation and then the door swung closed. I doubted that Scattergood could hear anything but his own voice and that of a cherished ghost of long ago.

'She never came to that church. I waited there until night had fallen but my Lisette never came. I searched high and low. She wasn't at the house nor any place I could think of. I guessed she had just lit out.' He paused as if in a reverie and it was some seconds before he remembered himself and went on. 'She had gone and I was left high and dry. I cursed her fickleness and after some time in which I was always sorrowful and once thought to take my own life, her name was poison on my lips. I left New Orleans, cursing her and womankind and swearing I should never give a goddamn about anything nor anybody again.

'It was maybe two years before I was in that region again and happened to hear that my Lisette had been abducted by someone who knew her as a whore and thought she was such a woman still and that she had been murdered by this fellow, as she tried to fight him off.'

His face, with tears shining in the lights, betrayed his suffering. I noticed that his beard had become unstuck at one side. I thought he had nothing more to say and that he was finished.

'Hope!' I called. 'It's me, Billy!'

And this time he saw me and smiled benignly upon me. I stretched out my hand. He walked slowly over to where I stood, his face a waning moon in the theatre lights. Once again, I thought he was finished.

'Come on, Hope,' I said, 'let's get out of here.'

He bent down and took my hand, but rather than letting me help him down from the stage, he found strength to haul me up upon it, where I stood, blinking in the brightness, at his side. I could feel the anger of the crowd.

'What is going on here?' demanded a stentorian voice in the crowd. Another boomed, 'Who are you, sir?'

There were other such cries and the speaker, fearing association with us, slipped away, leaving Hope and I transfixed before a great crowd whose mood was rapidly worsening as important men realised that they had just been made fools of. Hope, however, seemed only more determined to have his say, come what might. When he spoke again, it was not in the affected tones of his Dickens and nor did he sound like a riverboat gambler. His voice had a faint Southern inflection and a power of dignity.

'I thought I should never know the love of a woman nor

the joys of a family,' he said. 'I could not have anticipated that my joy was to be reserved and that I had only to wait the passage of years and then my cup would be filled. Gentlemen, I present to you Billy, the son who has been sent to me and in whom I am . . .'

'Get off the stage, you old fraud!'

'You'd make fools of us, would you?'

'Call the usher!'

I pulled Hope away but he would not be moved. He gripped the podium and still he spoke to an audience that I thought could become a dangerous mob at any instant.

'I have a son in my image and a wife whose love means more to me than I can say. I can't claim that I have always been a good man, though I can declare to you that neither Billy nor I had any part in that murder in Cincinnati, but I don't think it goes too far to say that in their love and my own for them, I see hope.'

I tried to pull Scattergood away as a man in dark clothes who seemed somehow familiar to me now hauled himself up upon the stage. Once off his knees he might have been the villain of a melodrama as he extended his arm and pointed out Scattergood to some voices off. 'That's the man!' he cried and there was violent movement among the curtains on the wings.

At that moment, Hope Scattergood's frame shook violently, his head jerked back and he began to cough, such an awful, racking fit, that the catcalls were stilled and Hope's terrible hacking filled the auditorium. He gripped the podium for support. His eyes caught mine and flashed his hopelessness as he was caught in another dreadful attack, a mad dog barking in an empty room. I tried to hold fast his shaking body, but he pushed me away and no handkerchief could contain the great gouts of blood that gushed forth and splashed heavily upon the boards. 'Get a doctor,' I shouted and a party of men arrived promptly upon the stage. I looked for a medical man in their midst but only saw uniforms, and, unmistakable amongst the braids and brass of the military, those of the New York City police.

Chapter Fifteen

I

WHEN SCATTERGOOD COLLAPSED upon the stage at the Steinway there had been uproar amongst the audience as the inquisitive surged forward to find out more. The police and the ushers fought to clear the building but people were jammed in aisles and about the doorways and minutes passed before a doctor could break the siege and examine Hope, who lay upon the bloodied planks, silent save for a noise that rose in his throat like bubbles breaking in a hot mud pool. The doctor looked him over and shook his head. 'You'll take this man to the hospital directly,' he advised.

'Cain't do that,' said an officer of the law. 'This here's a wanted man.'

'A murderer, if what the Pinkerton man says is right,' said a military gent.

'You want him to stand trial, you'll take him to a hospital first.'

'He's real sick,' I said. 'We didn't do no murder. He needs to go to a hospital.'

But someone manacled my hands and I became only a package for transportation. The doctor knew when he was beat and stood back. 'Well, you be sure he gets treatment the minute he's arraigned, if not before. I can't be held responsible. You do understand that?'

'Sure, Doc. Somebody give me a hand here.'

They bundled me after Scattergood, whom they lifted from the stage and carried out into the frosty night and deposited in the back of a police van. There was cheering and laughing when the van set off as those involved congratulated themselves on their capture of such dangerous villains. We rumbled down busy streets where drinkers could be heard spilling out of late-night bars and shouting at their friends and at the world. Though there was a grill at the back of the van and I burned to know the direction we were taking, I stayed beside Scattergood, whose breathing sounded as poor as it had when he had been at his worst. The van bounced on cobbles and potholes and I held Hope's head close and told him it would all work out. It was too dark to see his face and he never answered.

Then we had slowed up and the roads were even enough for me to let go of Hope and peer through the grill. We were passing a long and low-fronted building, dimly illuminated by the streetlights. It was unusual enough to capture my notice even in such extreme circumstance. Four great columns of an order I had seen nowhere else supported a great entablature and a decorated frieze ran above tall windows that were moulded in neither Greek nor Roman fashion but grand and imposing all the same. The van pulled up beside a building almost adjoining this last and the driver unlocked the door. 'Criminal Law Court,' he said as he and another pulled Hope from the van. 'You have arrived, gentlemen.'

II

The jailer led us over a bridge that connected the Criminal Law Court with the jail then down a dark hall and up flights of stairs and across another, dizzying bridge and on to a galleried landing, tapping his keys along the rails as he walked. He was inclined to talk, indifferent that I alone supported

Hope's weight and guided his faltering steps. 'In the old days,' he offered, 'this here was Collect Pond and over on the island was a gibbet. They filled it over and built this place.'

The indictment for the murder of Matthew Irving and our remand to the Tombs had been so speedy that I had barely time to take in the full horror of the scenes that had flooded upon us as we were conveyed from the courtroom through the jail. Now I am forced to recall that terrible time I find that I remember more than ever I knew I had seen. Behind the low facade, the building was long and high, with four landings, each with a row of black, iron-doored cells. We had seen below us coloured prisoners herded into dank and foul-smelling dungeons but little better was the hole into which we were ushered and whose door slammed shut with a report that still intrudes upon my dreams. It was as gloomy as any medieval counterpart, as if light hesitated at the small aperture high upon the wall. There were two rough beds, a table and chair, a tin jug and basin. There was nowhere to hang clothes: I learnt soon after that prisoners had chosen to hang themselves from hooks once provided rather than face another day in this dismal hole.

It was certainly a curious place and I suppose that had I been there on any other business than that of my own interment, I might have delighted in drawing comparisons with the Newgate of Jaggers and Wemmick or the Marshalsea of William Dorrit and it is indeed an interesting exercise now but then I was too stricken with terror to see it as anything more poetic than a forbidding, noisy and terrible hell.

'Right in there,' the jailer had said and crashed the door and left us to our meditations. I helped Scattergood upon his bed. He was still weak. He had been medically examined and such treatment as was thought fit, administered. And then he had, I thought, been given into my care and for this reason we had been allowed to share our captivity while the due processes of law were gone through, that marshals from Ohio might be sent from Cincinnati and in New York apply for the extradition licence that would allow our transportation back to that city, to stand trial for murder. The inquiry agent had attended the arraignment, a sleek-headed, pin-eyed gentleman who looked as slippery as a slaughterhouse floor. He represented the citizens of Cincinnati, he said, where these two 'wicious scoundrels' – he pointed us out – had committed 'the most wicious murder'. And not only were we wanted for murder in Ohio but I was in demand in Missouri in connection with a hotel robbery and Hope, I discovered, had unsettled business with the courts in half the states in the Union.

I covered Scattergood with a thin blanket and cleansed the blood from his face and hands with water from the basin. He was asking about my mother who had remained in her theatre seat and so had not been taken up with us. His sudden exertions at the Steinway Hall and his loss of blood had left him very much enervated and I begged him not to talk but to rest and recruit his strength.

'I never meant for this,' he was saying. 'I was lost up there, Billy. I didn't know what I was about. Forgive me.'

'Ain't nothing to forgive, Hope,' I said. 'Rest up. We'll beat this yet.' But after I had nursed him into some imitation of sleep, I sat down against the cold wall, pulled up my knees and wept like I had never done since my childhood.

Sometime in the night I must have got myself upon my bed and after I woke it was some seconds before I realised I was not on my old straw mattress at the Particular but in a secure cell at the Tombs jail. Keys rattled in the lock and the scant morning light showed the figure of a turnkey as he deposited tin plates upon the table. I asked him if a woman had called, asking for us.

'It's lady visitors you want?' he said with a chuckle. 'And perhaps you'll be after entertaining them in the Warden's rooms?'

This was O'Connell, a jovial man whose humour often masked concerns he had for certain prisoners, his family or some terrible thing he had seen on his way to the prison. I don't know which route he took but I remember thinking that if ever I was free, I should discover and avoid it.

'I saw a one-armed fellow board a moving omnibus today,' he was saying as I cooled Hope's face with a dampened cloth. 'Hadn't got the trick of the thing at all and fell in the street where he was struck by a man with an ass. It happened at the very spot I once met a priest with a prostitute, drinking from a bottle of rum. Having a crisis of faith, so he was.'

O'Connell mentioned a couple more unique incidents that he had witnessed that morning, or so he said, but then he had seen how things lay with Hope and when he spoke again, it was to offer his assistance. 'I don't know what they say he's done but it's our help he needs now,' he said. 'I might lay my hands on more blankets, if they would do him good?'

'My friend needs proper treatment.' I said. 'They've got to send him to a hospital. I never saw him so sick.' O'Connell knelt by Scattergood's side and felt his forehead. He touched his neck and pushed himself up. 'I'll see what I can do,' he said.

Scattergood rested uneasily throughout the morning. I found I had the freedom to walk as far as the pump room where I could refill my bucket with water and that I might, if I so desired, take my place in the mournful circling of prisoners exercising in the yard. I was clumsy with my bucket and dropped it from the iron steps. I went to retrieve and refill it but a jailer I came to know as 'Georgia George' put up his hand.

'Luther'll git that. You stay where you are,' he commanded, as a thin black man placed my bucket under the faucet and began to pump.

'There you are,' said Georgia George. 'You need anything, you git Luther to fetch it, you hear?' I thanked Luther for the water and climbed the steps to our cell, where Scattergood lay muttering quietly.

I had my eye upon the door all day, waiting for O'Connell to return. When he did, he seemed a changed man. Anger had dispelled his joviality and he said to me, 'Will you get this place cleaned up? Sure, it's a disgrace.' While I worked, he took off his cap and smoothed down his grey curls, expelling a mighty breath like an engine blowing off steam. 'I saw the Warden,' he said at last, sitting upon the hard chair by the door. 'He's not going to move your friend to the hospital. Not when he expects you both to be on your way to Ohio in a few days. It won't be his responsibility then.' He stood and took up his hat. 'He's no better, then?'

I shook my head. 'I'm sorry for that,' he said. 'At least he looks peaceful now. I've seen a lot of bad men pass through this place and he doesn't have the look of them.' Mr O'Connell closed the door as quietly as he could.

Not long after, Drummond, who had escorted us into the Tombs, began his evening rounds. As ever he was disposed to talk but the substance of his conversation made me wish that he had been born mute. He stuck his hands in his pockets and walked up and down the cell, sometimes going outside to peer over the gallery rail at goings-on below. He appeared not to notice Hope and to be using me only as a receptacle for his outpourings. I sat up when he said that he had heard the Warden discussing our case.

From him I gleaned that some other party, Silas Amory, I presumed, had been seen running from the fire in Cincinnati and he had been found and arrested but had sworn his innocence, claiming he was a newspaperman on the track of desperate fraudsters and he had lost no time in accusing we two of the murder that was perpetrated by himself. Drummond was phlegmatic about our fate. 'Well, of course, you do a thing like that, you have to pay for it. They'll hang you, I expect.' And then, in a clumsy attempt to palliate the doom he had pronounced, he said, 'But I guess it'll be quick and most like, you won't feel much. Now, here in New York we used a gallows operated with weights, which they all said was most scientific. That might be but I never saw a hangin' that way that I didn't think was a most terrible thing. One moment the condemned man has his feet on the ground, you see, and then down drop the weights and there he is, swinging high in the sky. What it must do to a man's neck!'

This was unpalatable food for thought as night fell and I

lay on my rough bed, denied the refuge of sleep by the cries of prisoners above and below and the ravings of Hope Scattergood as he battled with his own demons in the next cot. Countless times during that night I rose and cooled his brow or changed his position and told him again and again that everything was going to be all right. He didn't seem to know I was there and muttered to himself, often calling out for people he must have once known. The only name that meant anything to me was that of my mother.

The next morning, Scattergood sleeping, I joined the prisoners at exercise and found myself walking with Luther, who had brought my water. By way of breaking the monotony, I said, 'He don't like you over much, that guard?'

Luther grunted. 'G'orgia George don't like anyone much, least of all nigras. The South's full of folk like him.'

'Is that where you're from?' I asked, welcoming conversation.

'Savannah, once 'pon a time,' he said. 'Born on a plantation.'

I had never the experience of talking to a slave before. Not like I might talk to another man, anyway. I might have found it an uncomfortable experience had not justice, in its absence, made us each the equal of the other. I said that I supposed that it must have been a terrible life and suggested to him that the victory of the abolitionist cause was a miracle wrought by God.

'A miracle?' he said as we began another circuit of the yard. He tried the words again as if they were new to him. 'A miracle, you say.'

'A liberation,' I said.

'Lincoln leading us out of Egypt? Well, you look at it any way you want to. But this sure isn't what I expected.'

And indeed, Luther Wing's story was one of expectations disappointed on a grand scale. While others toiled in the fields, Luther had been taught to read and write, in order that he might fill some lowly office position and provide a temporary companion for Mr Henry, the plantation owner's child. When they heard the Yankees were coming, he said, the owner had locked up their slaves the same as they had their other valuables. The soldiers looted and razed the house but over-looked the slaves and it was the best part of a day before they escaped their confinement and stood amongst the smoking ruins of a gutted wing of the house half-expecting to see the owners reappear from some other part or to hear again the crack of the overseer's bullwhip. There followed uncertain times for Luther, in which he lived in shanties outside towns, selling bits of scrap metal and logs. After the war, his literacy got him work in a Freedmen's Bureau and only then had he begun to think that things might come all right. But then the Freedmen's Bureaus had closed. President Johnson, he said, had refused to save them. Luther's life got harder, the new Black Codes placing almost as many restrictions upon his liberty as he had known as a slave. He had made his way up North where he figured things would be better but the Northerners were cold and kept their distance. There was no work and he had been forced to steal. It was against his Bible learning but what was he to do? He wasn't cut out to be a thief and had been arrested the first time he had tried to rob a store. His liberation, he told me, would not be until several years hence.

Throughout the day I sat by Scattergood, who slipped in and out of a troubled sleep. That night I lit a candle stub and was surprised to see its glare reflected in eyes that were turned towards me. Scattergood was conscious. Moments passed as he took in the dim surroundings and then he said, 'Have I been here long?'

'Coupla days,' I said. 'How do you feel?'

'Like,' he closed his eyes as he considered, 'like something caught in the paddles of a Mississippi steamer.'

'Do you want to eat?' I said, for I had saved some food against such a case.

'Need a drink,' he said and I helped him raise the tin cup to his lips and as gently, laid him back down.

'What are they saying?' he asked.

''Bout us? It ain't good,' I said. I had no wish to acquaint him with our desperate predicament just then. I couldn't tell

260

him that we were to be sent back to Ohio and that Mr O'Connell and I were agreed that such a journey might be more than his weakened constitution could stand. Nor could I tell him that even if we both arrived safely, we looked certain of conviction. And yet, looking back, I think he knew all of this. Instead of pursuing the subject of our future, he talked of our past.

'I suppose you think I have led you rather out of your way,' he murmured. 'I never meant it to come to this, as you know.'

'I do know, Hope,' I said.

'Seems you should have left me on that stage in Louisville and I could have gone to my destruction without dragging anyone down with me.'

'Well, I won't deny I'd as soon it all turned out better than this,' I said. 'But, Hope, I don't regret nothing else. I wan't going to amount to much. Without you I'd have gone to the big city, made a fool of myself trying to get to see Charles Dickens and returned to Hayes, where I guess I'd have lived out my life wishing I was born good enough for Cissy Bullock's pop. You've given me greater expectations. I want more now. If I was free, I have the feeling that I might do anything.' I tried my best to stem boiling tears.

He raised himself up upon an elbow. It looked too great an effort and I tried to stop him. 'Leave me be, Billy, I want to look at you.' And look he did, his pale eyes burning faintly in the candlelight which shone also on globules of perspiration that dropped from his temples like wax from the candle.

'If ever I had a boy, if Lisette and me . . .' he closed his eyes for a moment. Then he said, 'I should have been mighty glad if that boy had turned out like you. You've been like a right arm to me, Billy. I'm sorry I led you from the straight and narrow.'

'You never took me nowhere I didn't want to go,' I said.

'The cons and the lays were all I could teach you, all I knew myself. Other folk have their own ways of making it up the mountain. They have their skills, their pieces of paper, their connections. All I had was what I knew. I am a conman,

Billy. You don't need me to tell you that. I trick and I deceive. Everyone does it, one way or another. Difference is that people generally like being taken by me. I only wish I had thought bigger. Politics. I might have been made for that game. I know that in my bones. It's my regret I didn't wise up to it sooner. But it don't look like I'll ever be anything but what I always was. A confidence man.' He paused and smiled. 'But a pretty good one, I suppose?' He laughed until his gaiety was smothered by the knell of another cough and he gulped water from the tin cup. When he had recovered he said, 'If we get out of here, we're going to have to do some thinking. About the future.'

'You're going to Switzerland,' I said.

'It's your future we need to think about,' said Hope. 'You've come too far to go back home.'

'I'm suspected of the robbery at the hotel,' I said but then I saw his meaning. 'Yes, I've come too far to go back. But where I'd go, I don't know.'

'It'll be up to you, Billy. You'll have to decide. You might take a clerk's job somewhere and get by here in New York.'

'I might,' I conceded. I wasn't fitted for much better.

'Or,' he said, as the flames of the guttering candle flickered about his pale and drawn face, 'you might leave the ordinary and the commonplace lives for those that want to live them and take on where I'm leaving off. If I knew as a young man what I know now, I'd not have stayed a small-time swindler. There's so much more, the world is bigger than I knew. You, Billy, you could go further. You only have to hold your breath and take that leap. Believe in yourself and so will others. Tell yourself you're as good as the best. No reason why it shouldn't be you who has the money, the power and all that goes along with it.'

They say that condemned men dream they are free and Hope's deluded fantasies spoke similarly of times and possibilities that I knew could never be. I could only humour my sick friend. Before I pulled the covers up over his slight and shivering frame, I kissed his brow. 'I'll take that leap for you, Hope,' I said. 'If ever I get the chance.'

On the third day, the door was opened and my mother stood before me. She buried me in her bosom and we both cried so noisily that Scattergood was roused from his troubled slumber.

'It's bad, isn't it, Ma?' I said, as she knelt by Scattergood's side and dabbed at his brow with a moistened handkerchief.

'I cain't pretend it ain't, Billy,' she said. 'There's evil forces massing before us. It's in the newspapers and they say they'll have the papers ready to get you back to Ohio, real soon. I've got the money you saved and I'll be going back too, don't fret about that.'

'What can we do, Ma? I'll take my chances but I don't think Hope could stand the journey.'

'I don't rightly know,' she said, which expressed the despondency we all felt, at bottom, no matter how many little attempts we made at lightening each other's load. So dreadfully certain was I of our convictions and subsequent fate that the mere possibility of our being condemned had ceased to be a source of terror for me. I was only curious about when this would occur and whether Scattergood would suffer unduly en route and what might become of my mother after it was all over.

'We need help, Billy. Is there no one?'

'No one,' I said. Apart from Elijah, the only people to whom I would ever have thought of turning for help were then with me in that cell. I had written an account of our predicament and sent it to Elijah, trusting that some good person would read it for him but doubting that he would be able to offer more than spiritual support.

I didn't see my mother for a couple of days but when I did, she was bright with inspiration and she could barely contain herself as she rushed into the cell under the curious eye of Georgia George, who waited to discover her purpose but finding she would not speak in his presence and only sat by the sleeping Scattergood's side and stroked his hand, he walked on down the gallery. Then she said: 'I got an idea,

263

Billy, came to me jest after I saw you last, oh, listen, Billy, I think we have a chance!'

I was ready to hear anything along these lines: 'What chance, Ma?'

'It's like he said. You said it all along, didn't you, my poor, sweet Hope?' And she stroked his brow but his eyes stayed fast shut and shallow breathing rattled in his throat.

'Ma, what is it?'

'Oh, Billy, surely you see? He said it himself. We have to go see Charles Dickens! He cain't refuse to help his own flesh and blood!'

I was disappointed. Was this crazy fool scheme her great hope of our salvation? 'Oh, Mother,' I said. 'What can that do?'

'I got to try it, Billy. You figure out where he is and I'll go see him.'

I squeezed her hand. 'Me and Hope appreciate what you're trying to do but there really ain't a chance in that direction. You'd never get to him and even if you did, he'd refuse to acknowledge he ever saw you in his life. You and him, why, he'll no doubt remember that as an indiscretion of youth and something he'd much prefer remained well and truly buried. He couldn't risk his reputation.'

'I thought of that, Billy. Though I can hardly believe it. The man you tell me was this Charles Dickens was so gay and merry, so full of life and so tender with me that I cain't think he'd desert anyone in their time of need.'

'People change, Ma,' I said.

'Possible?' she murmured and then she took my hand and one of Hope's which lay drooped upon the floor and said, 'I been put upon a lot in this life, Billy. One man then the next has kept me down and treated me like dirt. Reckon I've had enough. No one's gonna harm my boy, not while I'm here. And if that means I have to drag the name of this so-called great man through the mud, then by Heaven, I'll do it!'

I had never seen her so resolved and offered no demur as she told me what she was about to do. 'Firstly Billy, I don't reckon I'll have any trouble getting to see him. I have certain memories of that night, little particularities that only he and I can possible know about. I'll mention them in a note that'll leave him no choice but to burn the letter and admit me at once. You'll write it for me, won't you – no, wait, I shall write it myself.'

'You, Ma?' I said, but she hurried on.

'Second, when I get to see him, I'll leave him in no doubt that if he doesn't do something about clearing up this mess, right away, then I'll go straight to the newspapers with everything I know.'

'But would anyone believe you, Ma? Can we prove you were ever with him?'

'I reckon we can. I've been finding out about this man and it turns out he wrote up most all of what he done when he was here in the forties. I found out at the city library,' she said, shyly, I thought.

'I know of that book,' I said. 'But the library? Who helped you?'

'No one, Billy. I read it up all by myself. I been working real hard for a long time, reading to Hope, mostly. I did it all myself. And I found out that Mr Dickens told about putting up at some place that must have been our house in a book he wrote right after going back to England. I know for a fact that everyone in his party knew what had happened that night and I reckon there must be one who would spill the beans.'

'I don't know, Ma,' I said, doubt and hope warring within me. 'What could Dickens do, even if he were willing to help?'

'Get us a good lawyer and maybe hire us detectives, too. We know Silas Amory did this. It couldn't be so hard to get to the bottom of it if hearts were willing. And if Dickens was trumpeting your cause in the newspapers, I reckon that'd be the case.'

'And you don't think the newspapers might smell a rat and want to find out why Dickens was supporting a couple of swindlers accused of murder and reckon there might be a better story in following that line – and maybe finding something to knock Dickens off his pedestal?'

'Newspapers wouldn't do such a thing, Billy. Why, the whole purpose of a newspaper is to report the truth and the truth of this matter is that you and Hope didn't kill Matthew Irving.'

Nothing I might have said would have turned her from her avowed purpose but neither would I have wished to. Right then, this slim chance was all I could see standing between me and the gallows. And even if it was hopeless, a purpose would at least keep my mother from despair a little while longer.

She was gone for some days, during which time Hope Scattergood hovered on the tattered fringes of consciousness and very likely on the brink of death itself. I sent to the Warden, notifying him of how seriously ill he was but the sense of the reply was that the whole matter would imminently be the concern of the State of Ohio. On the following Tuesday evening, we were informed that we were to be taken back to Cincinnati on the Thursday morning and still my mother had not returned. There could be no doubt in my mind that whatever my own fate, a journey such as that would surely kill Scattergood. His only chance, and even that seemed a slim one, was to stay put and give his body the chance to recuperate.

All I could do was comfort and feed him when he waked and keep him cool in his periods of fevered sleep, though it says something of his condition that he should need cooling in that awful ice-box. My own sleep was troubled and I had vivid dreams in which I lived once again in the house of Elijah Putnam but in the places of Elijah and Rosalie were my mother and Hope Scattergood, who stood in the drawing-room with the golden sun pouring in through the windows and the house filled with love and happiness. And then, of course I woke to find the cruel reality of our predicament and that what had woken me was the rasping of Hope's short breath and I would quickly adjust his position and when I

266

slept again, my dreams were more disturbing. Once I saw poor Elijah running from a burning house.

Only Scattergood's varying state of health modulated the monotony. The turnkeys came and went with the changing of their shifts and the hours ground past. I sat upon my bunk and talked to Hope, though whether he was sensible of what I said, I have no idea. I talked to him of Switzerland. My mother had sent books that contained accounts of the travellers and I read to him of a strange and magical place where the air was sweet, where delicate flowers carpeted the valleys and daring men scaled the peaks. And if ever I had contemplated having a bully time when he got back, I did so then. The plan, I said, would be to make a little money and get on down South, where we would become successful businessmen or yes, politicians, if that was what he wanted and we'd have a big old house and all three of us live there in perfect contentment.

On the Wednesday night, Hope looked just about finished. The Warden had eventually acquiesced with my demands that he be again examined. Georgia George led in the doctor, saying that this prisoner was quite a famous deceiver and the doctor should not be taken in now. However, the doctor was not one to be regulated by a turnkey and had taken off his coat in preparation for making a full examination of the prisoner. I told him all I knew of Hope's worsening condition. I thought that at last he might be moved to a hospital and treated properly.

But any chance of that was destroyed by Scattergood himself who chose that moment to make one of his small rallies. He lifted his head, unwitting of what was going on or even of where he was and wished the surgeon good day. He traded introductions, established that the visitor was a medical man and attempted to sell him a bottle of his own patent medicine. That had been enough. Georgia George gave the doctor a look as if to say he had seen this trick pulled once too often. The doctor pursed his lips and pronounced the patient fit enough to travel.

That unmanned me completely. The next few hours were spent in the blackest depths of utter, hopeless despair. It was Wednesday and on the morrow or day after, I felt sure, I should see my friend die in humiliating circumstances and probably, great pain. I sat upon the floor, next to Hope, listened to his faint, whistling breaths and found that I couldn't even cry.

Some time that evening he was roused from his poisoned slumber by the cries of prisoners or by some pain within himself. He took my hand. 'Billy,' he breathed. I could barely make out his words in the brittle rattling of his exhalation and bent close to his lips. 'You'll do as I said?' he whispered. 'Go South. Make something of yourself.' I nodded and swore that I would. 'Do it,' he said as I tried to still his lips. 'For your own sake. Not for mine.' He slept again and anger flared within me. Were I only free, I repeated to myself, over and over again. How things should change. I should change. Nothing should and nothing could prevent me from becoming everything and more than Hope Scattergood could have wanted or even imagined. Silently, I raged against the injustice of the world.

In the middle of that night, I heard footsteps on the stairs and the tapping of keys along the rail. I leapt up.

The marshals were here. The warrant for our extradition no doubt took effect after midnight on Wednesday and it was surely long past that now. They must want us back in Ohio badly, I thought, grimly and immediately set about getting Scattergood ready for his ordeal.

I straightened his clothes and brushed the hair from his sweat-beaded forehead. He was barely conscious and had no conception of what I was about. As gently as I could, I began to pull on his boots. I lifted a foot and pulled on the first boot but his feet had swollen in the draughts and I couldn't get it on. I tried again but the more I pulled the more uncomfortable I was making him. I was pierced by his sudden cry but I was hardly thinking straight and went on with what I was doing. I was determined that he would leave the jail as he had arrived, in his sharp-looking, highly polished boots. Then he would still be Hope Scattergood.

I pulled again, harder. Slowly and awkwardly, the boot passed over his bloated ankle. Hope winced as I tugged again and cried out as the first boot finally chafed into place. I grabbed the other but his left foot was worse and no matter how hard I pulled, I could not force his foot into position at the bottom of the boot. I was crying with frustration and rage as the steps clattered along the landing and the key rattled in the heavy door. It grated as it always did and then swung open to reveal, lit up by Drummond's lamp, the Warden and with him my mother and a man whose face I did not recognise and yet I thought I knew, just the same.

My mother swept past them all and fell at Hope's head. I was relieved that Hope's other boot was now in place, the result of one final, almighty wrench. I said, 'He's all ready to go, Ma.'

She was silent while she stroked the hair at his temples. One of my other visitors made some interrogative remark. Then my mother stood up and I was enfolded in her arms. She brushed the hair from her face and lamplight glinted in her tears. 'Oh, Billy,' she said, 'cain't you see he's aready gone?'

Epilogue

I

CAN IT REALLY be so long since last I sat behind this desk and took up my pen? The calendar shows October but already it is the New Year. Between these dates Washington has made its claims on my time and I have enjoyed another wonderful Christmas with my family in Natchez. And now that I am here again with pen in hand, I shall account for it all in full.

I was met at the station by my youngest son, Thomas Ethan, in his sleek black automobile, which he loves better than I might a good horse. Tom had driven across Arkansas from Oklahoma to be with us for the holiday. Tom's doing just fine in the oilfields there. Katherine must have heard the horn because she was out on the porch to greet me as we drove up the tree-lined approach to Claremont, the old plantation house we bought right after our wedding.

My eldest boy, Arthur Philip, showed up with his wife Dora on the next day. Art is in munitions. I ask him where's the war but he says just wait, munitions are the coming thing. Dora and Tom's Emily spent the rest of Christmas Eve shopping and spoiling my five growing grandchildren. I had made my own purchases in Washington and in my rush to make sure I got exactly the right gifts, I forgot to pack up my manuscript and so it has lain here on my desk gathering dust while the inkpot dried.

II

The last page I wrote and on it, the last of Hope Scattergood. I have kept you waiting and by now you may be impatient to know the manner of my resurrection from the Tombs and how the fulfilment of two promises, one made to a friend and one my own, led me from the prison door to Capitol Hill. I should be interested too, were I not intimate with the answer. But having so nearly completed this review of my young life, I would much rather address another matter. It has ever been the object of this exercise that I gain some understanding of how I have become what now I am. However, courtesy demands I satisfy your curiosity before my own.

I had little curiosity of any kind as I was led out of the cell. I saw that Drummond and Georgia George were already preparing to remove Hope's body. His face, flatly-illuminated by Drummond's lamp, was changed utterly. I would like to say he appeared peaceful, as the newly-departed are supposed to when death unbuckles all restraints. But Hope only looked empty as if his knowledge and his know-how, his craft and his guile had been collected up by whatever spirit had recently claimed his own.

Gone too was the charm that had animated his every look. He stared at me blankly as I stepped over his corpse. My mother took my arm and our party followed the Warden down the iron stairs. We must have seemed more like a procession to execution than liberation. As Luther Wing could testify, some liberations are illusory. I barely registered the formalities of my release and only imperfectly recall passing through the final door and seeing a waiting cab. Something more than shock and grief was welling inside me. The past few days had stretched me like no rack could ever do and now at last, something snapped. I remember falling against the strong-smelling leather of the cab seat and that is all.

272

In the extremity of our plight, I had hardly noticed that I too was becoming sick. I had been too much anxious to eat and the deprivation of food and sleep together with the terrible cold were now exacting their price. I slept for two full days, if that is not too amiable a term for the dream-bedevilled fever that followed. When I awoke, I thought I was in heaven. Above me was clear blue sky where cherubim sported upon frothy white clouds. Dimly, I perceived this to be neither after-life nor hallucination but a ceiling decoration, painted in emulation of some Italian original. I was thirsty and had I the strength, I should have availed myself of a glass of water that was upon my chair. How long I lay there staring at the heavenly ceiling I don't know but I had time enough to review the recent past and to speculate on how I could be here and not in my dark prison cell. No one came and I was incapable of anything further. I grieved silently for Hope and his suffering. I wondered if now I were really, somehow free and that being so, I might be afforded the opportunity of honouring the pledge I had made to him.

Then I heard voices at the door and my mother walked in with the man whose face had seemed familiar before.

'You're awake, Billy? Oh, thank Heaven!'

'I told you the fever was broken,' said the man, whose voice also was known to me.

'Are you all right, Billy?' she asked as she stroked my brow.

I nodded. I would speak later. I watched as she turned to the man, who was of medium height and spare frame, and, I should estimate, somewhere above fifty years of age. His hair was slate-grey and thin and when he smiled, an action he seemed always struggling to prevent, I saw that several of his teeth were missing. I could bring to mind no one in possession of these characteristics and yet I felt certain that I knew him. She told me to sleep and together they left the room.

A surfeit of sleep caused me to wake as a thin grey dawn began to filter through gaps in the curtains. I closed my eyes and a thousand thoughts flashed upon my eyelids, ideas and answers briefly illuminating my darkness like today's flickering cinematograph. I had so much to ask, so much to discover. I neither knew where I was nor why I was there. Nor could I determine who the man was I thought I knew and who behaved as if he knew me. Everything about him I seemed to know so well, with the single exception of his eyes. These were quick and bright and yet I thought they should be neither.

I heard voices beyond my door and before my mother had crossed to the window and admitted the morning, I had spoken the name of the man who followed her. 'George Putnam.' He glanced at my mother as if appealing for guidance. 'You're looking much better,' she said and put a breakfast tray upon my table. 'I hope you will eat something. Meet Billy, George.'

George advanced tentatively. 'Hello, Billy,' he said. He smiled uncertainly, lips parting to reveal a mouthful of piano keys. 'I'm glad to see you're recovering.'

'Am I really free?' I asked as my mother sat upon my bed and buttered my toast.

'As a bird,' said my mother. 'You must thank George for that.'

'Elijah's brother? Then you got my letter?'

The man before me found something to interest him beyond the window. 'I received it but I could do nothing to help you,' he said. 'There were reasons why I could never secure you an introduction to Dickens. But all the same, I should have gone to you. I might have helped in other ways. It wasn't your note that brought me to you. Your mother did that.'

He took out his watch and opened the cover. 'I said I would wait and see that Billy was all right. There's money in the account. Draw on it for what you need and wire me if you need more. I have to go. I shouldn't be here with you. Like this. I must be getting back to Boston.'

He rose and turned to go but she caught hold of his sleeve. 'Billy must know,' she said. 'Better to hear it from you, George.' His eyes implored but hers were adamant. He sat upon the edge of a plushly-upholstered chair like it was the hardest stick of furniture in New York. His hands gripped his knees and he stared at a humming-bird woven in the design of the carpet. 'George,' she prompted.

He sucked a whistling breath through gapped teeth and released it as a sigh. 'Nothing can make up for what I've done to you. To your mother,' he began, in a voice that faltered often. 'But there's money in a bank account. Get you settled. As for work, I have friends who need a good man in Georgia.' But still he looked miserably uncomfortable and I think that had the window been open he might have used it, no matter how high.

'George, what's done is done. Billy will understand that.'

He summoned resolution from somewhere within and sat up straight. And then he turned to me. 'You know that I was Charles Dickens' secretary back in '42?'

I nodded.

'Well, I was in his employ but he treated me as a friend. To his great credit, he still does. You're using his hotel room while he's out of town.'

I was the wrong side of Charles Dickens' sheets now, I reflected.

'Tell Billy how you helped, George,' said my mother.

'I'm telling you I didn't do anything,' he said. 'It was Charley's doing. Such a good man. I went to see him when he arrived at Boston from England and it was like we had never parted. Then I heard he would be out of town, on his readings for several weeks and as I anticipated being away when he returned to the city, I was visiting him again to say my farewell when your mother turned up.'

'I did like we said, Billy. I wrote to Mr Dickens reminding him of the past.'

'I was there when she sent up the note. He showed it me there and then,' said Putnam and added softly, 'it was an uncomfortable moment.'

'He said I should come up to his room,' said my mother. 'I was frightened, of course. I didn't know what I'd say to him, only that I'd beg at his feet and threaten him with his ruination

275

if I had to. I knocked on the door and went in. It was a big room. Like this, only grander, maybe and the first thing I saw was the two men standing by the window, looking at my note. I knew I had no choice now but to proceed, no matter that my stomach was turning insides out and my heart was thumping like a stick in a washtub. I walked right up to them as bold as brass and said, "Mr Dickens, I must speak with you." '

The idea of my mother the washerwoman facing up to Charles Dickens was too delicious. I entreated her to tell me all but George Putnam declared that his train would not wait. My mother urged him to stay but George was resolute. He took his coat and hat and shook our hands. 'It has done my heart good to meet you, Billy,' he said. 'I am so glad that I was able to be of some small service.' With that he departed and it has ever been my regret that I never saw him again.

It was left to my mother to tell me of how a letter from Charles Dickens had persuaded the authorities in Cincinnati to make every effort on the behalves of those least deserving of their assistance. The police talked with anyone and everyone who had business in that quarter of the city on the night of the fire and such diligence was rewarded. A stoker was found who had seen Amory setting the conflagration. Presuming he was witness to only another insurance swindle, the man had boarded his steamer and had only recently returned to Cincinnati. Silas Amory had been identified. He had remained in custody there and shortly would be tried for the murder of Matthew Irving.

No more revelations were forthcoming. Though I pressed her to speak of her meeting with Dickens and to tell me more of George Putnam and of my earliest history, she only said that it could wait until I had recovered my strength. But the stronger I became as I rested up in Dickens' hotel room, the more close-lipped became the oracle and the less inclined I was to ask.

I spent a week in that room and my mother was absent much of the time, making preparations for our removal to

Georgia, where Putnam had secured me employment and had arranged accommodation for us both. I had accepted his offer almost immediately. It was a first step in my intended direction. I would go South, as Scattergood had wished. I think my mother would have gone anywhere so long as she was with me. If she chattered incessantly of our new life to be, she was now equally closed about the lives we had left behind. 'Some things,' she said, with finality, 'are best left just as they are.'

There was never more to be gotten from her than that. Soon I gave up enquiring about my past because it came to me that I no longer needed to know. Although Elijah Putnam had once filled some part of a father's role and the possibility remained that I was a natural son to Charles Dickens, that vacancy in my heart had been claimed by another. Although I had known him for so short a while and though he was now gone, I discovered that I desired no other father than that I found in my memories of Hope Scattergood.

III

As you will have gathered, I didn't return to Hayes with or without Charles Dickens and I have no doubt that Elijah Putnam's disappointment was great. He sent me a letter, dictated through Cissy Bullock, urging me to speed back to Hayes with Dickens in my train. The whole town was expecting as much. Nor did I continue to deal in theatre tickets or involve myself in any of the paltry schemes by which I had got my bread before the death of Hope Scattergood.

His death affected us both, my mother not least. In Hope she had found the love that had eluded her throughout her life and although I believe she had always known that her time with Hope would not be long, she was no less saddened when it was ended with his passing.

I took work in Atlanta or what remained of it, where all kinds of materials were in short supply. I used a loan from George Putnam to become a kind of middleman, dealing in lumber and building supplies and then paint and anything else I could find a market for. I made some money and invested it in foreign trade, a shipful of zinc here, copra there. Within a very few years I was what I might once have called a very rich man and was invited to stand for office. I have my money still, indeed the stock market has doubled, perhaps tripled it since then and my career in politics has enjoyed a parallel success. But nothing gave me greater joy than to wed the prettiest girl in the world, the daughter of a schoolteacher, who I sometimes think looks a lot like Katy Pearson. My mother resided with me until a few years ago, when she died peacefully, never having married. She lived long enough to enjoy the use of the carriage I swore she should have and to lavish her love on four grandchildren.

I believe that I have cancelled my debt of acknowledgement and my account of my friendship with Hope Scattergood is complete. Now the scales must be balanced and the credit or the blame for what I am become judiciously apportioned. And what am I now? I am powerful in a place where power is what counts. I have prospered in mercantile ventures to the extent that my family is provided for. I have achieved that for which those around me still strive. I know that the means by which all was gotten were legitimate. (Well-paid lawyers assured me that this was always so.) So why do I hesitate to recount my later years with the same clarity of detail with which I recorded my earlier life? And why do I have misgivings about myself that Billy Talbot never knew?

I have always believed that Hope made me what I am. From him, I thought, I learned to so manipulate people that they have been grateful to become my dupes. I had thought myself innocence corrupted or at best, that I was perversely educated by Hope Scattergood. And yet, now that I am forced to look closely, I question whether Billy Talbot was ever the artless child I would remember him now.

I recall dollars filched and Merriweather deceived and realise that like any other boy of that age, I must have committed the Seven Capital Sins daily. I remember too how quickly I swallowed my pride and made myself accessory to a confidence man and how much uglier were my crimes than those perpetrated by my preceptor. I saw folk happy to be taken in by Scattergood and saw also that he loved them for it. Hope thrilled audiences with his readings, brought glamour to a provincial ball and faith to the miners of a dying Kentucky mining town. My own deceptions only filled me with the sour notion that these people were fools getting no better than they deserved. Hope was a showman and people got something in return for what they lost to him. From me they got nothing.

And when Hope was no longer around to guide me I hid behind lawyers while I cheated and swindled and took part in shakedowns the magnitude of which he could have had no conception. Was I fulfilling my own promise or my promise to Hope Scattergood when I unleashed ruthless ambition and rose to the top like the scum in a pond? If I alone had enjoyed spectacular success by doubtful means then I might be justified in condemning myself and perhaps Hope too, for being my spur. But all around me I see men whose cloth has been cut to my own pattern and these people are respected and rewarded for their conniving and their duplicity. I am nothing unique nor the only one who salves his conscience by saying that all he does is for his country. This is what spawns my misgivings.

I have cut corners and taken chances, risking the money of others. I excuse myself because, I affirm, *I knew what I was doing*. Gamblers say the same, no doubt, but mostly I have been vindicated. My friends have grown rich on my specula-tions. But I have seen others crash, the lame left behind and the fallen crushed underfoot. I reason that in lining my own pockets, I have increased the coffers of this country and that the adventurous pursuance of wealth is practically a con-stitutional imperative. I know also that this nation was built by gamblers and speculators of one kind or another. Ships berth daily at Ellis Island, their desperate cargoes staking everything against future success in America. They follow the pioneers and settlers who gambled against hunger and thirst,

Indian attacks and lawlessness when their quest for better lives pushed this nation into unknown territories. It has all been a great venture and if I sometimes question what I have grown fat off these past years then please excuse what is only the naïveté of a boy from Missouri, who is grown old.

Enough. I have sat here at my desk so long that I am stiff. I can no longer stay the demands of those who await my pleasure behind closed doors, whose petitions I must hear before I make my final speech to Congress. Miss Tummel may have this and the world may do as it likes. I am done here, although I see that my account has a loose end. I am obliged to leave it so because I never did hear what became of Silas Amory. For a time I had presumed him hanged but then I began to see him or someone very like him on the floor of Congress or thought that I glimpsed him among the marbles of this great city. There are many here like him and some who put me in mind of Hope Scattergood. I suppose that, if I am honest, I must say that there are also those in whom I see something of myself. I see these characters not only here, when I am called to Washington DC, but wherever I go in this great country. From the new towns of the West to the cities in the East, from the Great Lakes to the Gulf of Mexico, or only from Ellis Island to Park Avenue, are all kinds of Americans assiduous and unflagging in their pursuit of fortune and fame or anything at all that might raise them above or distinguish them from their neighbours, this land appearing at times a striving, struggling mass of hope and aspiration, where the con man is king of the heap.

280

Acknowledgements

I think it will be obvious that much of the preparation for this novel lay in reading and rereading works by Charles Dickens, Mark Twain and certain other Victorian novelists and the book contains many references to and borrowings from them. I also read P.T. Barnum's autobiography, from which many of the details about the contents of his museum are taken. Mary Black's *Old New York in Early Photographs*, (Dover, NY, 1973) was also helpful. An overview of the role of the confidence trickster in America was obtained from Stephen Matterson's excellent introduction to Herman Melville's *The Confidence Man* (Penguin, 1990).

Setting a novel in another time and in another country is fraught with problems and I apologise if, after checking and rechecking my facts, there remain anachronisms or mistakes regarding the geography or topography of America and especially in the difficult matter of American linguistic nuances. Most of the former problems will, I hope, have been ironed out through research and with the kind help of members of Compuserve's writers and literary forums found on the Internet. I can only hope that my dialogue at least approximates Missouri dialect of the 1860s.

Compuserve members have given freely of their time and gone to some trouble pursuing details that I would have found difficult to nail down from this side of the Atlantic. A great number of CIS members have come to my aid and I regret I'm unable to name them all here but they know who they are and I thank them now. In particular, I would like to thank Jim Ruel, Hal Turrel, Diana Gabaldon, Patrick Bishop, Kay Mitchell and Lynne K. Perednia; also John Beaulieu, David Byrnes, Merrill Cornish, Rich Hamper, Bob Lee, Janet McConnaughey, Donna Penyak, J. Manning, Steven Ratterman and my sister-in-law Lesley Carlsen of Seattle. My off-line thanks to Sid Griffin. Also firing e-mails in my direction has been another person to whom I owe a special debt of gratitude, my editor at Fourth Estate, Leo Hollis.

Ross Gilfillan
Suffolk, 1998

www.ingramcontent.com/pod-product-compliance
Ingram Content Group UK Ltd.
Pitfield, Milton Keynes, MK11 3LW, UK
UKHW020844190325
456436UK00005B/190